DRIFTING INTO A SIDE-STREAM

HENDRIK ERASMUS

Order this book online at www.trafford.com/08-0568
or email orders@trafford.com

Most Trafford titles are also available at major online book retailers.

© Copyright 2009 Hendrik Erasmus.
Editor: Terry Nicholson
Cover Design/Artwork: Chung Hyun Noh
Cape Town Picture: Soon Young Lee

Note for Librarians: A cataloguing record for this book is available from Library
and Archives Canada at www.collectionscanada.ca/amicus/index-e.html

Printed in Victoria, BC, Canada.

ISBN: 978-1-4251-7752-2 (soft)
ISBN: 978-1-4251-7753-9 (ebook)

*We at Trafford believe that it is the responsibility of us all, as both individuals
and corporations, to make choices that are environmentally and socially sound.
You, in turn, are supporting this responsible conduct each time you purchase a
Trafford book, or make use of our publishing services. To find out how you are
helping, please visit www.trafford.com/responsiblepublishing.html*

*Our mission is to efficiently provide the world's finest, most comprehensive
book publishing service, enabling every author to experience success.
To find out how to publish your book, your way, and have it available
worldwide, visit us online at www.trafford.com/10510*

 www.trafford.com

North America & international
toll-free: 1 888 232 4444 (USA & Canada)
phone: 250 383 6864 • fax: 250 383 6804 • email: info@trafford.com

The United Kingdom & Europe
phone: +44 (0)1865 487 395 • local rate: 0845 230 9601
facsimile: +44 (0)1865 481 507 • email: info.uk@trafford.com

10 9 8 7 6 5 4 3 2 1

Acknowledgements

I would like to thank my mother Molly for understanding my long absences, my brother David for all his wildlife photos, and Mac for always staying in touch and for sending me background information for the book. I also wish to thank my sisters Dianne and Lorraine for walking me into shape before my departure.

I am also very grateful to my editor Terry Nicholson for polishing the rough edges off my writing, to Andrew Holmes for his invaluable technical assistance, and to my Kiwi friend Nigel Robson for the book's back cover photo.

Also by Hendrik Erasmus

SOARING ON AFRICAN WINGS

a travel autobiography

Table of Contents

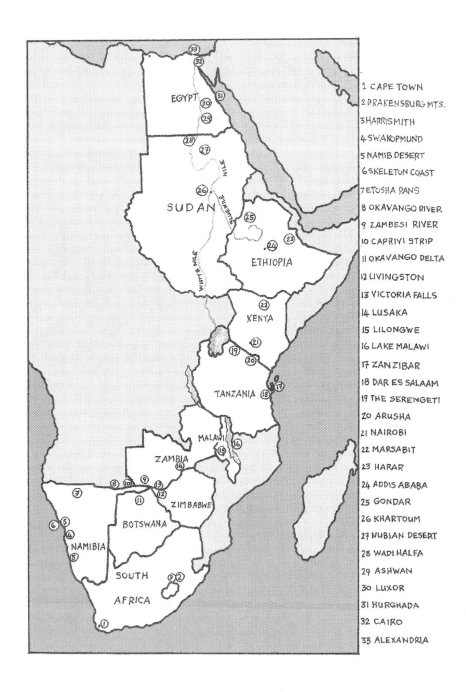

1 CAPE TOWN
2 DRAKENSBURG MTS.
3 HARRISMITH
4 SWAKOPMUND
5 NAMIB DESERT
6 SKELETON COAST
7 ETOSHA PANS
8 OKAVANGO RIVER
9 ZAMBESI RIVER
10 CAPRIVI STRIP
11 OKAVANGO DELTA
12 LIVINGSTON
13 VICTORIA FALLS
14 LUSAKA
15 LILONGWE
16 LAKE MALAWI
17 ZANZIBAR
18 DAR ES SALAAM
19 THE SERENGETI
20 ARUSHA
21 NAIROBI
22 MARSABIT
23 HARAR
24 ADDIS ABABA
25 GONDAR
26 KHARTOUM
27 NUBIAN DESERT
28 WADI HALFA
29 ASHWAN
30 LUXOR
31 HURGHADA
32 CAIRO
33 ALEXANDRIA

1

Prologue

THE WIND WAFTS down from the distant hills, carrying in its rejuvenating breath the heady aroma of impending rain.

Shadows fall across the fallow land, welcomed, yet fraught with menace.

There are dueling galleons in the darkening sky, the sun is outgunned now, and the crescent moon extinguished.

The firmament is volatile and shatters in flaming fissures.

Stark valley ridges of petrified granite kopjes bow in obeisance, as low, deep-throated rumbles of thunder roll off the lips of Enkai, supreme deity of the Masaai.

Abdala, a young livestock herder, urges his precious charges on towards the safety of the kraal, for the threat of electricity weighs heavily in the air, while the jostling cattle, finely attuned to the forces of nature, toss their heads and bellow in wild exuberance. He pauses momentarily to look up at the sky in awe, for high above him drones one of those wondrous, wide-winged, eagle-horses of the Mgeni ,(foreigners) gliding effortlessly through a gap in the swirl of clouds. All people know that Enkai is a dual-natured god. Enkai Norok - the Black God - brings life and happiness, but when he manifests himself as Enkai Nanyokie - the Red God - in his vengeful form, only a fool would venture into his domain. Abdala wonders who is rash enough to be up there chancing the wrath of the gods. Suddenly the darkness above cracks into a multi-pronged dazzle of fire, and a blinding flurry of rain drops is unleashed upon the parched plains.

'Attention! This is your captain speaking. Please fasten your seatbelts and kindly remain seated as we are now encountering an increase in atmospheric turbulence'. There is a strained calmness within Johannesburg bound Emirates Airlines flight 607's fragile cocoon as the airplane enters the turbulent equatorial thunder belt. Now that lunch has been served and order restored to the galley, the flight attendants patrol the aisles, smiling reassuringly at anxious faces. Up front in the shuddering cockpit, the cool-headed pilot navigates a narrow corridor through the tropical thunderheads. An old African hand, he dreams of calm, sunny blue skies as the beleaguered Boeing 777 runs the gauntlet of the heaven's shrouded titans.

'Here's your drink sir', says the smiling flight attendant. I take small sips from the tumbler of whiskey at my precarious window seat. The clouds are mutinous. I peer down through their muttering faces and catch brief glimpses of the African landscape; vast and desolate. A silvery streak of sizzling light whips by the aircraft's wing. If lightning were to strike us I imagine we'd flare up like a flaming roman candle. I take a deep swig of cool, soothing scotch.

I know that the journey I am about to undertake will lead diagonally up the length of the continent from Cape Town to Cairo, a seemingly endless overland trail. That is the only fragile certainty my mind will allow as it drifts off. Looking into the future is a confusing business, for prior to my departure from the Far East, upon a Korean friend's insistence, I consulted a local mudang (a female shaman). In a séance of chants and ritualistic movements she induced a hypnotic trance. Whilst drifting deep within the churning clouds of fortune, I beheld exotic images of Kathmandu and the wild beauty of the Himalayan Annapurna's icy heights, of haunting ruins of ancient India's holy sites, the teeming humanity of Calcutta, bobbing thoni boats on the heaving

Bay of Bengal, and the balmy, coconut fringed beaches of Goa. I could see myself, flying across the face of Asia to Bangkok. I saw the streets of Bombay, and a slow boat ride into the heartland of the Laotian Mekong; and I saw visions of the ancient mystique of Angkor Wat, and Phnom Phenn's horror of the Khmer Rouge.

This is mysterious, for my plan had been to travel through Russia, Mongolia and China via Amsterdam after crossing Africa. Yet despite the best made plans, a traveller is but a leaf in the wind, subject to the tides of life and fate. Thus, whatever my fortune may hold, I do not doubt that it is my destiny to face the wonder of the unknown, to see life in the raw and to endure the loneliness. Why don't you come along with me?

But first, let me introduce myself. My name is Koos van de Merwe, and I'm an international teacher, writer, humorist and perennial drifter. I was born in Southern Africa, a descendent of migrating European settlers whose ox wagons cut deep trails into the virgin earth of the wild, mysterious hinterland.

As a Sagittarian my sign is that of fire, and I am ruled by Jupiter, the planet of expansion, success, luck and opportunity - mythology dictates that I'm likely to be a man of the road. Chinese astrology seems to concur. I was born in the year of the goat, and therefore will have the nature of a wanderer, prone to undertake journeys of a more unconventional, spiritual nature. I suppose I should warn you though, that like the ram, I can be a bit of a butt-head, prone to act on impulse or emotion rather than rational thought, and therefore I may lead you down some rather wayward paths.

As a lifelong bachelor, I've been rather loose with women, money, alcohol and a few other intoxicating things, loving all, yet hooked on none. I'm a longstanding friend of Hendrik the author, but while we may be birds of a feather, he probably does not really approve of all my activities. Both of us have our spiritual moments, but are on occasion known to violate social, moral or legal codes of conduct. However he tends to have a religious inclination, and therefore is more conscience stricken than I am. I've asked him to tell the real story, with maybe a hint of discretion, but barring none of the basic good stuff.

The scotch is purely medicinal as my mind wanders nostalgically through memories of the recent past. I recall the time I took a break from my English teaching job, to spend a weekend with the Lee family high up in a retreat within South Korea's white blanketed Jiri Mountains. I remember the exuberance of the youngsters Ju Hyun, Chang Jun and Su Jin out in the fresh snowfall at dawn, and the ethereal, oriental femininity of the sisters Sun Sook and Sun Kyung in the fragile first light of daybreak. Then there's the warm remembrance of last night's farewell in Soon Young's legendary International Pub in Changwon, with the colourful Kiwis Nigel, Paul and their gorgeous Korean wives Young Hae and `Laura'. The renowned oil painter Choong Hyun Noh, and the handsome French Canadian Yannick – along with the lovely Hyun Ju - were also there, and of course the larger than life character, teacher, gambler, bouncer and DJ, the American, Big Jason.

We are expats who live in Changwon City, South Korea, and we think of ourselves as a kind of international tribe. Changwon is a place foreigners flow through, faces changing with the years. The teachers and engineers who live here more or less permanently, or come back from time to time, have a unique kind of kinship. The International Pub is our get-away from the stresses of working in a modern, industrialized Korean world. Within its warm, familiar old ambience, one can meet people from all around the globe, as well as local Koreans, always eager for a chat. Behind the bar you can often find the indefatigable Soon Young's beaming countenance - the `IP' - International Pub - is her hobby, she's really an extremely gifted artist. In the IP Soon Young is assisted by an ever-changing bevy of youngish beauties, who more often than not marry one of their customers. They are mostly would-be English speakers 'n bartenders, keen to meet people and make foreign friends. Min, a tough, softly spoken guy is Soon Young's assistant. He's the pub's jack-of-all-trades, a regular tinker, tailor DJ man.

Around the IP bar we form our friendships and alliances, but are all part of `the tribe'. There are special characters like Mr. Takasaki - or just Taka - the irrepressible Japanese man whose open friendly face shows the pleasure he gets from buying drinks for acquaintances and friends. He is often in the kitchen knocking up some special Japanese culinary delights, usually bringing the ingredients from Japan, then offering tastily arrayed dishes to everyone at the bar - everyone loves the guy. Some of the longstanding Korean regulars are: Dr. Jang, who, though in his 70's frequents the bar, even on his birthday, and can sometimes be found hiking high up in the local mountains; Prof. Jeong the lanky, sophisticated Korean academic and writer, who is often accompanied by his students from China, Poland, Russia etc; Mr. Kim, the ever-beaming pilot; Mr. Lee, the serious, well-read businessman; Mr. XXXX, the local drunk, who regularly has to be 'helped out'; the German speakers, the tall, quiet Ralf, and the handsome Sigi; the voluble Australians Matt and Michael; and the jovial travelling Dutchman, Reinier.

This morning's airport run with the artists Soon Young - the IP owner - and Mi Ok, who were just as hung-over as me, and the goodbyes, are a serious memory. Then the check-in, immigration, the blur of the flight from Inchon to Dubai, and now the final leg down the length of Africa to the OR Tambo International Airport, South Africa. The drone and thrust of the plane, combined with the flush of alcohol, fuel the heady emotion of movement away from the intense involvements of the recent past, into the tantalizing promises and the challenging uncertainties of the unknown.

2

The Shrine

South Africa

'WATCH OUT FOR snakes, this is puff adder and cobra country ', warns my mate Rod. 'And call us on your cell phone if anything happens, we'll be waiting all day' says his wife Rosalind, as I heft my day–pack and beat a path into the maze of black wattle trees. Beyond the ascending valleys of cattle pastures and steep, grassy, rock–strewn slopes tower the jutting cliffs of 'The Peak', Platberg Mountain's highest point and my personal shrine.

Engulfed deep within the stifling thickets, I pause to regain my sense of direction. Somewhere nearby a cow (or possibly a unicorn?), is lowing a soft, lost, mournful sound. Further away a horse neighs with a touch of hysteria, probably entangled helplessly in the undergrowth. Bush pigeons coo timeless melodies; intricate spider webs threaten entrapment, and the shrill chorus of cicadas' is overwhelming.

In the initial bushy mountain pastures, groups of stray cattle toss their heads, hoof the heather and moo threateningly, sensing an intruder. I stride silently by, confident but alert, on the look–out for Zulu cattle herders, belligerent bulls, territorial ostriches, or tsotsis – thugs . My weapons are simple but effective; a stout walking stick, a flick knife, and a catapult (catty), for the basic tenet of African survival is that a person must walk the walk, talk the talk, and never appear to be an easy touch. Besides the gift of the gab, my strong point is an uncommon turn of speed, which is usually one's best form of defence if confronted by an enraged cuckolded husband, but may invite attack from a threatening, randy cow.

Higher and higher, the forbidding granite cliffs of my boyhood temple reach into the unfathomable depths of the deep, pale-blue heavens. Hardy pink and red wild flowers appear between clumps of grass and rock, while pockets of azure- violet hued mountain agapanthus are blooming in a wondrous proliferation of colour. At this altitude the air is thin, with a pure pasture-flavoured freshness, but the temperature rises, as the late summer sun gains ascendancy, with occasional imposing galleons of puffed cumulus providing brief respite.

After an absence of around 30 years, familiar landmarks embrace me as though it were yesterday. A startling cacophony of hoarse barks rends the reverie, as an agitated troop of big marauding mountain baboons spot me and blow the whistle, clambering noisily up the rocks to a viewing point above. In the heat of the ascent, the sinuous flow of familiar outlines and the animated, near-human body postures provoke long dormant emotions of kinship.

An immense, near-impenetrable bush choked canyon dissects the mountainside, blocking access to the easier route up the back neck of the peak. I attempt the slanted rock bridge at the top, which forms the foot of the cliff face until it runs out – déjà vu – it comes back to me; oh shit, you have to jump at its end! You've got to throw your body across the void and stick like a leech to the opposite slope which falls away into the canyon - or you're a goner. My heart bounces in my chest and as I peer down, not relishing the difficult time consuming alternative, I launch myself across the divide and hit the further side with a jarring thud, and claw to a frantic stop on the lip of rich grass tufted overhang.

The mountain, not unlike a reluctant woman, yields itself grudgingly, and the peak I am pursuing is the local Madonna. Seemingly unattainable in the wild beauty of her desultory isolation, she bedazzles the climber with stupendous sights. I proceed up and over the neck, to enter the upward sloping, alien moon landscape at the top, with hammering chest and rasping breath. Through the tendril misty strands of an earthy vapour, the beacon appears at the peak's most daring extremity. I stagger forward and embrace it when I see where I carved my initials as a school boy. To my right, curled up in a valley below the breastbone of the mountainside, lies that old pioneering town Harrismith, where my forefathers rest, entombed in the peaceful setting of the tree shaded cemetery. Directly ahead, with an upheaval of emotion, I see my relatives' old homestead Bloemhof for the last time, not knowing that it is fast approaching the destructive, fiery turmoil of its own destiny. Far back to the southeast, the serene heights of Spioenkop, ancient battleground of the Boer and British armies, belie the reputation of death and destruction forever attached to it. On the horizon, across the shimmering, blue- grey vastness of space, lies the serpentine length of the unparalleled approach to the Drakensburg Mountains. In a moment of reverence I face Africa, and kneel with my hands on the old cairn of stones at the base of the beacon, and focus on the Great Spirit of life.

I take time for spiritual moments, to burn a sacrifice, and look out through a haze of green breeze far beyond the horizon. This is an old, old continent, supposedly the cradle of humanity. She has been alternately colonized, raped, and loved by European adventurers, who fought for territory for themselves, as well as their gods. In the north, Egyptian gods were sovereign in Arabic Africa in times past but they were compelled to submit to the influence of Islam, which jostled against Christianity from the south. The Africans lives were, and continue to be, ruled mostly by elements of animism and superstition, and as for earthly territory, tribes separated within diverse areas that their European conquerors claimed and named as countries. Thus they were named 'The Scatterlings' in the music of the South African musician Johhny Clegg.

The once teeming herds of wildlife that roamed the steamy jungles and endless savanna plains are now mostly fast dwindling refugees in ill-protected reserves. The vast space and the breeze makes me reflective, and images come to mind. Legends of the Skeleton Coast, the wandering sand oceans of the Sahara, the Namib and the Kalahari deserts, endless sculpted plains from the Makgadikgadi Salt Pans to Etosha, the unparalleled wonder of the Okavango Swamps, Mosi-oa-Tunya , the smoke that thunders', as Victoria Falls is called; Kilimanjaro's cloud-shrouded heights, the Serengeti and the Ngorongoro Crater; great lakes, and to the north, vast tracts of unblemished wilderness; and the powerful, thrusting lifeline of the Nile.

In recent years I have been grappling with life on the fringes of the mainstream, teaching English to Korean college students, preparing them to enter a life of corporate slavery in a rapidly changing world. Preparing them for fourteen hour work days, high stress, annual vacations of four working days, and weekends like birds in cages. Conformity and kowtowing are their keys to survival, and age determines the level of respect people are accorded in that society, marriage is in, single is not, youth is good, ageing is not, cigarettes and alcohol are OK, ganja and hashish are definitely not, while individuality is seriously uncool, and the questioning of authority is not tolerated.

The mainstream has its own relentless force, hammering through on its predestined course from source to end - birth to death. Misdirected governments are fuelled by ignorant mass cohesion, taking all along, willingly or otherwise. Within certain societies, freedom of choice is lost in the tide of fanatical, twisted religious fundamentalism, and in others, capitalism and materialism motivates the masses at the cost of spiritual values and the sanctity of the human soul. I have cut loose, and now it's time to hit the rapids, bends, and exhilarating thrills 'n spills, in search of the eternal natural calm in the peaceful reaches of the side-streams of life.

3

Cape Town - South Africa

THE COMBINED EFFORTS and experiences of the Portuguese seafaring legends Vasco da Gama and Bartholomew Dias prized open the long sought route around the tip of the African continent in the 1400's, and that enabled the Europeans to release their scurvy, rat infested flotillas on the unsuspecting Asians of the Orient. It is written that Jan van Riebeeck's arrival in Table Bay in 1652, to establish a victualling station for Dutch ships, heralded the first European settlement on the toe of the African continent. The British gained control of the area in 1795, which eventually lead to an exodus of Dutch farmers on epic ox-wagon voyages into the interior to escape the British rule. The `Boers', including my forefathers, endured many hardships as they travelled slowly in the unframed wilderness far beyond the comforts of Western civilization. They encountered, and often collided with, the southward migration of African tribes, and that gave birth to the legends of 'The Great Trek'.

The Cape Peninsula, the southwestern point of the continent, consists mainly of a dramatic, mountainous rock spine jutting into the wild Atlantic at Cape Point. At its furthest extremity, a lonely lighthouse overlooks a seafarers' graveyard, where howling tempests fuel the pounding breakers to spend their fury on the bleak, unforgiving granite cliffs. The barely submerged Bellows Rock is there, treacherous, and ready to lay to waste any unfortunate vessels that drift too close.

A popular tale is that of the Flying Dutchman, wherein the ill-fated captain Hendrik van der Decken, swore to sail to the ends of the earth, and is supposedly, still sighted on stormy nights. Then there is the fateful prophesy of Adamastor, (spirit of the Cape of Storms) warning of the doom that is certain to befall all who would presume to venture that way.

Cape Town by Korean artist Soon Young Lee

In its superb natural setting, Cape Town developed with a unique populace, as the original natives of the area, the Hottentots, were quickly assimilated into the emerging social mix of African, Malaysian, and a blend of European cultures. It is a fortune-seeker's haven, where the first sighting is sure to set fire to one's soul, as the traveller instinctively understands the uniqueness of the thrills and challenges ahead. According to Hottentot legend, the main city, which sprawls in the lee of the imposing heights of Table Mountain (Umlindi Wemingizimu) – The Watcher of the South – is flanked by Devils Peak to the left, and Lions Head to the right, and slopes down into the picturesque waterfront and dockyard areas of Table Bay. The Victoria & Alfred Waterfront quaysides are an adventurer's delight of bars, restaurants and open-air cafes, with squabbling seals vying for positions on the harbour ledges below. Seagulls freewheel above, enlivening the ocean-balmed breeze with raucous cries, while the movement of all manner of passing crafts, adds to the flavour of the ever changing seascape.

Cape Town, Tuesday, 23 April 2006. The years roll back as I stroll up through the blossoming humanity of buskers, artists, and beggars of St. George's Street Mall. It was around here that I once earned a living within the strict confines of the pinstriped legal profession, and roamed in my days of unemployment, seemingly in another life.

At the vibrant third-world market area, I squeeze through the colourful crush of tourists and vendor stalls in the bewildering maze of narrow lanes, until I find the right one, and enter a low shack flying a green flag, filled with smoking paraphernalia and herbal remedies. Here I am welcomed with a `Hi brother' and a warm three-clasp, African-style handshake. ` I've been looking all over for you', I say to the dread-locked Rasta-man. `God himself guided you to me, for I can see in your eyes that you are my soul-brother' replies the Rasta-man seriously, as he expounds on the Rasta's spiritual doctrine, and the inevitableness of our meeting. In the streets you may haggle, but this is the stall of the soul-soother, so the man slips me a bulging bank bag of the finest herbs from Swaziland, and pockets the R100 (about US $15) note concealed in my hand, as we embrace in the exchange.

`Sea Point, Sea Point!', the tattooed taxi tout cries, swinging from the partially open sliding door of the near full mini-bus as I wave it to a halt and jump in. The vehicle passes below the historic Malay, on the slopes of Signal Hill, and follows Somerset Road through and around Green Point into the urban crush of Sea Point's heady, stunning blue, oceanfront ambience.

I bail out in the centre and check into Lions Head Lodge – I have to get the Sudanese visa problem sorted out. The Sudanese have stubbornly resisted issuing a visa for the past 14 days, continually arguing moot points of the application, or requiring further irrelevant information. A phone call confirms that the visa will not be issued the next day, but maybe the day after.

In the Backpacker's Pub there is a massive, travel-stained man sitting alone at the bar with a beer dwarfed in his big hand. Christo speaks English with the slow inflection of vowels and grinding of consonants common to the Afrikaner, until he discovers that I am fluent in Afrikaans. He is dark haired with a short goatee, and burned brown by many suns, while his soft manner belies the steel below the surface, for despite his relative youth, he is a veteran of the African trails who is to be the leader of the overland expedition. 'Yaa, you will be the only other South African in the group' he says, 'and the oldest person, but you look alright, also with your army background you should be OK. We'll go on ahead, but when you get your passport back take an express bus to Swakopmund in Namibia, and we'll pick you up there', Christo suggests.

Outside, the evening sky is a luminous, brooding, dark speckled hen slowly settling upon its gold haloed egg and bathing the gentle swells of the shimmering Atlantic in a wondrous, deep-coppered hue. The second oldest member of the group arrives. Carie, a petite Canadian blonde with faded green eyes, is so hyped-up that she talks non-stop, and fast-tracks into the beers. I ease myself from the company to get out and burn a breeze on the deserted beach. Times have changed, I have to keep an eye open for muggers and be ready to palm the flick-knife. My cell phone buzzes, it's my mate Rod from up north who is almost as excited as I am, for the lure of the African wilderness is contagious.

Late at night, Sea Point is a bustling hub of activity. Night clubs, high-flyers in sports cars, hookers posturing suggestively in street bars, and beggars-cum-muggers mingling with revelers on the streets. At dawn,

Christo and the group of travellers will depart on the first step of an epic journey, zigzagging up the length of the continent to Cairo, while I'll be languishing in Cape Town because of the intransigence of the Sudanese. However all is not lost I reckon, for I am a free man with dollars in my pocket, about to cast off into a side-stream - and the allure of the night, with all its memories of yesterday, calls. I finish my beer at the Heartache 'n Vine Pub, ignore the inviting murmurs of the 'ladies', and jump into a jam-packed minibus cab heading into town.

My next stop is at a familiar old basement pub run by a former cockney acquaintance in the city bowl. There are two topless female bartenders working the bar, but my old cockney buddy is long gone. The music is overwhelming, while the clientele, a curious mix of locals and Russian and Oriental sailors is rough and loud, with eye-catching black and coloured hookers mingling freely. Later I extricate myself and walk out into the city to catch up on former haunts on Long Street, but have to back-off behind the cold steel of my knife blade as muggers threaten. I retreat to Cape Town Waterfront's furthest point; the pier at the entrance to the habour, where I set the breeze ablaze, and feast on the wonder of the view of Table Bay at night. Nevertheless, this cannot last forever, as man is a demanding beast, and I succumb to the lure of Sea Point's winking lights.

(Two days later) Cape Town, Thursday, 25 May 2006, 6 a.m. I groan and hold my head, while pushing myself upright on the couch as Hannes bustles in. Then it all comes back to me; last nights' meeting for a farewell braai, (South African for barbecue) with old friends Hannes, Maryna, and the youngsters GJ and Nadia - maybe I shouldn't have had the wine. Coffee and rusks, then hugs, kisses and waves and we are off to Hannes' office in Paarden Island. These are worrisome times, as the company Hannes is working for is slowly going under, and the Cape economy is not in the ascendancy.

Rising high above the city, Table Mountain, a forbidding colossus, is wondrously highlighted by rays of piercing translucent crimson, reaching across the verdant winelands of the Paarl Valley. The rising sun overwhelms the blue-lined barrier of the Boland Mountains to the east. To the southwest of the city is Table Bay, where Robin Island sits and smoulders in an undulating foggy vapour.

CHAPTER 3: CAPE TOWN – SOUTH AFRICA.

Cape Town bus station, 9a.m. 'Totsiens en alles van die beste ou pel!' (Afrikaans for: Goodbye and everything of the best old friend), a final handshake, then Hannes leaves as I heave my backpack into the luggage hold, and claim a seat on the top deck of the partially filled Inter Cape bus. It's 'take off' time again, and lines from that old movie 'Paint your wagon' come to mind; 'Wheels were made for rolling, mules were made to pack..., for I was born under a wandering star...'

The bus coasts smoothly away, snaking along its predetermined course and reducing Cape Town's radiant majesty to a diminishing oil painting. The traveller's disjointed emotions are wrenched into transition, from the rich cornfields and vineyards of Malmesbury, across the Piketberg and into the abundant fruit growing areas of Citrusdal, which lie in the shadow of the Cederberg Mountains. The landscape changes dramatically as the bus enters the arid region of Little Namaqualand, which is famous for it's kaleidoscope of color during the spring flowering season. To the north lies the vastness of Great Namaqualand, sparsely populated by the Nama, a Khoikhoi people.

Travelling, as I well know, is often an emotionally unsettling affair. South Africa has become a dangerous place, and one never knows when or where the tsotsis may strike next. To compensate for my often prolonged absences, I occasionally take time off to visit my ageing mother, who despite being in her 80's, still retains a sharp wit. My mind reaches back to a recent visit. Mom lives in a small cottage on my sister Marilyn's property. 'Let's have a sundowner on the patio' I say to Mom, and carry the drinks through the main house while giving her an arm down the steps. ' Anyway, everyone is away for the weekend, so let's enjoy the peace and quiet', says Mom, as we settle down to watch the typical Highveld thunderstorm activity through the trees directly ahead. Bo and Farah, the two gorgeous collies try to entice me out onto the lawn for a game of 'catch the ball', but it's Mom's hour and besides, I have a thick piece of biltong (deliciously spiced dried meat, a popular South African speciality) and a sharp knife on hand. Through occasional monster barks of thunder, with jagged streaks of lightning shredding the evening sky, the talk touches on old times and familiar family matters.

Bedtime at Mom's is a relatively early affair, and I eventually doze off on the couch, only to awaken to Mom's strident voice saying; 'Put that bag down at once, it's not yours, and what are you doing in my daughter's house?' I dash into her bedroom and see she is at the window shouting at a tall, well-dressed black man who has just emerged from the back door of the main house with a big, black bag in his arms. He drops the bag, uncertain what to do, but then points a gun at Mom who is totally unfazed, and continues berating him. I hurriedly push her down onto the bed before raising the alarm, shouting false threats about an immediate armed reprisal. Luckily the gang of tsotsis takes fright and disappears, for the cottage is unprotected and the wooden door and unbarred windows hardly worth a mention - and my sole weapon is a stout stick. The police arrive thirty minutes later. I meet them at the front gate and lead the officer and his men to the open back door of the main house, but they balk at this point. 'We do not go into unlit homes' the officer says, 'it's too dangerous, and besides, we may have to do this a few more times tonight'. 'But you're the police!' I protest, but to no avail, so I dash in, keeping my body low while turning on the lights throughout the house. A hurried search of the premises reveals that the TV, video, stereo etc. are all gone. But the tsotsis have left, and there is no loss of life or injury, so by local standards the robbery was a great success for victims and perpetrators alike.

Back in real time, the bus bypasses the Namaqualand villages of Garies and Pofadder, before stopping in Springbok, a central town lying between rugged mountains about 600 km's north of Cape Town. There the passengers disembark for a meal and toilet stop. Before long we are all aboard and on the road again, but a few kilometres further on an urgent call summonses the driver back to Springbok. Some old Namaqua guy got left behind. He has a foolish grin on his face as he finds his way to his seat.

Namaqualand, a place of random kopjes, desultory thorn bushes, and vast stony plains in slow motion, harmonizes with the setting sun in pastel shades of lilac, mauve, and pinky red. Soon the road is an illuminated funnel, sucking the bus into the vast, dark mysterious vortex of the wilderness.

Hours later there are lights up ahead and the bus slows to a halt. It's Vioolsdrift, the South African frontier town. All passengers disembark to have their passports stamped at the SA Immigration checkpoint. Then we take a short ride across the bridge spanning the Orange River, and into the town of Noordoewer, where everyone has to check in at the Namibian Immigration Office. For a certain pretty young Israeli backpacker, it's the end of the road, and all her pleas fall on deaf ears - `Entry denied'. She does not have a Namibian visa, so the bus driver turns back across the bridge and dumps her on the South African side. Her fellow passengers are aghast, and people wave to her and shout advice, as the bus takes off again, leaving her there beside the road, a forlorn figure, staring back at the bus receding into the night.

4

Namibia and Botswana

FRIDAY, 26 MAY 2006. Namibia. The pre-dawn desert chill brings a sluggish awakening to us bleary-eyed passengers, as the first light reveals the utter desolation of the bleak desert landscape. The mood turns to awed disquiet, for this is raw wilderness, far beyond the frontiers of civilization. In the night, we bypassed the Fish River Canyon National Park and the restricted diamond areas. To our left lies the vastness of the Namib-Naukluft Park, while to the right the Kalahari Desert stretches out seemingly endlessly into the emptiness of Botswana. Incredibly, Namibia and Botswana cover an area of more than 1,425,000 square kilometres, yet their combined populations are only around 3,600,000 people. Namibia, an independent country, previously known as South West Africa, was of course once a German colony and later a South African protectorate.

The desert towns of Keetmanshoop, Mariental, and Rehoboth are now behind us, and with a grey dawn breaking we enter the capital, Windhoek, at 6 a.m. Sitting across from me in a blue tracksuit and Adidas shoes is 'Phillip', a cool Namibian dude of the Ovambo ethnic group, who is seems to be a glib operator. First he tries to persuade a Canadian backpacker to let him arrange transportation to her next destination with his friend who has a car. She declines as she already has a bus ticket. Next he offers to take me to another friend who will sell me cheap gems; diamonds! He gives me his cell phone number in case I change my mind.

An hour later the Swakopmund bound bus departs, fleeing the molten face of the rising sun, heading westwards into the shimmering, sand-ribbed brown-dusted hue of the Namib Desert. I have a flashback; years ago sitting on the slopes of Muizenberg Mountain near Cape Town with my German-speaking friend Uta, both of us tweaked on weed. She draws a map of Swakopmund in the sand with a stick, describing the town in glowing terms. She was such a cool friend and I'll ask after her there.

Swakopmund (Namibia): By midday the undulating dunes of the desert finally give way to signs of civilization, as we enter the wide streets of Swakopmund, which apparently has a sizeable German population, and in layout and architectural structure, seems to be very European. We disembark into the hot midday sun, where I join a group of young backpackers and check into a room at a local youth hostel. At 300 Namibian Dollars my room seems rather pricey for Africa, as 1 Namibian Dollar is equal to 1 South African Rand, which is about US$0,14. A young European is a source of great amusement when he backs away from the reception counter, which is situated beside the pool, and goes over backwards into the water, with his backpack on.

As Swakopmund lies along the white beaches of the icy Atlantic's sullen swell, I decide to take a walk from Palm Beach along the Arnold Shad Promenade, and then leave the town behind for a coastal hike to the mouth of the Swakop River. The waves roll in, spitting and foaming up the white sand, so I take off my sandals and wade through the chilly surf. Later I relax high up on the deserted beach dunes in the slanting sun and catch a breeze, which opens me to the melancholy of the desert nomads' haunting songs of love, suffering, and indelible loneliness.

When I arrive back in the downtown area of Kaiser Wilhelm Strasse, I encounter a full-blown German beer festival, complete with couples in traditional costumes dancing on platforms to lively music. The brews are flowing, so I squeeze through the throng of local Africans and tourists, and join the revelers, drinking several mugs of draft beer as a show of good will. Apparently the movie stars Brad Pitt, and a very pregnant Angelina Jolie are in town somewhere, and the thuggish behavior of their bodyguards is grabbing the headlines.

Saturday, 27 May 2006, Swakopmund. It's time to move on, so I shoulder my heavy backpack down Roon Strasse to the Swakopmund Rest Camp just out of town, where I check into a cheaper, R150 per night, A-framed, self-catering bungalow. I wash my dirty clothes, go shopping, explore the area – all the normal backpacking stuff – but now it's evening, time to burn the breeze and see what this little town's really about.

I feast on a tasty take-away mince jaffel, as I stroll around the poorly illuminated streets, checking out the local scene. There are a couple of European, or backpacker style pubs, with the lyrics of the Eagles' `Hotel California' the rage, but it's at a more dimly lit, funky local African shebeen, (informal pub) that I take a place beside the bar and order a beer. It's a while before the locals pay attention, but they don't know what to make of me, as this is not the type of place that Euros are likely to frequent. Yet unknown to them I'm an African too, a white one. As a veteran of a thousand bars, I know the way. Be cool and relaxed, non-aggressive, yet fill your space with all the strength of your presence, avoid direct eye contact unless spoken to, smile and always keep a beer bottle in one hand – it helps to keep a harmonious beat. Before long I feel less conspicuous, and it's beer, skokiaan,(African firewater) and samba to the African rumba in the smoky haze. A really hot, but not so youngish Lolita hits on me for a drink or more, her name sounds like` Pewa' and she says that she's a Herero from up north. The crowd thickens, pulsates, the heat's on, there's passion and agro in the air, and it's all about the beat, but it's time to catch a sea breeze for the ride back home.

Sunday, 28 May 2006, Swakopmund. A credit card scam. I need some local currency, so I decide to withdraw cash using my Visa credit card issued by the Korean Foreigners Bank. There is a queue at the Nedbank auto cash machine, so I fall in behind a well-dressed African man. When it's my turn the machine simply swallows my card and won't return it. A tall African man in a black suit knocks and enters the booth. `I'm with the bank,' he says in flawless English, `we're having problems with this machine, please enter your pin again', he says while watching intently.

`Please get out of this booth right now' I say, ushering him out before entering my pin, and then let I him in again. He seems annoyed and taps around, but he's unable to fix it, so he shrugs and leaves without another word. Well it's Sunday, so there's not much I can do about it.

Monday, 29 May 2006, Swakopmund. First thing in the morning I stop by the bank, but to my surprise the bank teller denies that there was a card in the machine. The bank manager tells me that they've been having problems with credit card scams, so I call Korea to have my card cancelled, and report the case to the local police. They tell me that there is a scam going on, but they haven't figured out how the crooks get the cards out of the machines. Luckily, they did not get my pin number, so my money is safe, but I'm furious as I've lost my card. The police say that as I've not lost any money they cannot open a docket, and therefore cannot, or will not, do anything about it.

In the afternoon I discover that Christo and my fellow travellers have arrived in the truck, so I stroll over to meet them. Besides Christo, only three of them are to travel all the way to Cairo with me. They are Carie, the Canadian woman whom I met in Cape Town, and also Marieke, a pretty blonde blue-eyed student, and the impressive, young, good-looking engineer, Berend, both from Holland. `My friends call me `Beer', he says, giving me a warm handshake. Then there are Koen, also from Holland, Philippe from France, Christina -the baby of the group- Andreas, Ilka, Sandra, and the twins Iris and Doris, all from Germany or Austria. I can see it's going to be a big change in my life to be sharing part of the trip with this very lively and excited bunch of young people. I carry my backpack over for we are all to share 2 large A-frame bungalows.

In the evening we go to the Cape to Cairo Hotel for dinner, and then upstairs to the pub, which is crowded with backpackers. Windhoek Lager beer, and Jagermeister shooters are in, and pretty soon everyone is getting smashed, with big Christo our guide showing the way. The lively party continues till the early hours of the morning.

Tuesday, 30 May 2006, Swakopmund. Today is a major activity day despite the hangovers – quad biking, sand boarding and skydiving – all pre-booked. I opt out, preferring to head out along the coast, enriching the sea breeze with my special blend of legend.

Wednesday, 31 May 2006. The Skeleton Coast. There is a bank of mist rolling in from the sea, and it's the start of winter in Southern Africa, so we're all shivering in the early morning chill as we help ourselves to coffee, tea, cereal and self-made sandwiches. Christo has gotten the truck rumbling and is checking out the engine as we pack and choose seats in the back. The seating area inside the back of the truck is elevated higher than the front cab, with packing space below for the food-stuffs, and on the roof for the tents. There are metal trunks that slide in and out on brackets at the back, where one enters the truck. Each person is given the use of one trunk.

Then it's the thrill of the departure, with Swakopmund receding in a cloud of dust as we take to the narrow dirt road, winding northward between the desert and the deep blue sea. Our truck passes by the minor settlements of Wlotzkasbaken, Jackalsputz, and Hentiesbaai, where mere human survival seems to be a major feat, while the reason for settlement remains obscure. The spectacular desert scenery of the Skeleton Coast unfolds, contrasting starkly with the brilliant green-blue sightings of the moody Atlantic Ocean's sullen swells to our left. The treacherous coastline with its shifting sand banks, and eerie, disorienting fogs is notorious for shipwrecks.

The nom de guerre 'Skeleton Coast' seems appropriate, because of those who actually made it to land. They survived disaster wrought by the fury of the wild Atlantic storms, only to leave their bones littering the inhospitable dunes, to be honed to the tune of the emotional desert wind, and bleached white by the scorching sun. It is said that some hardy men survived and became legends, destined never to set eyes on their homelands again, but to adapt to, and enrich the ways of the Nama and Khoisan tribes that took them in.

The starkness and sheer desolation of the route have silenced the passengers, but when we arrive at the seal colony of Cape Cross their natural exuberance returns, as we spill out onto the hot sand, eager to stretch our legs. First we stop at the white cross, and read that Diego Cao erected it in honour of John 1 of Portugal in 1486. There is nothing here, no distinguishing feature, so it's not clear why they chose to place it here. The seal colony lies along the beachfront, below a protective stone wall barrier which separates us from the squabbling din and stench of the seals. Mangy looking desert jackals lurk on the outer fringes of the colony, scavengers on the lookout for unprotected baby seals.

I look back one last lingering time as we leave, for our next ocean sighting will be the tropical waters of the Indian Ocean, far to the north-east, across the width of the continent, on the Tanzanian coast of Dares Salaam. Later it's time for a pit stop, boys on one side of the truck, girls on the other. We notice a strange looking plant just off the road, which Christo says is a welwitschia, whose only source of water is moisture from dew and fog.

Our truck follows the dirt track through the desert for hours, until the sand gives way to scrub, and then we enter a high, seemingly deserted plateau of savanna, within a framed, ragged wilderness of low mountains. Later Christo turns off the road into the grounds of a solitary store, where we all disembark, eager to stretch and buy a cold drink. There are a couple of locals in the shade of a tree beside an outspanned mule cart, while a bunch of kids are playing beside the store. To my surprise, these African children are not speaking a tribal language, but a dialect of Afrikaans which I can understand.

By now, the passengers have become accustomed to the ever changing isolation of the superb natural setting. Some are playing cards, others reading or chatting, but it is Carie with her Canadian twang who's the real talker of the group. Philippe, the handsome muscular Frenchman, is a knot of pent up energy and excitement, moving or swinging between the seats in the narrow aisle, smiling broadly at everyone. With his happy-go-lucky nature he's a real catalyst, even though he speaks only a little English besides his native French. He doesn't have a day-pack, and many of his belongings are in a Pick-n-Pay plastic packet, which keeps spilling out onto the narrow passage way. The tall German twins Iris and Doris, with their protective friend Sandra, stick together and don't mix much, while there's a lot of ribbing and inter-cultural banter with sexual undercurrents between the others, for it's a long way to be cooped up together.

In the afternoon we spot springbok, kudu and giraffe between the thorn trees, before we pull into the Palmwag Campsite and park at our designated spot. Everyone rushes off to check out the camp grounds, while Christo tends to the truck and I erect the tent which will be my home for the foreseeable future. As a well seasoned camper I waste no time getting to the showers - late comers are likely to get theirs cold.

By the time I find the bar and hit a few cold ones, the others are leaving to climb a nearby hill to watch the sunset. When I ask the bartender for directions, he warns me to keep a lookout, for this is elephant country and there are no rules or fences here. The main group appears to be at the top of a viewing point, so I leave the path and follow a shortcut up a gulley to reach the summit. The sun dwindles slowly down between a myriad of jagged rock formations, formed by sun-scorched scarlet yonder hills.

Fast fading rays of light bathe the surreal savannah landscape in gentle pastel shades. The drifting, thinly misted valleys of gnarled and twisted acacia trees are silhouetted in a wondrous shroud of pink tinted mystique. Enthralled, my co-travellers follow me back down the barely discernable trail to the campsite.

The night descends suddenly in a thick cloak of inscrutable darkness, so we are happy to find a large log fire to guide us into our camp where Christo has prepared a delicious vegetable curry. Nobody wants to leave the fireside, as we huddle together drinking beer and listening to his tales of the trail that lies ahead, and in moments of silence the night sounds of Africa penetrate our awed reverie.

Thursday, June 1, 2008. Northern Namibia. Up at dawn, ablutions, pack the tents, breakfast, and we're off, heading east, north-east. The road winds through a seemingly endless wilderness of large forbidding hills and desolate valleys. Where have the people gone – have we discovered a new, uninhabited waterless world? These questions are soon answered when Christo drives off the main track and parks below a random jumble of granite kopjes. We follow the path and are soon scrambling higher up, climbing over the boulders and shallow depressions. This is an African art gallery, but alas, the artists have long gone – all that remains is the Bushmen's rock art, a memorial and shrine to the hunters and the noble animals they revered and killed. The giraffe seems to be the most celebrated animal.

In the mid afternoon we arrive at Ojitdongwe Cheetah Park, where we set up our camp alongside a fence separating us from the Cheetahs.

CHAPTER 4: NAMIBIA AND BOTSWANA.

Apparently this is a kind of cheetah refuge and rehabilitation centre, which takes in those that have been caught in traps or are under threat, and rehabilitates them until they are ready to be released back into the wild.

We have now set into a functional routine, with a roster designating two of us to take care of the daily communal chores, such as doing the dishes and helping Christo prepare meals. Everyone usually helps unpack the truck and set up the folding chairs and tables for mealtimes.

Just beyond the ablution blocks, we discover a small swimming pool nestled between the trees, and soon we are all eyeing each other as we dip into the cold water in our swimming costumes. Then we find the long, rambling bar area, where two real characters, the brothers Marco and Mario hold sway. As I enter, one of them is gleefully giving Christo a lively account of how he seduced a woman, in a colourful local dialect of Afrikaans. `En toe eet ek haar!' (then I … her!), he yells at the climax of the story, punching his open hand to emphasize the point. The beers are cheap and the atmosphere is great, so pretty soon a lively party takes off around our two laidback landlords.

However I have a date with destiny, and I slip out into the unlit grounds beyond our camping area, to follow the footpath leading by the tall wooden lookout tower overlooking the cheetah enclosure area, and climb up the steep staircase to the platform at the top. I savour my freedom, Hansa beer in hand, while looking around out into the darkness of the land. There are no other people within hundreds of kilometres, yet there is life out there on the silent, savage, savanna plains, where the scent of fear freely rides the restless wind, and the red-eyed shadow of death lurks on the fringes, ever stalking the unwary walking dead. But it's time to burn a sacrifice to the evening breeze, something to temper the glory of the night. Overhead, in mysterious celestial splendor, a brilliant, silver sliver of moon drifts across the skewed sky of a billion brightest stars. `Come', - it calls –` with you astride me we'll glide through the galaxies till we are way beyond the tilted rim' – I feel the magnetic power of the universe – a summons from the realm beyond – I reach out - but cannot grasp. Below, the cheetahs bark and cough, I return to earth in wonder.

Friday, June 2, 2006. Etosha National Park, Northern Namibia. Our first stop today is at Outjo, a rural Namibian town, where we step into the curious throng of local black people to check out the shopping and use an internet café. Once again, I'm surprised to hear how commonly Afrikaans is spoken by local black Africans. Then we're off again on the C38 national road, and before long we enter the Etosha National Park through the Anderson Gate, and almost immediately begin to see game; springbok, zebra, giraffe, and some elephant. So well do the animals blend in to the natural background, that they often have to be pointed out before the foreigners spot them. The game viewing is mostly on the fringes of the salt pan desert, which is roughly 130 km long, and 50 km wide at places. Now it is winter, and salt devils dance within the blur of the empty white salt plains, which Christo says are transformed into a wonderland for the animal world, and for pelicans and flamingo in particular, by the summer rains.

It is very hot when we arrive at the campsite in Okaukuejo, where we set up our tents and have a light lunch. An interesting feature of this camp is the scavenging jackals, and pretty soon Christo and I have to drive them off with our catapults, as they're capable of making ones footwear disappear.

In the cooler hours following midday, there is a buzz of eager anticipation, as we take off on a game drive through the park's arid bushveld of thorny scrub. Soon we come upon a small group of elephant doing their ablutions at a watering hole, indulging themselves in the timeless enjoyment their kind derives from getting really wet and very muddy. There are zebra, springbok, and giraffe, but where are the cats? When we get back everyone is really thirsty, so we stock up on some beers from the local store. With the setting sun casting a spell of melancholic magic on the camp, we gather wood and get a major fire going. Someone connects an iPod to the truck's speakers and then it's party time. Christo had picked up a batch of T-bone steaks at a good price, and soon the aroma of sizzling meat permeates the air.

Breaking news! 'There's a live sex show, come quickly!' We run to the viewing spot that overlooks the watering hole beside the camp, and that's where all the action is; two massive black rhino making out. It takes some time before they get to humping as the female is pretty feisty, provoking comments like,' Yea, just like humans – she's probably got a headache!', but the male perseveres and soon the air is hot with grunts and moans. This of course elicits further comments and giggles from our group members, as everyone attempts to get a good shot.

Later, as I'm bedding down someone tries to enter my tent. It's Philippe, who is a little drunk and unsure where his tent is in the stifling darkness. The expectant silence is profound as I'm drifting off, zipped up in my warm cocoon of a sleeping bag inside the deceptive safety of the tent. Not a sound can be heard within the camp, and outside, all of knowing nature holds its collective breath. Then somewhere out there under cover of night's murky muffle, a tumult of murder and mayhem rips the quiet. It's a lion kill, and throughout the earliest hours of the morning, the whole camp is mesmerized by a litany of full-chested primeval roaring that shreds the cloak of comfort, and chills the human soul. The rumbles resonate across the acacia-studded savanna plains. They are a blood-curdling challenge, and a warning from the dominant powers of the darkness. Later comes the ghoulish giggling whooping hysteria of the hyenas, and the yipping of the jackals. At dawn, the downward spiraling vultures will pin-point the killing ground.

Saturday, June 3, 2006. We arise in the chill of dawn at 5 a.m., and with the thrill of the lions' oration resonating within our subconscious, head for the rhinos' love nest, only to find it deserted. Then there is a movement out in the bush, and as I strain my eyes to unravel the African puzzle, two young macho-maned male lions emerge with the elegant, casual swagger that conveys their certainty that they are the kings of all they survey.

Next, we pile into the truck and take off into the dim light of the dawning day. The splendour of the African sunrise is a time when all of nature bursts into a spontaneous song of exuberance, in worship of its creator, and no visitor is left unmoved. Guinea fowls chatter in their distinctive click-clacking sounds, elegant blue cranes grace the creeks, a black korhaan calls out to its chicks, and overhead in a clear deep blue sky the martial eagles soar endlessly.

We round a bend in the road and suddenly they are there, tummy-up in the scrub beside our vehicle, a whole pride of lions in various extremely laid-back postures, often only revealing their positions by the flick of a tail or the twitch of an ear. Unlike other animals, they have no natural enemies (other than man), and can sleep off their full bellies without a care in the world.

It's time for breakfast! Christo drives off the road and parks beneath the widespread branches of a big old acacia tree. Everyone is now beginning to realize how difficult it is to spot the predators in their natural habitat, and we are careful to scan the surrounding bushveld continuously, as we boil the water and tuck into coffee, cereals, and sandwiches. Then there is a slight alarm, when someone spots three cheetahs loping by through the distant trees, but like phantoms, they are swallowed up in the natural blending of shades in the wild.

The Etosha Salt Pans which is a curious, white, flat place that melts into the distance in a blend of white dust and space (in the dry season), is matched only by its counterpart, the Makgadikgadi Pans, further to the south in Botswana. The surface at this time of the year is firm, and our truck has no problem driving out onto the pale, cracked surface. We stop and walk out away from the truck, which has an eerie abandoned appearance when we look back, rather like some weird looking shipwreck on a white lunar ocean.

Sunday, June 4. Etosha National Park. Wheels were made for rolling.... we pack and leave, heading eastward, passing by Rietfontein Halali, Springfontein, Noniams, Koinachas, all the way to Nambutoni Camp, where there is an old German fort; an impressive relic from former days. This area is the habitat of the mopane tree, with its distinctive butterfly-shaped leaf, and is home to the colourful mopane worms. These caterpillars are said to be rich in protein and they are eaten by the people. Luckily, nobody offers me a bite. Also prevalent in small herds, are the red hartebeest, the grassland antelope with their reddish-brown coats and outward curving horns.

While out on a game drive in the late afternoon, we spot a big lion and two lionesses lying on an elevated spot beside the road, staring off into the distance. Then the lionesses slink off into the savanna, stalking a lone giraffe a good distance away, with the lazy, whistle-blowing male trailing, and not making much of an effort to go undercover. They spend a good deal of time and energy in this pursuit, but all to no avail, as the giraffe spots them and gallops away.

CHAPTER 4: NAMIBIA AND BOTSWANA.

Monday, June 5, 2006. Northern Namibia. Our bags are packed and we're ready to go – it is with regret that we look back one last time as our truck roars off, leaving Etosha behind us, with only memories that are carried away to be held forever. Today the talk is all about the 'Hero's' theme party planned for tonight, for which we should all dress up in improvised costumes to look like some important world figure. In Tsumeb, a small non-descript town, there are signs of real poverty, from shifty eyed locals to ragged children begging with upturned palms. After doing the rounds we find a shop that sells clothing material, and the Afrikaans speaking female shop assistant is quite keen to help us. 'Who can I be?' I ask the others, in indecision. Carie studies me seriously for a moment and says, 'you're Ghandi', and that settles it, though I would have preferred her saying Brad Pitt, but that's the nature of the female eye. I buy a wide strip of white cloth and have my head shaved.

The next town is Grootfontein, a big dusty centre that once played a strategic military role in the days of the South African occupation. We hit the north-east route non-stop for a couple of hours, with the thorn scrub giving way to a more lush form of vegetation as we approach the Okavango River, which forms the border with Angola. From Rundu the eastward bound road enters the Caprivi Strip, a narrow stretch of land along the Zambesi River that separates Namibia from Angola, Zambia, Botswana and Zimbabwe.

Shortly before sunset we arrive at Ngepi Camp beside the Okavango River, across from Angola, - there it's known as the Cubango River - where we pitch our tents on the riverbank between the groves of tall african jacana, sausage, and sycamore fig trees. We are warned to take great care because hippos - Africa's no. 1 killers – after man - are a menace, as they sometimes choose to graze within the camp area after dark, and are liable to bite you in half if you get in the way. The two big young camp dogs give us a warm welcome, but we hear that their predecessors, Slim and Fatboy were taken by the crocs.

The camp has a marvelous bar just off the waterfront, with a pier and a protective cage for swimming in the crocodile infested water. There is another group of travellers staying over, and pretty soon everyone is congregating in the bar area, mingling and trying out the colourfully named list of shooter cocktails on offer. It's also Beer, the popular young Dutchman's birthday, so we're all in a celebratory mood. Then after dinner we appear in all kinds of 'hero's' costumes; such as Cleopatra, Arafat, and Philippe is dressed as a prostitute. 'Ghandi' arrives in his white robe, and later when the party gets too noisy, strolls off and gets really cooked on the quieter reaches of the river bank. Fortunately, he doesn't go rock 'n rolling with a croc or get his tenor stuck in a hippo's bass.

BOTSWANA.

Monday, June 6, 2006. The Okavango Delta. We break camp at dawn with most of us in the painful grip of a hangover, and drive east and then south until we reach the Botswana border. Immigration and customs are a brief formality, and then we head further south for another three hours until we reach Delta Dawn Camp on the fringe of the great swamp. Christo tells us that on entering Botswana, the Okavango River which has no sea outlet, empties into this vast swamp in the Kalahari Desert that swells up to about 15 000 square kilometres in peak season. 'Yaa' continues Christo, 'Besides the African people who live here, there are lion, elephant, cheetah, leopard, buffalo, rhino, zebra, giraffe, warthog, and all kinds of buck. And watch out for the birds, you will also see the fish eagle, the crested crane, and the sacred ibis if you have your eyes open. Keep your voices down and be careful, it's dangerous out there, but if you listen to your guides you'll be OK!' The greatest danger seems to be from dominant, territorial hippos, which are known to suddenly explode in a fury from the water, with their monstrous jaws agape, and bite boats in two.

The adventure is on; we transfer from the truck, taking only essentials such as food, tents and sleeping bags, and pile into 4-wheel drives for the trip through the lush vegetation to the lip of the marshland. There is a low buzz of excitement as we carry our stuff aboard the two motorboats, which are operated by smiling, white-toothed African men. We push off, and the boats follow the course of a narrow natural channel between dense banks of papyrus plants, that occasionally open onto islands. Several small herds of lechwe antelope that are feeding in the shallows and on the banks scatter when we appear. Feathered marshland dwellers announce their presence with shrill cries. Our drivers steer the boats with the assurance of experience, through a maze of channels, till we reach a low pier where there is a group of African men waiting beside several low mokoro dugout canoes.

We meet the polers who are to be our guides, and who assist us with the precarious transfer to the mokoros. There is Slea, the leader who will be with Beer and me, then there are, Morgan, Master, Captain, Cruiser, and RB. The mokoros enter a wide, flat area of the marshland, and in single file, with unerring precision, Slea and his team pole their way through the wonderland of reeds, water lilies and a myriad of other succulent water plants.

The poled mokoro dug-outs cleave the reed-fringed channels, as we float deeper into delta, dodging buffaloes and elephants, through a maze of lagoons and islands. We seem to be destined to be lost forever, following 'the river that never finds the sea', in the mysterious depths of the Okavango.

In the wafting morning mist, the free water spirits, Harun and Haruna dance in delight at the wild wattled cranes' elegant flight. In the hippo bulls rumbustious roar, the voice of the river god Tano, roams the reaches of the curving Cubango.

For more than two hours, we are close to heaven in a pristine water-world, with random bees, butterflies, and small birds for company. Slea's muscles ripple as he poles the dugout along with an easy, long-practiced motion, holding to his course despite the absence of any distinguishing landmarks. Our boat glides by a small verdant island with topi antelope grazing below an old baobab tree.

Later, as we approach a wider intersection between channels, Slea goes ` ssshhh', and places his finger across his lips while letting the dug-out glide slowly forward, as he points to our left. At first we think they're rocks, but then suddenly a massive hippo yawns lazily, revealing monstrous gaping jaws. In an instant everyone realizes how vulnerable we are in the fragile crafts, and no sound can be heard other than the water lapping around the boats, and distant birdcalls. Slow hand movements, and then cameras appear, as we grow bolder and go for the snaps.

Slea poling the mokoro through the Okavango

I remember reading about a recent real-life drama on the Zambesi River, to the north of here. Two tours guides were pointing out some distant hippos to the tourists in their boat, when one rose up from the depths below them and destroyed their craft, killing one of the guides in the process. The second guide, though injured, swam to the nearest shore to seek help, while the terrified tourists huddled together on a sandbank, exposed and defenseless until help arrived the following day - but that's an entire story on its own.

As the sun leans slightly towards the west, we arrive at an island clearing and moor the mokoros beneath gigantic jackalberry trees. It's all action as we eagerly disembark, unload, and carry our gear up to a clearing between the trees where we erect the tents. Slea and his men make their own camp in another clearing to our left.

After a quick lunch we are back in the mokoros again to explore a nearby island. The guides ask us to be quiet, and to follow their lead should we encounter any animals. They are only armed with pangas (African machetes), so caution and controlled retreat should be our strategy, with the 'each man (or woman) for himself' option, as a last resort. The game track we are following leads us through the verdant-virgin African bush, amongst an assortment of enormous trees, including the african ebony, the sycamore fig, and with the staggered array of stunningly photographic baobabs, which are objects of wonder. Heaps of fresh elephant dung appear on the path, causing us to eye our surroundings anxiously, as Slea and his men gather around and debate it, poking and prodding. 'No worry' he announces, 'maybe one day old, all OK'.

The sun weighs down on the crimson skyline, transforming the lily-flowered marsh world into a surreal, lilac laced pixy land. With silhouettes of the desultory baobabs frozen in immortal poses of demented ogres, we glide back to our camp in a mesmerized, silent wonder.

After a hot dinner around the blazing log fire, Slea and his team join us for drinks. They are all members of the Yei Delta folk he says, and pretty soon they begin entertaining us with melodic tribal songs and some lively, foot-stomping traditional dances. They are animated people, and their startlingly white teeth split their faces as they laugh and clap their hands in child-like fashion, while taking turns telling hilarious folktales about the hare and his barbaric uncle the baboon, and also the hippo. Later Slea claps his hands for silence, his face aglow in the firelight, 'now you do', he says to us. We go into a huddle, then, to the delight of the Africans, the comic Philippe hums a passable imitation of a violin as an accompaniment to Andreas and Marieke's elegant waltz. To round things off, Christo delivers a stirring rendition of the South African national anthem; Nkosi Sikele' iAfrika (God save Africa).

At bedtime most people wander off to their sleeping places, while Christo and I sip at a last beer beside the fire, and then decide to sleep right there. In typical African fashion, it is a very dark night, and once silence descends the continuous hippo roars can be heard reverberating across the swamp water throughout the night. Soft waves of lulling frog croak rise and fall as I drift off into my beloved parallel existence of dreamland. Suddenly I awaken partially, the fire's embers are glowing gently and there's the familiar smell of wood smoke, maybe I'll add a few small logs. When I push myself up and try to focus, my heartbeat accelerates dramatically, for there's a monster hippo looming out there on the fringe of the darkness. Frantically I try to stir Christo with my foot, but he's out of reach. 'Don't move' I think to myself. Then the beast comes forward, and when my terror is at its peak, I am shocked to see that it is only Marieke and Carie's tent. When I tell Christo the story in the morning he laughs and says, 'Ag Koos, I'm not afraid to sleep out with you man. The way you snore the animals will think we're wild beasts too, and leave us alone'.

Wednesday, June 7, 2006. Botswana. Exit from the Okavango Swamps. At the first light of day, the raw thrill of the fish eagles' call, in tandem with the hippos' didgeridoo, awaken us to the virgin glory of the delta's dawn. Anxious to 'seize the moment', high on pure oxygen, we set off for a pre-breakfast hike on our own island, following a couple of our guides. Buffalo dung on the ground, mmm, nasty customers, but our guides pronounce it to be several days old. Slea and his men point out the animal tracks, and identify those of the warthog and kudu, while from the prolific bird-life we get sightings of the painted snipe, a fishing owl and the lesser jacana, with guinea fowls abounding in the bush.

This is my idea of heaven, I don't want to leave, but from somewhere out there comes the undeniable call of the road, which is "… a wild call, a clear call, that may not be denied." (J. Masefield.)

When we arrive back at the edge of the swamp, Carie says goodbye in her way, by jumping into the water. Then we backtrack to immigration and all the way back to Ngepi Camp in Namibia.

NAMIBIA.

Wednesday, June 7, 2006 continued. Ngepi Camp. In the evening, we all gather in the pub after dinner, for a ride on the shooters and beer express to bliss and brain damage. Maybe we're suffering from `overload', as we've been subjected to a never ending kaleidoscope of natural beauty since the first day. For many of our group, animated conversation is the only way to get things into perspective, and there's no better setting than an African riverside pub. `Ghandi' later leaves the rowdy gathering to listen to the tales of the breeze along the river, with the camp dogs as company, and hippo bass and frog choir the nocturnal melody.

In the darkness the Okavango (Kubango) murmurs, swells and twirls, spurred by ferocious subtropical storms in the uplands of central Angola, it is a life-giving force, dissecting the savanna plains and nourishing all along its path. It runs through Namibia before descending into Botswana via a series of rapids known as the Popa Falls, to form a paradise within the Kalahari's wastelands. From its pure origin, it grows rich in alluvial deposits on its course to the delta, destined to bring life force to the swamps, before meeting its ultimate goal as a sacrifice to the sun god in the dry season.

`Ghandi' instinctively feels that the key to all of life lies within the flow of nature's pure liquid elements. With his body supposedly consisting mostly of water (or maybe alcohol), he feels the persuasion of the living river, and ponders on his own goal and destiny. Where is he going and why, and to what end? What will happen when his frail human body ceases to breathe? Will it be recycled? Will his life force be judged by a higher power, and found to wanting, or will it be elevated to a higher spiritual plane, or maybe just cease to exist? Does his real-life existence, as that of the Okavango, have a meaningful purpose, and ultimately like the evaporating waters rise up into the heavens to become part of a whole, to be reborn as pure, fresh rejuvenating raindrops, or some form of life upon the face of the earth?

He senses the latent presence of the Great Spirit of Life, a true but curious force, which in some mysterious fashion derives and lends its very real and potent power through ones belief therein. It seems that in the passing millenniums, people have gradually lost their direct spiritual bond with the natural elements. In an attempt to reestablish the link, the great, central force of life may have imparted elements of itself to its chosen ones, to reconnect with the evolutionistic, materialistic natured humans. He tries to imagine what it must feel like to be God. To send your emissaries out into the fields of life to enlighten human souls in anticipation of the golden harvest, and for the next two or so millennium the people are at each other's throats regarding which emissary was the real deal. In the ongoing `brawl, the emissaries' original messages of love, humility and forgiveness, have mostly been overlooked.

Thursday, June 8, 2006. The Caprivi Strip. In the early morning we follow the route through Divundu on the `golden highway' into the Caprivi Strip. We're in transit and the natural energy of my co-passengers threatens to boil over at times. Carie talks non-stop, Philippe moves up and down the aisle, grinning broadly, while others stretch, chat, play cards, do their diaries, or just watch the passing landscape.

Our truck enters Katimo Mulilo, a small town that was a South African military base in the 1970's, where as a young man I was part of the armed forces. We were trained to guard and patrol the jungles and marshlands of the Zambesi River border with Zambia, to combat armed insurgents in what now feels like a former life. We stop in the centre where I persuade Marieke to pose on the landmark toilet inside the gigantic, hollow baobab for a photo. Then our vehicle leaves the main route and heads southward till it reaches the Botswana border.

BOTSWANA.

Wednesday, June 8, 2006 continued. Chobe National Park. Our first stop is immigration, and then we proceed in a southerly direction. It is very dark when we arrive at the Chobe Park, where Christo parks in a clearing and we pitch our tents between the surrounding bushes. After dinner the 'hippo opera' lulls us to sleep.

Friday, June 9, 2006. Chobe National Park. Today our truck is given a rest as we board a few smaller open vehicles at 5 a.m., shivering in the early morning chill. In the dissipating darkness of dawn's half-light, one's eyes have difficulty distinguishing between shadows, objects, and animals, but everyone is on a razor edge of alertness, as this is prime viewing time.

We stake out a watering hole and as we are waiting, the parting bushes reveal the seldom sighted sable antelope approaching in single file. Magnificent animals, dark with white bellies, some weighing more than 200 kilograms, many have ringed horns longer than a metre, arched backward. Stepping softly through thick thorn-wood thickets, they draw near, as the leader continuously tests the air until they've had their fill of water and seemingly disappear.

We help ourselves to a light lunch, for Christo is down with diarrhea and vomiting, so we try to make him as comfortable as possible in the circumstances. The camp has an internet café with a really slow connection, the curse of most of rural Africa. My attempts to email photos are to no avail.

In the evening we board a river boat on the Chobe River for a sunset cruise. It's a big craft and there are several other groups of travellers aboard, with most people, including ourselves, dipping into the beers. At this juncture the river forms the border with Namibia. From the boat, the game viewing is spectacular, with herds of elephant and buffalo dominating the riverbanks at different places, while hippos can be seen in the water and on the smaller islands, feeding and splashing about. Barely submerged crocodile submarines lurk offshore, while splay-legged giraffes, and skittish herds of Kudu with their magnificent spiraled horns drink warily. Then, as the magical fiery setting of the Chobe sunset envelopes the boat, it slowly returns to shore in the shimmering twilight.

When we arrive back at camp, Christo is still incapacitated, so I take charge of the dinner preparations as we're having steaks cooked over the hot coals. Without him to direct operations, it's all a bit chaotic but we manage to connect the lights and get dinner done.

5

Zimbabwe

SATURDAY, JUNE 10, 2006. Christo has recovered sufficiently to drive us to our next destination, the ill-fated Zimbabwe. When some of us go to the toilets at immigration, the toilet paper consists of newspaper, neatly torn into squares, and so the foreigners slowly begin to understand the term, 'Third World'.

On our approach to Victoria Falls our truck suddenly comes to a halt, for crossing the road, seemingly in a state of agitation, is a small herd of elephants, hurrying off into the bush.

Then Christo pulls off the road again, and when we are all standing outside he points into the distance and says; 'listen'. We look ahead and see what appears to be a cloud of mist rising out of the hills in the distance, and hear a sound something akin to far-off cannon fire. It's Mosi-oa-Tunya; 'the smoke that thunders', as the Victoria Falls is called locally, working up a good head of steam.

With the continuous thundering sound in our ears, we enter the small town and set up our camp at the Victoria Falls Rest Camp, a vast tree shaded area with a restaurant and ablution blocks.

CHAPTER 5: ZIMBABWE.

Politically this is a very uncool place, as the 82 year-old dictator Robert Mugabe has brought this once thriving African economy to its knees. In former days Zimbabwe was called the bread-basket of southern Africa, but it now has to import food and has the highest inflation in the world. Mugabe set this all in motion by having white farmers ejected off their ground, and installing his cronies who have let the once verdant fields fall fallow. Instead of incorporating the white farmers into the agricultural system as advisors and managers, they were left bitter, homeless and unemployed, with no other option than to leave the country. Of course political opposition is barely tolerated, as Morgan Tsvangirai, the leader of the opposition found out recently, when he was arrested and brutally beaten by the police. Due to an unemployment rate of over 80%, Zimbabwe's southern neighbour, South Africa, is being overrun by illegal immigrants.

Christo stays behind to service the truck, while we set off to view one of the world's greatest natural wonders, the Victoria Falls. As we draw closer, the volume is deafening, akin to a million pounding Zulu war drums in tumultuous disharmony. The spectacular view awes one, as you dodge clouds of spray in the shifting winds, to see the sweeping torrent of the mighty Zambesi River drop more than one hundred metres down wide, mist-shrouded gorges in thunderous volumes of frothing, seething water. It is indisputable that nobody could survive a plunge over the edge and down into the steamy horror of the smoking abyss.

For each particle of racing water, the giddy ride over the lip of the precipice is the culmination of a long, eventful journey. It's the passing of a threshold, leading to an inevitable process of purification, renewal and change. It is not unlike the mortal human suffering a near-death experience, resulting in a spiritual awakening and renewed awareness of life. Immortal accounts of visits to these falls have been written by famous earlier travelers, such as Livingston, Selous, and many others.

Christo exchanges money for us on the black market. For US$10 I get 29, 000 000 Zim dollars, it's insane as I have to carry the money in a plastic bag as it won't fit into my wallet. We all spend a long time in the bathrooms trying to make ourselves presentable, for tonight we are to have a farewell dinner together, as this is the end of the road for most of the young Europeans who will be catching flights back home from here. Only Beer, Marieke, Carie, and I are to continue on the overland trip with Christo.

When we set off to the local Spur, I barely recognize some of the group members, with the flashily dressed Philippe easily taking the best dressed prize. It's hard to really enjoy your meal in a country where most people are hungry, yet we tuck into the restaurant food with relish, and seizing the moment, we order several bottles of wine, and drink nostalgic toasts to each other and to our intrepid leader. It takes an inordinately long time for each of us to pay his share of the bill, as one is counting out millions of dollars, albeit in large denominations.

When everyone heads for the casino section, I decide to burn the breeze downtown, and in the grip of a mellow haze, hit a few shebeens, where, despite the country's economic woes, the bars are crowded with local black people. Later, in the absence of street lighting, I'm hard pressed to find my way back to camp, as I wander through the dark streets with the thunder of Vic Falls dominating the evening quiet.

Sunday, June 11, 2006. Enter Zambia. In the morning I hand my pile of dirty washing to a grateful washer-woman. Instead of cash I pay her with the white 'Ghandi' robe I wore to the hero's party as an exchange. I need more local currency, so I secure the services of Lucky, a charismatic young local man to guide me. We enter a backstreet money exchange where bank notes are not counted, but weighed on a scale. Then I buy vodka and beer, after which Lucky sells me a bag of the local herbal remedy to ensure my wellbeing along the African trails.

A serious little African man stops me on the road, he says he's Mr. G. H. Hamanayanga, of 01-237225 Lusaka, and he's looking for a white farm manager for farm number 2815 Zinaba. I tell him I'll let him know if I find someone suitable.

Back at the camp there is great excitement as we all watch The Netherlands beat Serbia in the soccer world cup, to the delight of Beer and Marieke. Then the time of sadness is upon us, as I join Christo on a ride to the airport to drop off our co-travellers.

When we hit the road the truck seems quiet and empty, with only remnants of our former partners' presence remaining. Then we pass over the bridge across the Zambesi River, from where we have a spectacular view of the Victoria Falls, before we attend to the Zambian Immigration formalities.

6

Zambia

SUNDAY, JUNE 11, 2006 continued. Our truck passes many shacks, including the Heroes Restaurant & Grocery and the New Deal Tavern, before we turn off into a campsite beside the Zambesi River. We set up our two tents at dusk. There are only four of us, with Carie and Marieke sharing while Beer has decided he's going to sleep in my tent. Christo dosses in the truck. There is a place in the camp where we can exchange our dollars for the Zambian Kwatchas, before we try out the local fare in the camp's restaurant. We wash down the rather expensive (for Africa) food with Moosa beers before retiring early, as Marieke is not well.

Monday, 12 June, 2006. Via Livingston. We ply Marieke with medicine, as her condition has worsened overnight. Our departure is delayed as Christo is awaiting a cash transfer from South Africa, while Beer is also feeling under the weather with a slight case of diarrhea, and an unbelievable claim that he did not sleep well due to 'Ghandi's' snoring.

We prepare a bed for the white-faced Marieke in the narrow space between the lockers and the seating area, before driving to the town of Livingston, where we stop for some shopping. Then we're on the road again, via Chisekesi, Zimba, and Choma. The signs along the way read; Basic School, Chabota Supermarket, and I.P. Phiri & Sons. It's a long transit northwards, and the hard-ribbed road gives poor Marieke no respite, with an extra big bump causing the pile of mattresses to topple off the overhead lockers and bury her before I come to the rescue. We pass Mazabuka village, and enter the Manali Hills at sunset, but Christo misses the turnoff to our campsite in the dark, so we turn back later to spend the night in the Eureka Camp grounds. We set up camp and Beer moves back into his own tent.

Tuesday, 13 June, 2006. Lusaka. In the morning we drive into Lusaka, a modern looking city with wide boulevards lined with red flowering trees, where we stop at a shopping centre to buy supplies. We stock up on beer, vodka, wine and rum - bloody alcoholics!

Today is a transit day on a terribly bumpy pot-holed road that gives poor pale Marieke no relief. Beer is also not doing too well, with slight diarrhea, while Carie still fills all the empty space with chatter, and 'Ghandi' remains silent in his far-off world of the nowhere-man.

The truck zigzags between potholes, pounding along at a top speed of 40 km per hour. We pass by minor settlements with small shacks bearing grandiose names such as the Kacholola Shopping Centre, Nakolix Enterprises, Waleta Holdings, and Sakala Brothers. There is a turn-off to the right to Mozambique but we're heading north-east towards Malawi.

In the late afternoon we take the turnoff to Chipata, passing Only God Knows Grocery en route to Mama Rulas' Camp Ground, where we are welcomed by the unlikely combination of a Jack Russell and a Great Dane who are inseparable. Later, in a crowded bar we watch Brazil beat Croatia in the soccer world cup.

Wednesday, June 14, 2006. South Luangwa. We leave the main road for an atrocious dirt road heading north-west, in the general direction of the Congo (Zaire), towards the South Luangwa National Park. This is rural Africa, scenic with many small villages of round, thatched-roofed, mud-walled huts clustered together amidst groves of sycamore fig, palm, or papaya trees. Small, near-naked children run after us with arms outstretched, palms up, only to be swallowed up in the wake of our dust. The truck's shocks are incapable of dealing with this kind of abuse, and the whole vehicle bucks at the velocity of a pneumatic drill, while sometimes achieving a top speed of up to 20 km per hour. The only way to cope is to brace yourself with your legs while holding on with both arms. At a minor settlement, Christo suddenly pulls off the road, and we shudder to a halt in a cloud of dust beside JP & Sons Grocery & Bottle Store. With bruised butts and parched throats we stagger into the cool, narrow interior of the shop, as a small crowd of locals gather to watch. 'Habari', (Hi in Swahili) we greet the startled shopkeeper. 'First aid, we need first aid, where are the beers?' Soon we are downing chilled drinks on the shop's steps under the veranda. I venture out onto the clearing between the vendor stalls and purchase a bag of 'Vetkoek' - deep-fried dough balls- which my co-travellers partake in with some misgivings.

In the mid-afternoon we drive by a small herd of buffalo before arriving at Flat Dogs' - slang for crocodile- Camp on the banks of the Luangwa River. The camping area lies between the tall mopane, sycamore fig, and sausage trees, rife with flitting lovebirds, grey-headed parrots, hornbills, barbets, and broad-billed rollers. Light-fingered vervet monkeys gambol everywhere, and have to be driven off occasionally with a few catty shots. This campsite is situated beside the South Luangwa National Park and is not fenced in, therefore herds of elephant are known to stroll through at times, and hippos are said to invade regularly after dark for the rich grazing. Christo will sleep in the truck, and Carie, Marieke and Beer are going to erect their tents high up on the only available tree platforms, while I'll be camping at ground level. The camp supervisor comes over and says I must not keep any food in my tent, and I should not react or make any noise if I hear movements outside my tent at night. The surrounding area is also, of course, the habitat of big cats such as lions and leopards, but the nocturnal habits of the hippos, elephants and hyenas are of greater concern.

We find a marvelous bar beside a swimming pool, and before too long we are getting soaked, washing away the dust within and without. At sunset we stroll down to the riverbank to watch a large pod of hippos luxuriating in the Luangwa's loamy water. Within the sunset's golden wake, distances and shapes slowly lose their defining reality, but the game of life and death continues as a kingfisher falls from the sky, striking its prey below the river face in a feathered blur of liquid motion. With the whereabouts of all the hippos becoming unclear, the startling call of the fish eagle resounds in the twilight, as we retreat to our campsite and build a cheerful log fire beside the truck.

After a good dinner, our once weary group members gain a new lease on life around the bar, mingling with the handful of other travellers. Later 'Ghandi' detaches himself and wanders off in the general direction of his tent. He does not stop long there however, but waits for his eyes to adapt to the dark, before walking down to the border of the camp, and then strides out into the darkness beyond. He is possibly a little crazy, definitely foolhardy, so his behaviour now is not entirely unexpected. Then again, in mitigation, he is a veteran of night-hiking in the bush, and is very alert and alive right now, with all his senses probing for any hint of danger. By his reckoning, nothing bigger than a hyena would be interested in chewing on his skinny arse. Away from the contamination of the camp lights, he sees his surroundings in minute detail, and moves slowly forward through the tall trees and low scrub, until he reaches the river bank where he sits on a log and melts into the natural melody of the Zambian night.

Africa will talk to you if you take the time to go out there and listen. 'Ghandi' closes his eyes, cups his hands and blows a salute to the breeze, to changing reality, to life on the edge - to the moment! The Luangwa pulsates with the rich life forms it harbours. Occasional hollow hippo hurrahs halloo back and forth across its surface, while a lonesome fishing owl hoots, by rote, its familiar haunting 'who – hoo'. The wind carries the loony, hiccupping whoops of hyenas from afar. In the nearby trees, the high-pitched, click-clucking chatter of roosting guinea fowl pierces the solitude. A solitary pigeon coos intermittently, frogs croak a soothing lullaby, a cricket's shrill, needle-thin serenade stirs the air. Time stands still, mind stretches, unconnected letters float to the surface forming words. The silent spaces are speaking, saying something important. Sixth sense alert! Something's wrong!

What's the matter? 'Ghandi' starts from his reverie; there's a monstrous form cantering slowly towards him. It appears, disappears and reappears along the undulating river bank. It's a hippo! For an instant, he considers climbing the smallish tree beside him, then reconsiders and runs for his life. Nobody puts on a macho act when there's a hippo around, and few can match Koos for speed when there's one on his tail!

I blunder into camp all out of breath to find the others sitting around the low, glowing embers of the fire, grinning owlishly at me, as if they're used to me coming in out of the dark like this. 'Have a drink', slurs Christo, and pours me a good shot of rum as I open a beer. We see the ladies, and Beer, off to their tree platforms while there's still a good chance they won't fall off, before he and I dig into the remnants of the bottle in the fading fire light. I ask Christo about his life. 'When I was younger I used to do a lot of drugs', he says, looking deeply into his drink. 'But I was getting nowhere, so I decided to cool it, and now I'm happier with my life'. 'I don't do drugs', I say, 'but when I'm on holiday I like to smoke a little weed to put some colour into the scenery, it's harmless and is very relaxing'. 'Yaa, I know, me too, but only on occasion these days', says Christo, 'I just have to be careful, because I'm responsible for my passengers and don't want any problems or complaints.' He tells me many stories about life on the trail, and despite his obvious love for the outdoors, I can see that he's unfulfilled. He had a love affair with a European woman but his lifestyle doesn't allow permanence. I worry about him, as he's very intelligent, and though he's a qualified motor mechanic, he should be an engineer.

The camp is deathly quiet after I've zipped up, and I'm falling asleep when I hear the movement of some very big animals out in the night close by. Then it strikes me, ' oh shit – I forgot to get rid of the apple in my bag!'. I hurriedly find it, take a quick bite, then partially unzip the front of the tent and toss it as far as I can. My sleep is a sound but disturbed one. In the darkest hours of the night, a lion roars several times in the near vicinity, and in the early morning, large bodies are moving near my tent again. Before dawn I hear a tinkling, and the sound of far-off female giggling, ah, I guess some ladies are too scared to come down in the dark and are having a pee from the tree platform – maybe to repel invaders?.

Thursday, June 15, 2006. South Luangwa National Park. It is very cold when we leave on open game viewing vehicles at 6 a.m., huddled together and wrapped in our sleeping bags. At daybreak, the wild wood pigeons' lilting lyrics filter through the shady trees of the miombo woodlands of the park. Mounds of earthy smelling dung and broken tree branches mark an elephant crossing. The crisp air has a refreshing, savanna-flavored aroma. Clusters of wildebeest, zebra and giraffe emerge warily from their nocturnal haunts. Around a bend in the road, we come upon a buffalo cow nursing its glistening newborn calf. Skittish impala antelope skip by, undulating through the scrub, while chattering red-arsed baboons chase one another up and down the trees.

We stop for coffee and biscuits on the bank of the Luangwa River, and disembark to stretch our legs and take a leak. On a sandbank below several monster crocodiles are basking in the sun. A pod of hippos floats lazily in the water. We hurriedly board the vehicles again when, downstream from us, a small herd of elephants emerges from the trees with a high pitched trumpeting, as the matrons drive the calves down to the water's edge.

In the evening Beer has a crisis when he wants to retire to his tent on the tree platform. There are several large hippos grazing nearby. The night watchman accompanies us out into the dark, flashing his spotlight about until we spot them. He then picks up stones and hurls them in the beasts direction, while shouting loudly and waving his arms, instructing us to do likewise until they move off grunting grumpily. Right – now I know how to kick a hippo's butt!

I decide to take my nocturnal stroll in the opposite direction to the departing hippos. Once again, I proceed with the utmost caution, scanning every foot of the terrain ahead, scrutinizing every shadow, until I'm alone, way out in the darkness surrounded by bushveld. I get involved with the blowing breeze, listen to the night sounds, try to imagine being lost out here in the wilderness, and wander off. Passages from the autobiography of the explorer Frederick Selous written in the 1800's come to mind. Once, while riding on his first hunting expedition somewhere in this area, his horse tossed him and took off with his rifle and gear. He spent several days and nights out in the bush with no jacket or matches for a fire, a young, inexperienced Englishman, unarmed and alone, before miraculously recognizing a hill and finding his way back to the camp. Thrilling but scary! I glance around, there are no distinguishing features and the landscape looks exactly the same in every direction. In a moment of madness, to silence the challenging voices of the night, I close my eyes and twirl. Then I take stock, and when doubt sets in I retreat back in the direction in which I suppose the camp lies, and soon the welcoming glow of light warms my way.

In the early hours of the morning, we are shocked out of a dead sleep by a tremendous caterwauling out there in the dark – a baboon kill by a leopard! The sheer thrill of the survivors' terror cuts through the night. Once again, some big animals pass by my tent, as I lie motionless in my sleeping bag. Later, a strong-smelling, fearsome beast sniffs and scratches at the entrance of my tent.

Friday, June 16, 2006. Southern Zambia. Today is a long wearisome transit day, as we have to contend with the atrocious road back to Chipata. First stop is at the JJ Hiporama Shopping Centre for supplies and fresh bananas. After a brief lunch break at Mama Rulas, we pass through customs at the Mchinji border post.

7

Malawi

FRIDAY, JUNE 16, 2006 continued. Lilongwe. The road carries us through the ineffably beautiful scenery of the ever-changing landscape. An interesting feature is that the traditional mud huts are square and not round as in Zambia. We pass by the usual local business enterprises consisting mostly of shacks along the way. There's `God is the answer' Tea Room and Gica Joe Corner Shop, before we pass Dwangwa Village and arrive at a campsite in the modern-looking capital, Lilongwe, where we change dollars for the Malawian Kwatcha.

Saturday, June 17, 2006. Central Malawi. This country has that carefree sub-tropical flavour that comes from a lush, green landscape with plentiful papaya, mango, and tall palm trees.

We stop beside a market area at Salima Village. It's time to try Chichewa, the local language; `moni' for `hello' and `mtengo bwanji ?' for `how much?'. We wander through the stalls, curiously checking out the wares, while we similarly attract a lot of attention. In Korea the locals often say `waeguk saram' when they see a foreigner, while here we frequently hear `mzumu', which means `white foreigner'. I buy peanuts and fresh peas then take out my camera for a picture. When we depart, Beer spots some guy taking off with my camera case, which

I had accidentally dropped. Luckily, nobody comes to his aid when I catch him and take my property back.

The road winds by scenic mountains and green fields with crops of tea, coffee, corn, and cassava, and then subjects us to refreshing views of the startlingly blue Lake Malawi. This is a small, but more densely populated country, and many people are walking beside the road, while there are frequent mud-hut villages nestled between the tall trees.

Then the truck stops abruptly. It's a roadblock of heavily armed uniformed men. A bored-looking, flamboyantly dressed police officer climbs into the back of the truck, struts up the aisle, and declares loudly; `open all your bags. I want to see what's in them.' He starts in the front of the truck and slowly works his way to the back where I'm sitting. Christo previously said that his truck had never been searched before, and of course there is absolutely NO WAY I want any nosy policeman looking too deeply into my bag. In an instant of inspiration, I place my Korean hand massager, a ring of hard studded rubber at the top. When he gets to me, he immediately grabs it and tilts his head in question. I keep waving him closer, until our heads are almost touching, then I cup my right hand and whisper; ` I use it for sex - the women love it', and wink, man-to-man, while nodding my head knowingly. He's fascinated, and pretends he understands when I attempt an impossibly complicated, impromptu explanation on how it works. We are on hand-shaking terms when he departs, and of course, my bag is long forgotten.

The campsite at Kande Beach is very cool, lying on the shore of the lake, shaded by giant Red Mahogany trees. It has a shop, a pub and restaurant, ablution blocks and bungalows. Christo is pretty chuffed, as part of the deal is that he gets a free bungalow. After lunch he invites me in, lights up, and offers me a big, fat, spliff. `Care for one of these?' He asks, grinning at my reaction. `Yaa', he says. `It's part of the overland trip's tradition. Every group that stops over here gets stoned, this is a safe place.' He shows me a big gourd of weed he bought at the gate on our way in. Well, when in Rome...as if I need prompting.

Later, in a mellowed mood, I drift down to the beach, enjoying the warm sunshine on my body, the lack of urgency and the joy and freedom of life on the side-stream. On the beach, I remove my sandals and look around, taking in the marvelous view. Across the lake, in the hazy distance is Mozambique. I read somewhere that Lake Malawi is about 365 miles long and 52 miles wide. As I stroll along I come across Beer, Marieke, and Carie relaxing in the sun. 'Watch out for sunburn', I warn them. 'Your bodies are all very pale'. We chat, and then I wander on. It strikes me that we do not have a particularly warm relationship. I guess I've been a bit preoccupied. Beer and Marieke have made it clear to all from the start that they intend to be faithful to their respective lovers in Holland, while Carie drinks and talks a lot, always seemingly out to try to prove that she's one of the boys, but is kind of distant with me. I make a mental note to try to be friendlier, even though we're worlds apart.

Later just before sunset, I meet a local Rasta man who goes by the name 'Rob' and is an artist. He tells me that the lake contains more than 600 kinds of fish, and that most of them are varieties of a colourful evolutionary species called cichlids. He warns me that as most people are really poor it's best not to go for walks along the lakeshore late at night. Later we go to check out the artwork in his place on a street lined with colourful arts and crafts shacks. The traditional artwork on display is of an extremely high standard and I regret not being in a position to buy souvenirs.

Sunday, June 18, 2006. Kande Beach, Lake Malawi. A guide comes to pick some of us up for a church service in the early morning. He leads us through verdant cassava fields to a small rural, village church. He tells us that all the ground belongs to the local chief who allocates fields to different families, which is the traditional African way. It's a very 'colourful' church service, complete with singing and dancing. The uncomplicated simplicity and obviously true devotion of African worshipers shames most outsiders. Several members of the community feel compelled to share touching, real life stories. Their genuine love of life and the true light of faith that radiates from their faces are inspiring. They even have an interpreter for us. When it's time for collection someone gives a live chicken, all trussed up, as an offering.

After lunch Christo informs us that it's a tradition for all the men on the trip do something crazy with their hairstyles at this point – the women are spared. Christo and Beer get shaved 'mohawk' style while

I get the skinhead look, as I don't have enough hair to support such a spiffy style.

In the afternoon we gravitate down to the beach, where an overnight wind had blown up some really good surf, which is rolling in with big curved wave formations. Pretty soon I'm body surfing near perfect waves, with Marieke and Carie trying to follow suit, while Beer drifts off to sleep on the beach.

Before long I'm enveloped in a wonder water world, riding perfect wave after wave. As I swim back into the surf again, I spot Marieke waving frantically at me. She's shouting something about not being able to help Carie, who's drowning. I launch my body sideways and strike out towards them, just as a wave breaks over us. For a terrible moment it's as if I'm stuck in the trough and cannot reach them. Then Carie suddenly appears before me, and I take hold of her just as another wave breaks, pushing us under again. I hold her around the waist, and propelling myself from the lakebed, I lift her high up, giving her a chance to breathe. Then as we break free in the sucking swell, I take her wrist firmly in my right hand while she locks my grip with her other hand. In an instant our eyes meet and I smile encouragingly. Then comes a tremendous struggle through the seething waters. To her credit she keeps calm and never attempts to cling to me, which is every rescuer's nightmare. I look back and see that Marieke is struggling valiantly to keep up, but she shakes her head and flashes me a smile when I offer my free hand. When we reach the shallows everyone is OK, but I'm a bit buggered and lie down in the sun, while the girls return to camp.

We have an afternoon lie-down, and as sunset approaches, we all gather in the enclosure where our truck is parked. Christo is steaming a 'space-cake' in a big, heavy African pot on the side of the wood fire. It' a chocolate cake recipe and is loaded with 'weed', so we all open beers and watch Christo's 'bake' with eager anticipation. Beer rigs up the wiring to connect the iPod, and soon the party is on, with the drinks flowing freely, while Christo and I share spliffs.

When Christo shouts, 'come and get it', we place the cake on the folding table, cut it into slices and help ourselves. They all have one slice and watch wide-eyed as I devour five – it's a good cake and I have a sweet tooth! The general verdict is that it doesn't have much punch, but

Christo and I just grin, as we know that taken orally, weed takes about an hour to kick in – and so it does! Later Marieke wanders over to where I'm standing and rubs my smooth head, beaming broadly at me as my ugly mug cracks into a wide grin and I wink at her. This sets us both off, and every time we make eye contact we start laughing till we're rolling on the ground holding our sides. This gets the others going too, except for Beer, who wanders back to his tent in a serious frame of mind, and later approaches Christo and asks if he can be taken to a doctor as he's having mental problems. He says his thoughts are scattered, he's feeling light-headed and kind of spaced out. 'Congratulations!' says Christo. 'You're stoned at last'. With his problem diagnosed, Beer relaxes and has another beer, while exploring the newfound space within his mind. Carie becomes quiet and introspective, as she dwells on her near-drowning experience, but with some prompting she puts it behind her, for tonight we're celebrating life, not death. Hammered, we stagger through the black veil of darkness to the light fountain of the waterfront pub, where the party continues. The pool game is a shambles, as we're too cock-eyed for sharp shooting but who cares, we're all having fun!

Monday, June 19, 2006. Kande Beach. In the morning we're seriously hung over, but gather ourselves in time to meet a guide who promises to lead us to the local school. There we meet Mr. Dixon Chirwa of Kande Private Secondary School (Box 10, Kande, Malawi, tel. 265 1357268), who tells us of the tremendous problems they face in an impoverished society where most parents cannot even afford the annual school fees. Another problem, he says, is the increase in the number of parental deaths due to Aids related diseases. When he takes us into the elementary school area, we are swamped by young children wanting to touch us and have their picture taken. They also touch our hearts, and we are all so moved that we make donations far above what our budgets really allow.

In the evening we meet Sickner, Chief Fukamapili's son who is a well-spoken, intelligent man. He says that they belong to the Tonga Tribe, which has 25 chiefs. He tells us of the many problems they face in the modern world, amongst others, that there is only one doctor for every 50,000 people. Later they serve us a simple, but delicious meal of rice, beans, spinach and sweet potato.

Tuesday, June 20, 2006. Chitimba Beach, Lake Malawi. Our truck follows the road through the lush vegetation as it heads northward, passing over scenic mountains to rejoin the lake's curving coastline at Chitimba Beach. There we find that another group of truck-born backpackers has already established themselves. They are also going north to Zanzibar Island before they will turn back towards southern Africa. There is a bar and a restaurant right on the beachfront, where many people are hanging out. Others are playing games on the beach. We soon get a frisbee game going and later cool off in the lake.

In the evening, after supper, we join the boisterous party in the open-air pub area. A voluptuous, big-boobed, emerald-eyed, German sounding woman catches my eye, so I push through the crowd and shamelessly hit on her, and she seems to enjoy the additional attention. Her name is Janita, and she's an East German surgeon visiting Africa for the first time. As the stirring spirit of Bachus spurs me into action, I take her by the hand and lead her away from the crowd to a low-burning log fire on the beach, where we can sit close together and talk. Janita is not a procrastinator however. She suddenly grabs me behind the neck and begins to kiss me passionately. Maybe I need to add an element of speed to my seduction technique!

Wednesday, June 21, 2006. Northern Malawi. We hit the road some time after 6 a.m. with most of us nursing serious hangovers. Our course follows the coastal route northwards, via Karonga where we stop to buy supplies at a local market. To the east, the granite fanged heights of the Nyika Plateau fall behind as we reach the northern border and check out through the Malawian Immigration office. We cross the Songwe River and proceed to the Tanzanian Immigration office.

8

Tanzania

WEDNESDAY, JUNE 21, 2006 continued. Iringa. We each have to pay US$50 for a Tanzanian visa. Though there is a demarcated 'baggage check' area, thankfully nobody threatens to inspect our things, so we pass through and take the northbound road, which leads by coffee and tea plantations to Mbeya. From there the road takes an east, northeast twist and begins to climb upwards as it enters a stark plateau. We are now beginning to leave the Christian south behind, for many Islamic mosques can now be seen in the small mountain villages.

In the late afternoon we arrive at 'the old cottage,' as the Iringa campsite is called (I believe the original farm house is somewhere close by). It's in the middle of nowhere, and as the setting sun drops, so does the temperature. Surprise!! The truck bearing Janita and her group arrives and she pitches her tent in the bushes close to mine. Later we manage to stroll off together for a romantic interlude in a grass hut that serves as a bush pub. Then we leave, armed with a bottle of wine to an even more private location.

Thursday, June 22, 2006. Dar es Salaam. It's really cold when we leave at 6 a.m. in the pale light of an African dawn. Around midday the truck begins to descend into 'Baobab Valley,' via a narrow road. It's a spectacularly scenic place, where thousands of baobab trees cover the surrounding hills and the deep valley in an absolutely unique setting. Halfway down the steep decline we pull off the road for a pit stop. As we chat beside the road another truck comes labouring upwards from the opposite direction. When it draws level with us, a dark-skinned man leans out and aims a tautly drawn catapult at Christo's face from the passenger's seat. 'Do you want to die today?' I call out to him. He lowers the catapult, and showing a mouthful of startlingly white teeth, laughs uproariously, as the truck continues on its way.

In the afternoon we enter the ancient city of Dar es Salaam, and drive through the slums until we reach the city centre, where we park and go shopping. The moment we step out of the truck we are besieged by would-be moneychangers, guides, salesmen, etc. First stop is to change our dollars to the Tanzanian shilling. It's a big, crowded, unruly city, and we are glad to get back and proceed to the oceanfront. It is also apparent that we've entered the sphere of Islamic influence, as many men wear white robes with a fez on their heads, and several mosques can be seen. We drive to the waterfront and onto a car ferry, which transports us across a narrow straight and drops us on an island.

The Mikadi campsite is situated behind the pub/restaurant area on the beachfront of the sparkling blue Indian Ocean. This is our first view of the sea since leaving the Atlantic Ocean at the Skeleton Coast in Namibia.

On our arrival, I stroll out under a green canopy of trees to select a secluded spot for my tent. Suddenly the foliage above me shakes and parts, as a huge coconut smashes through and hits the ground near me with a mighty thump. I'm startled and look up to see that it fell from the top of a very tall palm tree. A black man appears from somewhere and rushes to my side, pats me on the back and says happily, 'Hey you much lucky man, this nut he hitta you on the head you pretty dead guy'. He picks up the coconut and disappears. Shaken, I pitch my tent far from the tree.

We spend the afternoon on the beach, swimming in the clear, blue warm swells of the Indian Ocean. The beach is littered with bright seashells, and there are numerous cowries, the true jewels of the ocean. Small crabs scurry from cover to cover, while overhead seagulls glide and dive with raucous cries. This is the perfect antidote to 'travel ache'.

More backpackers arrive, and in the evening I'm delighted to find Janita at the bar. There is a festive feeling in the air, in this near perfect setting, as everyone washes off the trail dust with beer and shooters. There are several good Tanzanian beers available, including Mosi, Ndovu, Serengeti, Kilimanjaro and Safari Lager. The smiling black bartenders keep saying 'Hakuna matata'; Swahili for 'no worries'.

As the evening degenerates, I lead Janita down to the beach for a touch of moonlit romance, then as passions flare, we retreat to the safer confines of a more private retreat.

Friday, June 23, 2006. Stone Town, Zanzibar Island. Christo and most of our group are too hung over to prepare breakfast, so we order coffee and toast in the bar area. Carie is nursing a bruise on her face. Apparently, a pole she was leaning against, late last night, failed to give her the support she needed.

We pack and make our way through the city's early morning traffic to the Ferry Terminal, where we buy tickets and board, carrying only our backpacks. Janita joins me, and soon we exchange our seats for the open air at the back of the boat. Beer is also there sitting in a corner. He has a hangover and is feeling really sea-sick. I pass him my Korean hand-massager, which seems to help, as it stimulates all the natural healing reflexes within the palm of the hand.

The powerful ferry cuts a swath across the iridescent blue-green swells beyond the harbour, throwing waves of spray up in its wake, as it gradually leaves the African shoreline, and heads out into the great deep sways of the warm tropical waters. Flamboyant Arabian dhows, with their lateen sails billowing in the breeze, can be seen in the distance, while shoals of flying fish shimmer in the sun rays. Our craft passes the well-forested Chumbe Island, with its whitewashed lighthouse, before our first sighting of Zanzibar Island.

The so-called Spice Island is said to have once been a major slave-trading centre, with its Old Slave Market at the heart of operations. It has been controlled successively by the Portuguese, the Arabs, the British, and it now belongs to Tanzania. The number of passing dhows increases, as we sail up the coast towards Stone Town, the capital, and soon we catch glimpses of fascinating architectural structures of former ages, that dominate the waterfront approach.

The harbour waterfront where we disembark is a rough, boisterous place. A local man, resembling the fabled Ali Baba, fortunately guides us to immigration, where we have a long wait in the hot, crowded street. Then we follow our guide into a fascinating labyrinth of ancient white triple-storied houses, with balconies that boast beautiful pillars or patterned facades and carved wooden shutters. We pass through two-metre-wide streets, by doorways with carved wooden pillars of urns, and flowers, and bright bazaars selling artwork, beads, carved giraffes, and elongated statues of Maasai warriors. At the Narrow Street Hotel, our smiling landlord checks us in, and we go up to our rooms and bounce on the soft beds, shower, and head out onto the streets again to catch up on a bit of local history.

In an attempt to atone for this island's shameful past, an Anglican Cathedral was erected on the site of the former slave market, with its altar placed directly over the former slave whipping post. An indelible heartache pervades the silent stone carvings of men and women shackled together by their necks. Yet this belated show of collective guilt and repentance cannot erase the lasting harm to the African psyche. In most places, education is rudimentary. Internationally, discrimination against people of African descent continues, most African countries are ravaged by Aids, while the perpetually upturned palms across the continent say it's payback time. Maybe it is, but development of self-sufficiency would help them far more than aid. According to reports on the internet, 500 million Africans still subsist on less than $2 a day, while factions of the political class and their business cronies have become extremely wealthy. International non-governmental agencies estimate that conflicts are costing the continent $18 billion per year. This ongoing cycle of violence hinders growth. Imagine if that money was used for better education and health, and to combat the HIV/AIDS crisis.

The muezzin's call sounds through the narrow streets, as we aim to the west of Stone Town. The balcony of the Africa House Hotel offers unsurpassable views of the island's sunset, with its oceanfront vista of heady coconut palms and flying dhows marvelously silhouetted by the dying sun. It is there that I find Janita, in the grip of sombre reflection, with a cocktail in her hand and questions in her eyes, for tonight we should say our farewells, possibly forever. Now we'll have fun warmth and laughter, but what will tomorrow bring? However, nobody is allowed to be melancholy for too long when Koos is around, and I soon whisk her off to the splendid open-air seafood eatery, in the vendors' market at the waterfront. There, you can select your own seafood, to be barbecued and served at rough wooden tables lined with benches.

Behind us, the old city is a play of dancing shadows and mystique, with white-robed figures flitting surreptitiously though the unlit alleys, seemingly engaged in mysterious cloak-and-dagger activities. Doorways are barred, and dim light gleams through shuttered windows. I gently guide the apprehensive Janita out into the darkness for gin and tonics, at a waterfront place called the Mercury Restaurant, before our passionate leave-taking in her room at the Safari Hotel.

Saturday, June 24, 2006. Zanzibar. Sugar and spice and all things nice. Abdul our guide picks us up at our hotel and leads us to Creek Road, where we catch a dala dala (taxi) to the spice plantations at the centre of the island. There we enter the aromatically flavoured red light district of the culinary senses. Abdul picks a leaf and offers it to me. `Smell this' he says. I inhale its familiar fragrance but can't place it. `Now you taste,' he says. `Ah' I've got it! `It's cinnamon!'. He introduces the spices in their raw state by offering bark, small branches, or leaves for us to taste and smell. We sample ginger, cloves, nutmeg, coffee, vanilla, pepper, cardamom, green light red lipstick, turmeric, lemon grass, saffron, cumin…There are teak, jackfruit, dorian, breadfruit, coconut, and a myriad of other trees. It brings to light how far removed we've become from the natural world. Never again will I use supermarket purchased spices without being transported back to the cool plantations of Zanzibar.

In the afternoon we cram into an old dala dala, which whisks us off across to the further side of the island. The driver cruises along tracks at random on the wide bumpy dirt road, and only veers back to his side when an oncoming vehicle threatens. The road leads by scenic villages of wooden structures lying between clusters of coconut palms. Children chase chickens through the trees, people sit chatting on stoops, and in the general course of things, life appears to move at a slow pace.

The driver takes a turnoff to 'Sunset Bungalows', but stops when the track seriously deteriorates, and that's it - we have to walk the rest of the way. The road passes over a crest before dropping down through verdant thickets to white, coconut palm-lined beaches.

Sunset Bungalows is made up of wooden structures tumbling down several terraced levels to the beach, where the cool, tree-shaded restaurant and pub lie. There to meet and show us to our respective bungalows are Christo, and Sula, the tall, sultry, German-accented manageress. As usual, Marieke and Carie are sharing, with Christo and Berend together, while I get bungalow no. 4 all to myself.

To be let free in the tropics, cut off from CNN's daily horror show is pure human delight! There is fresh coconut juice to quench the thirst, and the sparkling blue swell of the Indian Ocean's warm waters for a swim to heaven. The magical sunset heralds the coming of the night with its clear, unblemished ceiling of sparkling, silver stars. Local island men drag several logs of driftwood up the beach for a bright bonfire. A local herbalist offers me his wares, the menu offers cheap seafood, while the bar offers cold beer. I think I could hang out here for some time. To the side of the pub there is a pool table, where locals take on tourists in animated games, while others gather around the fire where an island man is playing a guitar and singing soulful ballads in Swahili.

Sunday, June 25. Zanzibar Island. At the first light of dawn I set off, passing several vendor stalls selling souvenirs and beautiful African arts and crafts, to follow the pristine coastline in a northerly direction. I burn a toast to the breeze and take in my surroundings, as I allow my mind to drift, enjoying the freedom of the moment. To my right, the beach is bordered by a low cliff-face, which runs parallel to the seafront. Lazy waves roll in from the left, sending their sparkling, foamy wash jetting across the sloping white sand. Overhead exuberant seagulls coast on puffs of pure ocean breath, while polished cowrie shells with unique markings nestle between the colourful clutter of seashells that mark the tide line. In a former age before human values went askew, these precious jewels of nature served as a monetary currency amongst the tribes.

A coastal settlement appears ahead. It's Nungwi, which is at the northern tip of the island. In the afternoon I try to return here with

Beer and Marieke, but we find that the tide rises right up to the cliff face, and have to scramble up and follow a path through the thickets and rocks. It's Christo's birthday, so we buy him a bright green t-shirt with an African motif.

In the evening, we treat Christo to a great seafood dinner of lobsters and wine. He puts in the hard hours in the heat of the truck's cab, is calm in the face of threat or danger, and is never too tired to help out. `Speech, speech', we call out as we drink a toast to him. `I want to thank yous all for a blerrie lekker (S. African for bloody nice) party, jislaaik (S. African for gee whizz) yous is all blerrie good oues (S. African for guys) and I'm enjoying this trip with you!' he says, beaming at us over his raised wine glass. When we revert to beer and shooters, the party degenerates a bit. Later I invite Christo to my bungalow to burn a traditional African sacrifice to the breeze. Thereafter I'm kaput, but he still makes it back to the beach.

Monday. June 26, 2006. Zanzibar Island. In the morning we take stock – all members hung over but alive, though Carie has lost her teeth aligner and there's a bit of memory loss all round. Christo leaves to take care of business in Dar es Salaam.

Today it's business as usual for the locals. Many women are tugging at ropes, hauling fishing nets ashore and others are harvesting seaweed, while the men are tinkering with their boats and fixing nets. I start to wonder who is the better off. These fisher people are at the bottom end of the international social ladder, yet from here, it looks a bit more relaxing than working out there in the main stream.

Bodysurfing in the Indian Ocean with many fruit and coconut juice breaks is the ideal remedy for the after effects of alcohol abuse, and after lunch time I'm a new man with a plate of fish, chips, and salad under my belt.

After sundown, I'm having drinks with the gorgeous Sula when we are joined by Rachel, a Congolese refugee who makes a living as an artist. She is a bubbly, well-spoken, stunningly good-looking African woman, continually bursting into pleasant peals of spontaneous laughter. Later she and I stroll up to sit on the porch of my bungalow and drink beers as we chat, and the subject of her past comes up. Her dark soulful eyes change to a deep abyss of fear, as she talks about her homeland, the Congo, which is rich in mineral wealth, but has been racked by civil wars ever since independence, as various factions and personalities vie for control. Once, when she was a teenager, returning home through a forest, she found that her village had been plundered and burned to the ground by militias. Her family members had been hacked to death with pangas. Tears stream from her eyes and her body shudders uncontrollably as she recalls the horror and her subsequent flight and rape by soldiers. I'm horrified at the stark reality of her tale, and hold her hand, trying to lead her away from the terror of the past to her current life. Africa has moulded her from a naïve village girl to a tough, independent, worldly-wise woman with a radiant soul. Had she been a white western woman, she would have enjoyed trauma counseling, and protective care, but as a rural black African woman, nobody gave a damn if she drowned in the deep end. Listening to her makes me ashamed of the way the world is, and ashamed that I've done so little to make it a better place. Overhead, the rising moon-face weeps and hangs its head in despair.

I start to wonder what on earth we are all doing and what can be done to improve things. I imagine each person on the continent being presented with the choice of either the present situation, or the continent's current national boundaries being eliminated, and the greater part of the chaotic continent being controlled by chosen academic experts in various fields of government. It seems to me that democracy does not work on most of this continent. All that happens in many countries is that a small group of people seizes power and imposes a kind of dictatorship, under the pretext of democracy, without regard to tribal law or basic human rights, which are often violently opposed, resulting in prolonged, bloody civil wars. It would be interesting to see how many people would prefer to continue in the current way if they had a viable choice.

Each person on the continent should have access to the truth; that all of black Africa was once ruled by tribal monarchs, and that modern states are a colonial creation with scant regard to tribal lines, a situation exploited by those in power. Then a referendum should be held as to whether the majority wants to continue with the status quo, or (for example) if the continent should be divided into wider tribally-related areas, run by pools of African-born experts. A government of people with special expertise chosen from all these regions should have final control over this loose federation of states. I imagine a new Africa free of weapons and strife, a place where natural resources as well as tribal culture are protected and nurtured, a continent with a billion dollar tourist industry.

One of the first steps would of course be to collect all weapons in a central, (initially) UN controlled armory, as the continent is brimming with firepower. Defence should fall under the control of a federal-style government.

But this is all a pipedream, because the biggest failure in the region in the last few decades is the weakness and inefficiency of the United Nations, due to the nature of its composition. It has also been rendered powerless because the USA chooses not to support it in real financial terms, but rather pursues its own ill-informed, blundering international policies. For example; why on earth is the international weapons trade allowed? Why isn't every nuclear weapon in the world being dismantled and destroyed under UN supervision? If we had a strong, wisely backed UN, the whole world could be changed in a relatively short time. This could be a reality. A strong UN, administered by the world's top experts, (not bureaucrats) in every field, could change the whole complexion of the current world. For it to become a better place, we need to move away from the age of professional, movie star-like politicians, to leaders chosen from and by pools of academics. Ultimately, major national and international decisions should be made by groups of informed academics, rather than politicians, who are controlled by self-interest seeking groups.

Tuesday. June 27, 2006. Return to Dar es Salaam. Once again, the call of the road cannot be denied, and it's with heavy hearts that we say our goodbyes, then we leave in a taxi at 10:30 a.m. The taxi drops us off in Stone Town, where we use an internet café and go shopping.

The ferry is late and there is chaos at the harbour, as crowds of people surge, all trying not to be left behind. The trip back is rough, and I lead Marieke, who is feeling sea-sick, to the back of the boat, where she huddles in a corner.

It is very dark when we arrive at Dar es Salaam, where Christo is waiting for us in the truck to take us back to the Mikadi campsite.

Wednesday. June 28, 2006. Dar es Salaam to Arusha. The road, which by African standards is a good one despite the rather severe speed bumps, leads us in a northwesterly direction. Then we drive into an ambush near Nkata, a small settlement where men with guns block the road and get into an argument with Christo. They claim he was speeding, and produce some antiquated gadget to back up their claim. He has to pay an on-the-spot fine of 20,000 Shillings.

The road leads across bushy plains with small villages nestled between the hills. Nobody talks, even Carie is quiet. Everyone seems a bit travel-lagged, as `Betsy', our jealous truck, continually wrenches us away, carrying us off into the unknown, each time we grow familiar with a place.

Christo wants to treat us to lunch, so instead of the fare we usually prepare along the road, we feast at a wayside buffet at 11 a.m. Later, Christo points to the right, where magnificent, towering white-capped peaks, and the azure vault of heaven elope within a cloud-shrouded halo. It's Mt. Kilimanjaro, the pride of Africa.

Betsy runs by fields of aloe, coffee, corn and sunflower. Big billboards proclaim; Tropical Mint, the coolest mint, and Fruit Drops. Many shack shops line the road with the Pambazuko Bar very prominent. Later, the dwellings increase, until we enter Arusha, a large, sprawling third-world town lying in the shadow of Mt. Meru. Several kilometres beyond Arusha we pull into the rather crowded Snake Park Campsite, where we pitch our tents.

There to meet us, in a big spanking new truck are two South Africans; `Sean,' (not his real name) and De Ville. De Ville is to drive Betsy back to South Africa, while Sean, a veteran of the more dangerous North African route, is to take over as tour leader. Christo will accompany us in an apprenticeship role. Sean, a very big, tough looking, English speaking South African, from the rougher side of Johannesburg, is a sharp contrast to the equally big, gentle-natured Christo. With these two leading the way, we feel we could push right through Africa into Afghanistan via Iraq. Both of them are tattooed, wear shorts and T-shirts, and walk bare-foot, no matter what the terrain or weather conditions are like.

CHAPTER 8: TANZANIA.

Thursday. June 29, 2006. The Serengeti. There to meet us at 6 am. is Lawrence, a perpetually grinning local Rasta man in a partially covered 4-by-4 who is to be our guide. Christo and Sean will remain behind to service the trucks.

The trip through the rural agricultural regions of Tanzania to the densely forested rim of the Ngorongoro Crater takes around 2 hours. Lawrence, a chatty laid-back guy from Arusha, is a specially trained wildlife guide who loves his job. He says that about 2.5 million mammals migrate annually from the plains of the Serengeti to Kenya's Maasai Mara.

We catch brief glimpses through clumps of gigantic old trees down into the crater, before the road descends to the plains beyond, passing by scenic Maasai kraals of mud huts and thatched grass. Tall Maasai warriors carrying shields, spears, and balled clubs, and decked out in their colourful red-styled tribal gear stride proudly along the wayside, while groups of women toil by, burdened by impossibly heavy loads of firewood. These 'warriors' soon piss us off however, as the moment we aim a camera at them they storm forward threateningly, demanding money, and Lawrence, who is not a Maasai hurriedly hits the gas. 'The Masaai' says Lawrence, once inhabited the inner crater but were relocated to the Ngorongoro Conservation Area by the British Colonial rulers. This area provides protection status for wildlife whilst allowing human habitation.

Lawrence parks near the Serengeti 's entrance to do the paper work, while we buy cold drinks and climb up a nearby hill to a viewing point. Cheeky hyraxes and lizards play on the rocks, while in the surrounding trees there is a lively profusion of birds, such as barbets, lilac-breasted rollers, black-headed weavers, long-tailed starlings, and cooing, ring-necked doves. The din of cicadas rises and falls, as the eastern sun reaches through the trees.

As we enter this vast primeval African place, Lawrence tells us that 'Serengeti' means 'endless plain,' in Swahili. To the right a far-off high range of stark hills forms the horizon, while around us the rolling savanna begins to reveal its precious, camouflaged charges. There are herds of wildebeest, zebra, gazelle, and hartebees in abundance, with ostentatiously plumed ostriches and cocky secretary birds stalking through the long grass. The terrain slowly changes with small rocky granite kopjes appearing between the umbrella-like acacia trees, where long-necked giraffe feed. A large herd of elephants brings us to a stop as they cross the road in an unhurried, loose formation, leaving their trademark dumps of steaming dung, as they swagger off between the trees.

After we've left the main road on a narrow side trail en route to our campsite, we suddenly come upon a pride of lions relaxing between the acacias. There are two majestic looking black-maned males, several lionesses, and a couple of cubs gamboling through the bushes. With the sheer number of animals we've seen today this must surely be lion heaven. However, like the farmer they have to 'till the fields' in order to reap the harvest.

In the late afternoon we arrive at an unfenced area with many tents and two small ablution blocks. We pitch our tents on the outer fringe, as all the inner spots are taken. At around sunset we make a massive log fire, and then queue up alongside the mess tent for a bowl of hot food. A senior guide calls for quiet. 'Do not leave the camping area for any reason' he warns. He goes on to say that two nights ago a big male lion was seen from the toilet area, which might mean that it may be an old one looking for easier prey. People peer fearfully out into the black veil of the night, and some point flashlights, probing for the baleful red twin reflections of the beast's eyes.

As the logs burn down to a glowing amber furnace, most people finish their drinks and hurry off to bed. Lawrence and I chat quietly, drinking beer and adding sticks to the fire, while listening to the rhythms and sounds of the night, which he is an expert at identifying. Beyond the fringe of fire-light, out in the inscrutable darkness there is an intense mélange of animal emotions at play. They range from the near- human apes' fearful lookout for the furtive leopards' flitting shadow, to the scurrying rodents' supersonic heartbeat at the descending wing-beat of the tawny, taloned owl. The slavering, wild-maned lion pads silently behind his slinking female death-squad cohorts, determined to dash in and deliver the coup-de-grace to some desperate victim. Expectant hyena and jackal scavengers continually probe the cadence of the night with ear and nose alert, eager for the sumptuous smell or delightful sound of death. Out on the wavy savanna plains, adoring mothers lovingly lick their helpless newborn offspring of quivering life, nudging them to their first giddy steps as the stalking cheetah closes in. The cycle continues eternally, yet animals, unlike humans, kill only for survival and do not use weapons. There is no doubting that we are by far the most fearsome of all the beasts.

Friday, June 30, 2006. The Serengeti. At the first light of day there is a general bustling within the camp, and by 6 am. we pile into the Land Cruiser and take off. We are soon rewarded with a view of a cheetah leading her four skipping cubs through the bush. Then we are mesmerized by the sight of the sun's golden rays glistening on the wide, menacingly curved horns of poker-faced buffalo feeding in the meadows. When under threat from lion prides, the mean-tempered males often counter-attack with deadly results.

Every visitor to Africa dreams of seeing the so-called `big five,' of lion, elephant, leopard, buffalo, and rhino. Lion and elephant are the most exciting. The lion is king by virtue of its power and volatile regal persona, while the highly intelligent, but unpredictable elephant is liable to charge your car and roll it into the shape of a squashed beer can. Buffalo are often sighted in vast splendid herds, while one has a lesser chance of seeing the endangered rhino. However, the furtive leopard is the really tough one to spot in its natural habitat. Its classic pose is the languid laid-back position, draped over an acacia's branch at sunset.

To see such beasts in their natural glory, free from fear of mankind, awakens one to an ancient longing: that we could return to life in such a pristine world, to live in harmony within an unspoiled environment. It was the so-called, `great white hunters,' who were largely responsible for the near extermination of most of the larger African animals. Even in these days, American and European `sportsmen,' or trophy hunters, pay large amounts of money to kill near-defenseless animals with high-powered weapons.

`There it is – leopard!' shrieks Carie, pointing to a hillside as Lawrence hurriedly brings us to a halt. `Where?' I enquire as we all peer out. `I see it too!' someone else shouts, indicating vaguely upwards. Out come the binoculars. I climb through the sunroof and scan the hillside but only see rocks. It's probably another false alarm. Then as we are returning to the campsite for lunch, we spot one sitting motionlessly on a rock, staring into the distance. A superlative hunter, master of the ambush and scourge of the baboons, it is a solitary animal, larger, but less lanky than the cheetah. Lawrence says that though it prefers smaller antelope, it's capable of killing a 900kg eland. Then in a fluid, elegant flow of muscle, it suddenly alights from the rock and bounds up a nearby acacia to blend in on a wide-spread branch, with only its dangling tail giving it away.

After lunch we pack our tents and drive back through the park and head back towards the crater. Lawrence pulls off the road in an area of granite kopjes, gnarled trees, and thorn bushes. 'We need lots of firewood for tonight' he says, so we spend an hour gathering dead branches and logs to load onto the roof.

We find a large flat area with ablution blocks, within the montane forest at the very rim of the Ngorongoro Crater, where we erect our tents near the truck. The sunlight dwindles through the tall trees, and it grows surprisingly cold, so we build an enormous log fire and open some beers. 'Don't walk out into the dark!' we are warned, 'this is leopard terrain.'

Saturday, July 1, 2006. The Ngorongoro Crater. We awaken to cold and wet tents. There was an unbelievably high amount of condensation during the night, soaking the interiors of all the tents.

'The Ngorongoro Crater is the world's largest of its kind, around 8,300 sq km says Lawrence, as he steers the skidding Landcruiser along the muddy track that descends 610 metres down the steep inner slope of the crater. 'It was formed millions of years ago, when a giant volcano exploded and collapsed on itself. Nowadays it's home to more than 25 000 large animals'.

The road leaves the damp forests of the crater rim as it emerges in the valley's bush lands, which later change to grasslands, as the welcome sun peeps over the crater rim. This must surely be a predator's heaven, for we encounter vast herds of zebra, wildebeest and antelope, all seemingly in magnificent condition.

'The Ngorongoro has the densest known population of lion' Lawrence informs us, as we eagerly scan the savanna, but it's only when we enter a vast, flat area that we spot them. They appear in single file, seven full-grown lions and three cubs, gamboling along without a care in the world. One curious female detaches herself, strolls over to our vehicle, and rubs her side against it before catching up with the pride. It's obvious that they're on a mission, and not strolling along in a random direction, so intriguing questions arise - who planned the excursion? - and how did they all agree to it?

At lunch time, we have a picnic at the Ngoitokitok Spring, with its leering elephant skulls, which feeds a large, green marsh. We are following a circular route back, which takes us by the salty Makat Lake, within which several large hippos are hanging cool. On the banks, horns aglow in the flaming sunrays, a herd of ruminating buffalo is gathered, while flocks of elegant, pink-blanched flamingo tiptoe through the rippled shallows.

Out on the open plains, we see the aftermath of what must have been a dramatic showdown between African titans. A dark-maned lion and two lionesses with bloated bellies are spread-eagled beside the partially eaten carcass of a big buffalo bull. Yet the final act remains, for a steady stream of hyenas are loping in, and whooping themselves into a red meat crazed frenzy, while edging ever closer to the prize. A lethargic lioness mock-charges and for now the cackling hyenas retreat.

A lion feeds on a buffalo (Photograph by Dr. D. Erasmus)

Then we slip-slide away up the rim, load the tents, and hit the humpy dust trail back to the Snake Park Campsite, where we are saddened to take leave of the cool Rasta man, Lawrence.

Fatigue sets in. The whirlwind action-packed schedule of changing venues and menus takes its toll. `Ghandi' takes out his first aid kit and treats Beer and Marieke for persistent diarrhea and fatigue with his acupuncture needles, while treating himself for his ongoing ailments.

A friendly South African middle-aged couple and their pre-teen son pull in beside us in a well-stocked off-road vehicle. The father, delighted to meet some of his countrymen, freely hands out sachets of that South African alcoholic delight, Amarula Cream, which hits us hard.

It's time for us to get to know Sean. He and I have already had a long chat, but as a group, we decide on a buffet dinner for general ice-breaking. We all hit the camp's bar, which is staffed by ex-pat South Africans, for pre-dinner drinks. When we take our seats at the outdoor table, Carie orders two bottles of sparkling wine, and from there everything slowly spirals into a late night party with an, `oh shit, I can't find my tent' ending.

Sunday, July 2, 2006. Northern Tanzania. In the early morning we share a very basic breakfast in a bruised, hung-overed silence, before taking seats in our new truck. The road heads northwards, passing many shack-based businesses, such as Mwambo Florida Shop, Lasakachika Shop, Irangi Shop, Mosco Shop, Duka La Dawa, and Sharons Hair Beauty Salon. There's the Golden Chance Bar before a police check point, and then a sign, `accident ahead', partially blocking the road, but we never see one.

The traffic, consisting mainly of trucks, thickens and slows down as we approach the Kenyan border. There is a proliferation of shacks, including Little `Tunu', The Negotiator, and In God We Trust.

Then we check out at the Tanzanian Immigration office, and enter the no-mans-land mayhem of hustling, clutching salesmen between the borders, before passing through the Kenyan Immigration office. Christo brings the truck and somehow we reconnect beyond the border.

9

Kenya

SUNDAY, JULY 2 continued. From southern Kenya to Nairobi. There is a grand mosque beside the road in Namanga, the frontier town, and then the road leads by a church in a tin shack, which seems to signify the rise of Islam and the fall of Christianity, as one heads north. The traffic is a mixed bag of trucks, bicycles, and caravans of heavily packed donkeys and camels. The roadside is dirty, with crowded open-air markets and shacks.

The northbound road passes through desolate semi-arid country, where wild antelope and ostriches can be seen foraging for food in the scrub. We pass through a town called Kadjiado, and later drive by Kitengela Township. Then the truck is brought to a halt by the curious sight of an unhurried procession of wild donkeys crossing our path in single file. A bloated dead hyena beside the road adds to the grimness of the surroundings.

As we approach Nairobi, the traffic picks up and the landscape changes dramatically, with cultivated fields and the colourful red flowering flamboyant trees along the roadside.

Our truck pulls into the Karen Campsite on the outskirts of Nairobi at 4 p.m. As this is the end of the second stage of our trip, it's time to get our house in order. We put up the tents, clean the truck, and then Beer and I do a massive clothes wash together. Although we are just slightly below the equator the night is surprisingly cold.

Monday, July 3, 2006. Nairobi. We begin to meet new members who are joining our group. There is Valerie, from France who travels a lot and never gets close to anyone, Alexandra, a friendly young woman from Germany, Jess, a seemingly cool dude from the USA, and a very young, annoying couple I'll call John and Mary, from England.

During the day, some of us join Sean and Christo on a trip into Nairobi to buy supplies. We enter the city via Kenyatta Avenue. Kenyatta, who later became the country's president, was of course one of the leaders of the Mau Mau rebellion against the British colonizers. The road intersects with Uhuru (freedom) Highway, as it runs into the rather cosmopolitan, pleasantly landscaped city of about one million people. This is not what I expected after reading Paul Theroux, the renowned American writer's rather negative book, Dark Star Safari. It's a typical bustling African city, with the usual street vendors and hustlers, so it's best to watch your wallet and your back.

In the evening a large group of travellers arrives, and the late night carousing of their two drunken Australian tour guides is an annoyance.

Tuesday, July 4, 2006. From Nairobi to Nanyuki. We drive into Nairobi again to pick up a German ex-pat couple who live in Southern Africa at their hotel. They keep us waiting, and Sean and Christo are furious because they've joined us despite being warned about the age limit, which is recommended due to the physical nature of the arduous trip ahead, and the necessity that each traveller is able to cope. They look to be in their late sixties, and the woman, whom I'll call Olga, is feisty but obviously frail, while the man, who I'll call Heinz, is tall and proud, giving the impression that he's used to having everything done for him.

The city is dirty. A group of men wave at us. When I wave back, one of them gives me the finger. A van packed with men pulls up beside us at a red light. They shout and gesticulate, as one of them thrusts an upturned palm through the open window. I lean out and place a million dollar Zimbabwean note in his open hand. There are yells of jubilation -I feel guilty. Then our truck hits the northbound road, passing over the central highlands, as we're in transit across Kenya.

Hours later we stop at the equator, where a sign says 'This sign is on the equator'. Nanyuki. Altitude 6389 ft.' Here we see a former science teacher conducting an experiment with a floating object in a cup of water. Each time he moves the cup across the equator line the floating object twirls in a different direction.

In the afternoon, we arrive in Nanyuki and set up our camp in the grounds of the Sportsman's Arms Hotel, a sprawling survivor from colonial days. Vendor stalls line the dusty streets beyond the hotel, while there are shops, banks, and an internet café on the main road. I buy two huge avocados as well as some local herbs from a friendly, young, local guy called Junior.

After dark, Sean, Christo and I take a nocturnal stroll to feed the breeze, before joining the others in the bar to watch world cup soccer. The black barman, Pius, reminisces about serving British officers in former days.

Wednesday, July 5, 2006. Nanyuki to Marsabit. There is a marvelous view of Mount Kenya (5199m) when we depart at 7 am. Alongside the road we see Erasto House, with a sign, 'Pool game available', and the Sisikwasisi Keg Bar. Little children walking along the roadside to school stare and wave at us, as we pass through the hills and cultivated fields of the Timau district. Though private cars are scarce, the driving of the taxis and buses is 'fierce'. Like most of Africa, there are settlements consisting mainly of shacks or mud huts along the road. We see The 3 in 1 Hotel, and the St. Eusiubus Catholic Church, with a giant-size painting of Jesus.

There is a crisis, as Christo has lost the No.27 spanner, which is essential for vehicle maintenance, so we drive into Isolo, a small settlement where we separate into groups to enquire at the myriad of shops. The surprised shopkeepers are helpful, and miraculously, someone produces the type of spanner we need. We have a crowd of kids in attendance by the time we depart.

The northbound road leads us into wild, isolated country, where soaring wide-winged tawny eagles glide gracefully across the clear blue skies. Out in the stony, thorn-bush scrub we catch glimpses of wild camels, long-necked gerenuk, the tall, thin, gazelle-like antelope, ostriches, and dik-diks, which are graceful dwarf antelope that are the size of a small dog.

In this hostile, waterless terrain, most living things have either horns or thorns, and those that become victims of the scorching sun leave their skeletons littering the landscape. Sullen men holding rifles stare menacingly at us from the shade of a thorn tree. Sean says that there is an ongoing livestock war in the area, between Turkana militiamen and their Borana Tribe rivals. This is not a good place for a breakdown!

Later in the afternoon we leave the desert behind, as we enter Marsabit, which lies in a scenic setting between green hills at the foot of Mount Marsabit (1702m). On the way to our campsite, on a lonely windswept hillside beyond the town, we pass through colourful throngs of tribes people. Beer and I build a flaming log-fire beneath the thorny acacias, as we wash the trail dust off with cold beers. After dark Carie complains bitterly when a thorn penetrates her sandal.

Heinz and Olga are proving to be totally inept each time I show them how to erect the tent, and as their self-appointed helper, I foresee hard times ahead.

Thursday, July 6, 2006. Northern Kenya. The northbound road passes through wild desolate country. To the west lies Uganda. Somalia forms the eastern border, and Sudan is to the northwest. Ethiopia lies directly ahead. These are not friendly surroundings.

Sean brakes to avoid hitting a large troop of baboons crossing the road. There are no trees to be seen, only sand, billions of stones, thorny scrub and barren hills. This is the un-policed frontier country of bandits, smugglers, and cross-border cattle raiders.

The road through Northern Kenya

There are no signs of human habitation, though we do come upon brightly dressed, nomadic goat herders, who throw rocks at Heinz, who insists on hanging out of a window and aiming his enormous camera at everything he sees.

We see strange sights, such as groups of white goats inexplicably standing in circles and an old man - maybe an alchemist - all alone sitting under a large thorn bush, staring into the distance, and stray camels roaming in the desert. Suddenly we come upon an enormous crater to the left, alongside the road, and get out for a look at the barren lunar-like landscape. With the wind whistling an eerie, wistful note, emphasizing the end-of-earth-like solitude, many are hasty to re-enter the warmth of our truck, and leave this lonely forsaken place forever.

Our truck thunders through the ever-changing wilderness on to the Ethiopian frontier town of Moyle. We see women in burkas bent double under enormous loads of wood, and men holding rifles watching from lean-tos at the roadside. There are kids sniffing glue.

We pass through the friendly Kenyan Immigration office and then walk across a bridge to the Ethiopian side.

10

Ethiopia

THURSDAY, JULY 6, 2006 continued. Moyale, southern Ethiopia. We drive up the bustling main road of Moyale with its colourful stalls, shacks, and mosques. Goats roam freely, and kids chase after us with upturned palms shouting, `you, you'.

Sean turns into the grounds of a semi-deserted hotel, where we erect our tents. When I help Heinz and Olga with theirs, they only get in my way, as usual. There is no running water and the toilets don't flush, yet there is a restaurant that sells beer, which we all seem to be in need of. A moneychanger exchanges our dollars for Birr, the local currency. The local language is Amharic, and few people seem to understand any English.

While Sean and Christo attend to the truck, we split up into groups and wander out into the streets. Beer and I accompany Jess into a barbershop where he has a shave. Many of the men wear white robes and a fez, and wherever we go there is always a sizeable crowd, mostly in colourful but ragged dress in attendance, watching our every move. Many kids shout `you, you' and we continually hear the word `ferangi'. This country is unlike any we have encountered along the way. Usually one attracts many stares and comments, but here we have a personal, enthusiastic entourage dogging our footsteps wherever we go.

As the sun descends westward we retreat back to our camp with the muezzins call wailing weirdly through the streets. Supposedly, about half the population of Ethiopia is Islamic.

Sean has purchased a big bag of the green leaves we've seen many people on the streets chewing. He says it's a mild natural narcotic called `chat', and that it will give you a `buzz' if you chew lots of it.

Later in the evening as we're sipping beer and chewing on chat leaves beside our fire, three uninvited men in white robes join us, with the leader giving us an extremely loud sermon in broken English, apparently to the effect that we should convert to Islam. Nobody converts, and the three men leave in disgust.

During the night we hear singing from the mosque, dogs barking, donkeys braying, and the sinister, high-pitched, ghoulish giggle of hyenas. It rains lightly.

Friday, July 7, 2006. Southern Ethiopia. There is a thin strand of relatively good tar road leading northward into a sandy landscape of green bushes and big termite mounds. Staggering cactuses with groping hands reach into the sky. Beside the road there are piles of wood or bags of charcoal for sale. The only kind of traffic we encounter is crowded buses with water containers and bags of charcoal loaded on their roofs. This informal charcoal industry seems to be taking a toll, as trees seem to be scarce.

Ethiopians drive on the right of the road, USA style, while our truck is designed for the left, with its steering wheel on the right. Oncoming trucks and buses hold to the centre of the road and only veer slightly to their side at the last moment in a scary game of `chicken'. Sean is a master at this game, and as the passenger side of our cab faces the oncoming traffic, the co-driver holds a protruding stick out of the window, which forces the oncoming vehicle to give way or lose a mirror. Alongside the road we see an upside down tar truck with its content spilling out. There is no sign of the driver.

CHAPTER 10: ETHIOPIA.

When Sean pulls over to the left we encounter the 'singing wells of the Borana', a semi-nomadic tribe who survive this harsh environment by retrieving nature's precious water from wells that are up to 30 metres deep. We follow a path down the steep hillside to the deep gouge in the earth below and peer over the rim. A loud chorus of singing rises from the depths of what seems to be a well within a cave. Men form a human chain down a rickety ladder and toss buckets of water up at a mesmerizing pace to fill the troughs at the top. Even the animals have to wait their turn to drink. We are not welcome, and there are shouts of anger when Heinz points his intrusive camera at them.

As the road leads up the ascending hills of the Abysinian Plateau, we enter an eerie bank of mist, then daylight regains its strength within the descending valley, as the sun breaks through in blinding shards of light. Women carry jerry cans of water on their backs with no destination in sight. Ragged shepherds holding guns guard herds of goats and camels.

We stop for fuel and use the toilets at the Yabello Motel, before trying small cups of good, strong Ethiopian coffee. Someone tells us that Ethiopia is the original home of the coffee bean. When we leave, our truck stampedes a herd of goats, sending small shepherd boys scampering after them.

The landscape changes to valleys of lush meadows, with grazing cattle and mud huts amidst groves of banana trees lying between the verdant, green hills. Waving kids run after us, idle men chat in the shade, and women work in cultivated fields, or carry baskets or babies along the roadside.

Christo, who is driving, slows down as we pass through many small villages chaotically congested by multitudes of people and randomly parked cars and trucks. Everywhere kids chase after us shouting 'you, you, you'.

In the afternoon, we pass a naked man who is walking along the road just as we reach Dila, which is a major centre in the south. We stop beside the large, sprawling Hoteela Lewi, which has a restaurant with outdoor tables, where we order cake and delicious fresh mango juice. 'Don't point your cameras at people, first ask if it's OK, use body language. Many people in this country don't like to have their picture taken and might become aggressive', warns Sean. We all stare at Heinz, who is the main culprit. Out in the hurly-burly of the crowds we soon split up and distance ourselves from him and Olga as he ignores Sean's advice and once again attracts the hostility of the locals.

Later, when we rendezvous at the truck, all of us are ravenous so we decide to eat in the restaurant. The main dish is Injera, a kind of sour bread, which is made of millet flour and yeast, and looks like a sponge bathroom floor mat. It is served with Wat, a spicy sauce containing meat, beans and lentils. I order Beg Key Wat, delicious goat stew, to go with my Injera. Later when we want to pay the bill, they grossly overcharge us but we each only hand over enough money to cover our order and a tip. Carie insists on paying the claimed amount, which causes a heated argument amongst us. 'I don't care – it's just money', she keeps saying, but our point is that people like her encourage the locals to overcharge travellers.

There is a brief debate as to whether we should make a dry camp along the road, or chance the dangerous drive through the dark to our destination beside Lake Langano. The decision to push on is unanimous, despite the danger of the dodgem-style duel with death on the deadly Friday night roads of Ethiopia.

It's very dark by the time Sean turns off the main course down a dirt road bordered by a low range of lonely hills. There is a far-off grumbling, and flickering light illuminates the distant horizon, warning of an approaching front. Upon entering the Lake Langano area, we find that there are large groups of young men camping everywhere, and we see armed soldiers patrolling through the trees. As we erect our tents, the first drops of rain begin to fall. I put mine up super-quick, and discarding niceties, I tell Olga to get out of the way and sit under a tree, as she keeps getting in the way when I try to help them. Heinz is only slightly less inept. They are exhausted, and retire almost immediately.

Sean leads some of us through the downpour to a large, dimly lit building which is the local pub. Inside we find a hoard of young, hard-drinking Ethiopian men clustered around the bar area. The music is loud as we push our way through to the bar front, drawing a lot of attention, but no welcome. We are drinking beers, seated in a corner away from the main action, when a couple of passing men stop and stare at us. One of them who is obviously very drunk says, 'white bitches,' loudly. We all fall silent, then Christo chuckles as Sean gets up and says menacingly, 'we are not Europeans, we are South Africans - we don't take this kind of shit from anyone.' They hurriedly withdraw, but the mood is spoiled and we gravitate back to our tents.

Despite the rain, the din of Ethiopian-style R&B music and raucous shouting continues throughout the night, as these dudes have come to party.

Saturday, July 8, 2006. Lake Langano. Thankfully the rain has stopped. Hordes of people, mostly men, arrive by car or truck, presumably from Addis Ababa, and pitch their tents along the lake's shoreline. We are objects of curiosity, and by the time we eat our breakfast, we have a throng of onlookers. Then it's time to get some exercise with a game of frisbee on the beach. Sean and I wander up the lake's rocky cliff-backed shoreline, dodging a herd of cattle being shepherded by several small boys, to catch up on the peaceful tidings of the breeze. It's a pleasure to get away from all the people, including our co-travellers, some of whom are becoming increasingly annoying.

In the afternoon several of us go for a long walk away from the lake, and find a local shebeen between the mud huts on a green hillside. A chuckling middle-aged woman serves us beers in the shade of a thorn tree. There are two 'slaughter' goats tied to the tree, and the atmosphere is enlivened by the persistent bellowing of a bull. Local customers emerging from within the shebeen wave and shout greetings, 'Tenaystelegn', (hello), so we wave back and have a relaxing time.

When we return in the late afternoon the locals have erected an inflatable soccer playground on the beach near our tents. Teams consisting of five players on a side take each other on in hotly contested duels. The very skillful Beer, and all-elbows Carie, jump in and join opposing teams, causing much mirth as they consistently foul each other.

After dark the din is unbelievable. Beside each group of campers, there is a car with its music system playing at maximum volume, and the carousing young men are hitting the liquor hard. Later, several of us gravitate up to the pub to play pool. Carie is getting pretty wasted, and keeps paying when the bartenders overcharge her. She shouts 'I don't care', when we reprimand her. It is obvious that she's becoming a problem.

The lighting within the tavern is really dim, so we don't notice at first that she has wandered off. Then Christo spots her in the centre of a thick throng of men, several of whom have their hands on her. She has a seemingly bewildered expression on her face, as if unsure what to make of all the attention she's receiving. Sean immediately takes charge. 'She's pissed and doesn't realize they'll soon have her out the back into a tent for a gang-bang ' he says. 'Koos, you're the oldest, and you don't look so dangerous. Will you go in there and bring her out? If they resist the rest of us will come in hard'. I look at them, our 'cavalry', Sean, Christo, Beer and Jess. Although they are stout-bodied individuals, they are 'thin on the ground'. 'OK' I say, and stroll over to the further side of the tavern and shove my way through their massed bodies. The man who has his arms tightly around Carie is startled when I suddenly appear beside her, and all attention shifts to me as they press in even closer. I smile a wide, shark-toothed grin, and say in the deepest voice I can muster, 'it's time to go home Carie'. I pull the leader's one arm off her and place my arm around her shoulders, while looking across her head into his eyes. 'This is my sister, and she's going with me now, so please take your hands off her.' He holds her firmly by the arm as I try to pull her away. I stop, turn back and look deeply into his eyes, smiling all the while. 'This is my sister, let go of her NOW!' Our eyes lock for a long moment as my smile dips. Then he slowly lets go her and the throng reluctantly parts as I lead her away. We finish our drinks and depart.

Back at the truck it becomes apparent that she's very drunk and wants to wander off again. Sean is really angry, but luckily Marieke manages to get her into her bed. The noise never lets up and none of us gets much sleep throughout the night.

Sunday, July 9, 2006. Awash National Park. At about 8:30 we're ready to go. The northbound road slowly leaves the green, lush vegetation of the south behind as the terrain changes to sand, rocks, bushes and desultory thorn trees. Groups of women work in cultivated fields and men with oxen are plowing.

Some of the villages are dominated by dome-shaped churches and others by mosques with antenna-like minarets. It is impossible to maintain your speed in the urban areas where the roads are thronged with people, darting kids, donkeys, and goats.

An open truck loaded with camels lurches by, then around a bend we come upon the scene of an accident. A truck has overshot the curve and hit a tree, but the only casualty seems to have been a donkey, now dead, that was in the wrong place at the wrong time. Further along the way there are two very small boys herding goats in the wilderness.

At around midday we enter Awash National Park, and as far as we can ascertain we are the only visitors there. According to the information we receive at the entrance, there are leopards, cheetah, and hippo in the park area, and therefore we are advised to exercise extreme caution. It is a flat place with alternate acacia woodland, and grasslands. Along the way we see several grazing oryx and a couple of graceful little dik-dik bounding through the trees.

Sean follows the rough track that leads through the dense vegetation along the banks of the Awash River, and parks in a superb setting beneath gigantic acacia trees.

The first thing we do is release a small tortoise we named Katie, that I bought from small boys at a roadside stop. Then we select spots to erect our tents. I choose a place right above the steep riverbank, which drops about two metres into the water. Then when Beer comes over to check my place out, he spots a monster crocodile lying in the shallows below my tent. I'm not comfortable with this and drive it off with a few pot shots from my catty.

An old African man arrives and offers to lead us to a waterfall. There we see a torrent of muddy, brown water cascading down rapids to plunge over a major drop. In the trees there are flashes of the brilliantly-coloured, pink-throated, ruby-plumed carmine bee-eater, and the turquoise and purple-winged abyssinian roller.

In the late afternoon there is a celebratory mood in the camp, as we revel in the peace and quiet. Heinz also tells us that it's Olga's birthday and hands out beers. With the river bordering our camp on one side, and a semi-circle of dense bushes enclosing us, as well as wide tree branches forming a covering overhead, there is a cosy feeling as John and the females set about preparing a special dinner. Beer and I gather firewood while Heinz and the exhausted Olga, who is not well, are reclining in their unzipped tent. The folding tables and stools are all set out, while Sean and Christo are doing truck maintenance.

Marieke has an idea. 'Let's have toasted marshmallows for dessert', she proposes. We search the truck but we don't find any marshmallows. Unwilling to abandon her idea, she has another brainwave. 'Koos!' she cries, 'don't you have bananas in your tent? Let's cut some up and toast them'. I'm the banana man – everyone knows I always buy a bunch wherever we stop. 'OK, I'll bring them', I reply, and stroll over to fetch them. As I walk back beneath an overhanging acacia branch, we are all startled when a large baboon utters a hoarse primeval bark, as he drops out of the tree and bounds toward me with bristling fangs and arms extended into formidable claws. His body language screams, 'give me that banana!'

This is an extremely dangerous animal, capable of ripping a big dog to pieces, and it may possibly be rabid. In an instant, I become aware of a whole gang of apes that have surreptitiously occupied the surrounding trees, and I realize that I'm being challenged by the alpha male of the troop, while his mates are on standby, ready to ransack the camp. In southern Africa, I've had encounters with baboons before, especially in the Cape Town area, where they are growing bold and dangerous because foolish tourists feed them, thereby condemning them to death. The general notion however, is that they pose a threat to children and women, but for an adult human male to be attacked in full view of the tribe is uncommon.

As it bounds toward me, something happens that the ape may not have foreseen. The human loses its temper and counter attacks. As a former boxer, I prefer to fight a bigger, clumsier opponent. It's the smaller, broad-shouldered, well-balanced ones that give me problems, and no sane man would want to go head-to-head with a baboon. I instinctively know that to retreat is not an option, so I surprise the beast by dropping a few choice curses as I go into a crouch, turning my left side toward him. Clutching the bananas to my chest with my right hand, while raising my left, I take a few short steps forward, and begin flicking fast karate style kicks into the space where I estimate he will arrive. The ape pulls up short and begins to circle me, trying to force an opening by catching me off balance, but I never let up and keep pressing forward, kicking with vicious intent, slowly driving him back. He keeps gliding away, casually, just keeping out of reach, like a young Muhammad Ali. There is a turning point when we reach the edge of the clearing and he shifts sideways, glancing over his left shoulder. Then he quickly shuffles off towards a tree as I bend down and pretend to throw a stone at him, but he escapes with his dignity semi intact.

Then suddenly it's over, and everyone is shouting at the same time, but I feel weak-kneed and need a drink. 'Why didn't you throw a chair at the bloody ape?' I demand of Christo. 'Ag Koos, you two was doing such a lekker (nice), close two-step that I didn't want to spoil it' he laughs. 'I'll never try to take your bananas away from you again', Marieke jokes, but I'm still angry, and grabbing my catty I pursue the apes until I get a shot, hitting the big one on the backside. His roar rends the air as he swings away through the trees, and I reckon he'll think twice before invading a human camp again.

After dinner, we place small pieces of banana on sticks and toast them over the fire, drinking beers as we listen to the night sounds, while being lulled by the mesmerizing beauty of the glowing log fire's ever-changing face. Apes are afraid to venture out in the dark. It is their nemesis, and the leopards' favourite hunting time.

Monday, July 10, 2006. Harar. Everyone is feeling refreshed after a good night's sleep, so we're up and away just after sunrise. A scenic range of blue-hued mountains lines the horizon as we drive towards Awash, a big, congested town. We stop and enter a café but for some unknown reason the owner refuses to serve us.

We pass a shriveled, naked woman walking along, mumbling who-knows-what to herself, and see two men sleeping beside the road at different places. In the distance lying far out within the harsh thorn-bush surroundings, weird, pinched hills come into view. Troops of baboons forage in the scrub, as three majestic oryx gather in the shade of an acacia. A large tortoise on a mission crosses the road. It must be a loner for it's heading out to the nowhere space, into the heartland of old mother Africa. Imagine going with it! Maybe one day it'll tell its grandchildren how, long, long ago, it was crossing a flat barren place when a monstrous animal that roared like thunder came to a stop before it; and how elongated pieces of spam in two-legged shapes appeared from its rear, and flashed the sun at it.

Sean turns off the main road in a northeasterly direction into the mountains, passing through Aberekati, a small village where the pace of life seems to be rather slow. The road keeps to the high ground, winding through many small towns amidst cornfields and tea plantations. There is a proliferation of strange-looking drumstick-shaped trees.

The place we choose to stop for lunch has a good view of the terraced mountainside falling away into the valley below. Once again, we're quite an attraction, as a crowd of local villagers gathers around us. Passing trucks hoot and some even pull over to have a better look.

Buses pass our truck on blind bends, going at suicidal speeds. Further along there is a truck lying on its side in a ditch. In the small villages perched on the mountain edges, people, goats, and donkey's form a crazy mishmash of colourful life.

In the afternoon we arrive in Harar, an ancient walled hilltop city with fortress-style walls and numerous ancient mosques. Sean says it's the fourth holiest city in Islam, and that it's been the centre of the Islamic faith in the horn of Africa for a thousand years. We park next to the hotel where we are going to stay, which lies beside the crowded Crystal Market, where one can purchase fruit, vegetables, chat, spices, camels etc. Christo and I will share a room while Sean is to sleep in the truck.

Alexandra joins me on a walk through the bustling market area where we buy mangos and bananas. Then we enter a cool tearoom and try out our phrase book Amharic, `hulet shai ebakah' (two teas please). The male attendant seems to get it and brings us a pot of delicious cinnamon flavoured tea.

After dark we get a couple of cabs to take us through the narrow serpentine alleys to the outskirts of town to see the phenomenon of Mulugeta, one of the hyena men of Harar. We join a small gathering of tourists and locals under an old tree beside a small mosque, where people are peering out into the darkness beyond the headlights of a car that illuminate the scene. Mulugeta, the 'hyena man', tells us that after a great famine in the 19th century, the people of Harar made a pact with the hyenas. The hyenas would not kill children or livestock, and in return, they would be fed. He walks out into the clearing and calls out into the darkness beyond. Soon more than 30 luminous pairs of eyes can be seen on the fringe of the light. When Mulugeta calls out a name in a commanding voice, a glowering beast with glowing eyes emerges into the light and catches the piece of raw meat that is tossed to it. This process is repeated many times. Then he sits in a chair, calls out a name, and dangles a piece of raw meat from his mouth. In a blur of action, a loping hyena accelerates to snatch it from his jaws as it dashes by. He continues until there is no meat left in the bucket, and the hyenas retreat into the forests beyond. We are happy to make a small donation for this is a tradition worth continuing.

Tuesday, July 11, 2006. Addis Ababa. Just after 7 a.m. we take to the road again, backtracking through Awash, then rejoining the north bound route. Once again the traffic is fierce, and soon we see a large crowd gathered around a truck, which is lying on its side down an embankment. Another bus, jam-packed with people, overtakes us at a high speed. Later we find that it was unable to negotiate a curve and went straight up the mountainside, and is now stuck in a deep ditch, with all the passengers milling around it.

After a lunch stop beside the road our truck won't start. Christo and Sean tinker with the engine to no avail, and say that it needs a push-start. As we begin pushing it, the black-browed sky winks coughs and weeps, catching us in a torrential deluge. Luckily, the engine starts before we're soaked, but heavy rain pounds down from the darkening heavens, and disturbingly, the surrounding countryside seems to be awash in water.

The thunder and lightning is intense, and poor Christo, our driver, is having a 'baptism of fire', as the traffic thickens on the approach to

Addis Ababa. The road passes over a bridge which is under threat from the throttled, swollen river, before it continues through the shack-like shops within the outskirts of the city. I see the Sputnik Music Shop; and Taita Hotel displaying a sign, 'over 100 years old', which it looks, as do most other buildings in the city. A clothing store has curiously incongruous white manikins displaying clothes.

With Sean navigating, we pass through the turmoil of rain and traffic in the centre of the city, and follow Ras Abebe Arregay Avenue to the historic Ethiopia Hotel, where I have a large old room with a hollow bed to myself.

It is still raining when some of us venture out into the streets in the evening. Despite the wet conditions, we still run the gauntlet of beggars and hawkers as we check out the lively street scene. We randomly choose a restaurant and order Wat and Injera. I go for the Bug Wat, which is mostly lamb stew. The locally brewed alcohols are pretty lively. There is the Arakie, a heady spirit, and T'ej, a mead made from honey - both best to be treated with extreme caution.

Wednesday, July 12, 2006. Addis Ababa. Today we are free to do as we please. After having a good breakfast at the hotel, Beer, Alexandra, and I take a cab to the Merkato, which is supposedly one of the biggest open-air markets in Africa.

One can easily get lost within the narrow passages of this teeming, mega-bazaar, where one needs good bargaining skills, and you can get run over by convoys of goats or donkeys. Beggars and street children hassle us. A group of policemen patrolling on foot warn us to be alert for pickpockets or muggers. We go into a shop to have passport-size pictures taken for our next border crossing, but there is a power failure before they are developed, so we have to while the time away in teashops for a few hours.

Alexandra wants to experience an Ethiopian sauna, so Beer takes a cab back to the hotel while I accompany her. We have to queue to get in, but it's not a good idea, as I find myself squashed into a rather crowded area with a group of men who are all staring at me, the only Caucasian. I exit early and find Alexandra has absconded too – for the same reason.

Next we jump into a cab, asking for the Giorgis (St George's) cathederal, but the taxi driver is on a mission of his own, driving off elsewhere. We can see on the map that he's going the wrong way, so I get him to turn back and drop us at the Piazza, (De Gaulle Square) from where we can walk. First we go into a small museum, before a zealous little man leads us through the Cathedral. It's a grand place, which he says was built to commemorate the victory over the Italians in 1896, at the battle of Adwa.

Later in the afternoon, Carie and Marieke ask me to help them find a phone so that Carie can make an international call. Out on a crowded street, a big, smooth-talking local man approaches us. 'Hi.' My name is John, I'm the best tour guide, blah blah blah...' 'Thanks', I answer, 'We don't need one, we're only looking for an international phone'. 'No problem' says John, 'Just follow me'. He leads us across a busy street and then enters some back street complex built mainly from clapboard. John continually says 'No problem', until I quip, 'When someone keeps saying no problem, that's when I usually expect one'. He leads us into an office, where a woman has an international phone with a meter in an adjoining room. She gives Marieke the rate to the Netherlands and I tell her to synchronize her watch with the call, as I do not trust these people. She speaks for just a few seconds under 4 minutes then cuts the call. The meter says 6 minutes and the woman wants to be paid for 6 minutes. The argument gets heated, and when I intervene, John grabs me by the shoulders from behind and tries to drag me out of the room, still murmuring 'No problem'. In an instant I see red, and swivel, catching him with a crunching elbow blow to the midriff. He goes down on one knee, but manages to get up, clutching his ribs in apparent agony, and disappears from the scene. The woman has Marieke by the arm and is trying to pull her back into the room. I take the due amount from Marieke's hand and throw the money on the woman's desk. Then I take hold of Marieke's other arm and literally drag her free while cursing loudly, with Carie fleeing before us.

Sean suggests we have dinner at the Ethiopia Restaurant, which is renowned for its ethnic food. The main group sets off, but I wait for Carie and Marieke who're a bit late. We endure the usual harassment of the regulars as we hurry out on to the dimly lit street, hoping to catch up with the others. I've noticed that some guys get money from tourists by intimidating them. One such guy is persistently in our faces and I warn him to back off, but each time we step around him he runs forward and blocks our path again. The third time I shoulder barge him, sending him rolling. Another local man gives him a kick for good measure, then falls in beside me. This guy's name is Afewerk, and he's a gardener, specializing in herbs. He's charismatic, and accompanies us all the way to the restaurant as he and I discuss the deal.

This is to be our last dinner in a restaurant for some time, so it turns into quite a festive occasion. When we leave a soft rain is falling, washing the faded facades of the shabby buildings that line the streets of this old city that was founded in 1887 by Menelik the second. According to a popular Ethiopian folk story, Menelik the first was the son of King Solomon and the Queen of Sheba.

Thursday, July 13, 2006. Northern Ethiopia. We leave after 8 a.m. in a soft pall of misty rain, yet it takes a while to extricate ourselves from the old city's maze of poorly sign-posted roads. There is a fairly good strip of tar road leading to the northwest, up thickly forested hillsides and across stout stone bridges bottlenecking the swollen rivers. There are small settlements with huts and kraals made of mud and stone. Women till the fields, and there are oxen pulling ploughs.

When the road turns abruptly to the west, the tar ends as the route falls off the plateau. Christo gears back when we enter a blinding belt of mist as the road keeps plunging. Our truck edges its way downward, slipping, sliding and going into heart-stopping skids, yet somehow managing to cling tenaciously to the muddy track. It's a driver's nightmare. Through occasional breaks in the mist, we see that the road is hewn out of rough sandstone cliffs, without the protection of barriers on the sides. Around a blind hairpin bend, a break in the mist offers us a scary view of a bus wreck lying on the steep mountainside. It must have skidded over the edge higher up and somersaulted to its current precarious position. There is no way of knowing when it happened. It may well be full of long dead bodies. Later we see a 4-wheel drive vehicle lying upside-down on a slope, and then yet another bus wreck.

Throughout the descent, the tension is tangible, and there is a deathly silence aboard. Then we break into a spontaneous cheer when our truck reaches the bottom, where a long bridge crosses the Blue Nile River, which lies within a spectacular gorge. There is a roadblock with many armed soldiers, who warn us not to take pictures, but we have to shout at Heinz who doesn't get it.

Immediately after the bridge, the road begins to ascend, up and up through barren, bleak landscape. Later there are rocky fields where men plow with oxen. Women can be seen carrying large pitchers of water held on the smalls of their backs. When we drive over the crest at the top of the escarpment there is a dead donkey lying beside the road. Then we enter Debre Markos, a large chaotic town, where we are held up by two bulls engaged in a ferocious duel in the middle of the road.

The road passes through several small, crowded villages with the inevitable boys chasing after us shouting 'you, you!' as we head to the northwest.

Directly ahead, there is a massive build-up of cloud spectacularly highlighted by the sinking sun, when Sean and Christo decide on a place for a rough, overnight bush-camp near a village. The word spreads like wildfire, and by the time our tents are up there is a very large ever- increasing crowd in attendance, closing in from all directions. We take a rope and span it around the perimeter of our camp, literally pushing people beyond it. Everyone feels rather uncomfortable as we go about preparing for dinner and having to push our way through the throng to go about our ablutions in nearby thickets, with precautions having to be taken to ensure the safety of the females.

Heinz wanders into the crowd and gives an impromptu speech, while taking pictures to his hearts content. Several of the younger people can speak a little English, but the majority can't.

Then, as darkness descends with undue haste, there is an ominous, deep growl of thunder, as the sky splits into jagged, flaming lesions. The rain comes suddenly, in a vast sweeping torrent, which is a further complication, but at least it drives the crowd away. As it is often impossible to buy beers in parts of the country, we have a large stock of gin and some squash, which everyone tucks into liberally. We somehow manage to cook and devour a good dinner, after which all the newcomers retire to their tents.

With the soaking rain streaming down, the bush-whacked, road-dog crazies Christo, Sean, Carie, Marieke, Beer and I hit the gin hard, reveling in our newfound isolation. In the spirit of the moment, Sean goes into the truck and prepares a fitting toast to the occasion, which even the girls partake in, and then promptly get the giggles, which are contagious. There we are, all wet and huddled together, howling with laughter under the truck's propped-up side-cover, when we see a bright light shining at the top of the embankment leading down from the road. `Oh no', somebody says, `they're back again!' In the spirit of the moment Christo grabs one of the pangas lying on hand, and whooping like a Zulu warrior, he charges up the steep slope, brandishing it above his head like a maniac. When Sean goes to his rescue, he finds several policemen pointing machine guns at a sheepish-looking Christo, and has to help him to explain that it was only a joke. The policemen had actually come to see if we were OK, so Christo and Sean, both pissed, give them hearty handshakes all around. When they depart the party continues. Later, as Carie's legs go, she has to be helped to their tent beside mine, where I can hear them talking and giggling themselves to sleep.

Friday, July 14, 2006. Bahir (Bahar) Dar. We depart under cover of a dark, rainy morning at 6a.m. and soon see a crushed 4-wheel drive vehicle alongside the road. I sit at the front of the seating area beside Marieke, as the roadside view unfolds in a never-ending kaleidoscope of goats, donkeys, ancient trucks, colourfully dressed people, and the `you, yous' twirling into our vision. As bright sunrays suddenly break through the murk, we see three goats sunning themselves on the top of a high rock.

This is a very religious country. We hear the wail of the muezzins call from a mosque, and in the next village see a procession of people in white robes, singing on their way to a church. Off the road people bathe in muddy streams.

The road crosses the Wetet Abay River where there is a large lumberyard. In this country, the fast-growing Australian eucalyptus trees are cultivated like a crop. Then the road is blocked by a group of men beside a truck, who are pushing each other around in some dispute.

In the mid afternoon we drive into Bahir Dar, a small city on the southern tip of Lake Tana. The Blue Nile originates from Lake Tana, and flows through Ethiopia into Sudan, where it merges with the White Nile in Khartoum to form the Nile proper. The city has a semi-tropical feel to it with its hibiscus tree lined avenues and dense lakeside vegetation. Christo turns into the grounds of the Ghion Hotel / Simien Lodge, where the manager says we can erect our tents inside a large shed. The first thing we do though is to put up all the tents out in the sunshine and hang our things out too, as almost everything is wet or damp. It is an old rambling colonial style hotel, where one can enjoy meals out on the veranda. The lake lies down a pathway shrouded by enormous trees. Sean and Christo will be sharing a room in an outbuilding where we can shower.

Later, many of us wander off into the rather scruffy town, gravitating toward the sprawling, third world market area. Each group has its own entourage of enthusiastic hangers on – except for Jeff and I - as I've developed an effective discouragement technique. After checking out the market area we hit the sidewalk cafes, ordering delicious fruit juices and cinnamon tea with cake.

Saturday, July 15, 2006. Bahir Dar. The muezzin's call from the large mosques lying beside the lake awakens us at daybreak. Sean and I take a stroll down along the waterfront to take in the fragrance of the breeze. The air is alive with the calls of the red-chested cuckoos, known as the 'Piet-my-vrou' in South Africa. Weavers' nests and hulking vultures decorate the trees, while pelicans and several kinds of water birds are searching for tidbits in the shallows.

After a good breakfast on the hotel veranda, we board a boat for a tour to the island monasteries on the scenic Lake Tana, which is dotted with 37 islands. We pass by young African fishermen, who wave to us. At the first island, the guide leads us up a steep path, through a plantation to a large round building built of stone and clad in mud and straw. The inner walls are decorated with colourful paintings depicting biblical scenes.

In the late afternoon I accompany Marieke and Carie to the market area to buy gin and fruit. When we go to an internet café I'm horrified to read that Australia beat South Africa in the Tri-nations rugby.

After dark there's a lively thunderstorm, but thankfully our tents are under cover, as they all tend to leak a bit. We gather in the hotel bar for drinks before retiring early.

Sunday, July 16, 2006. From Bahir Dar to Lalibela. Today may be a holy one in the Islamic world, as there is a chorus of loud singing coming from the nearest mosque. The hotel offers a rather good breakfast of banana, mango, toast, and bacon and eggs, which we're happy to pay for rather than having our usual fare.

By 9 a.m. we're packed and hit the road. Beyond the city the road heads in a north-easterly direction. Alongside the road there are three goats sunning themselves on a rock, and once again there are people bathing in a muddy river. Many people dressed in white robes are gathered in a churchyard. In prolific spurts of life, green mielie (maize corn) heads break through the soaked brown soil in vast fields of nourishing earth. Shepherds herd cattle in verdant green fields. Racing streams of muddy brown water snake across the plains. Boys wearing strange, high woven hats drive their cattle across the road. To the east, weirdly shaped mountains enliven the horizon. In a field there is an abandoned soviet era tank, its turret pointing into the distance.

Then Sean slows down to turn off the tar road onto a gravel route heading due east towards the far blue mountains. The route gradually ascends the plateau, keeping to the narrow mountain ridge as the sides fall away in spectacular terraced layers with endless stone walls. Towering mountain sentinels stand guard over valleys of cultivated green fields.

When we stop for lunch along the roadside, the usual crowd of curious haphazardly dressed locals gathers around us. There are grinning ragamuffin children and a solemn man hefting an ancient .303 Enfield rifle.

On the road to Lalibela

High up on a flat section of the plateau, the road leads through Gobgob, a small village where there is a signpost to the Dibuko Veterinary Clinic. Later, when we pull over for a pit stop, Sean calls for attention. 'Listen up' he says, 'do you want to sleep in a bush camp, or would you rather that we push through in the dark to Lalibela?' The decision to continue is unanimous.

As the sun besieges the rear skyline, the road plunges down into a vast thorn tree world. Then it changes to tar and begins to climb again. An interesting feature in the small settlements we encounter is the many double storey huts built from wood and stone.

When nightfall overtakes us in a descending shawl of darkness, the lonely peaks of the Debra Maruhn Mountains reach longingly into a gleaming sky of distant glittering stars. The moon, unattainable and aloof, hangs precariously dipped on a far-off horizon.

We pass by a settlement, as the winding road rises sharply up to enter Lalibela, which lies at an altitude of 2,600 metres, on a rock terrace surrounded on all sides by rugged, forbidding mountains. Christo parks at the entrance to the 7 Olive Hotel, which is built on the side of a hill with a grand view of the town below.

Heinz and Olga check into the hotel, with Christo and Sean sharing a complimentary room, while the rest of us erect our tents on a strip of lawn between the guest rooms and a thick hedge. Nobody feels like the usual fare, so we meet for a hot dinner in the hotel dining room.

'Tell us about Lalibela?' someone asks as we gather on the patio for after dinner drinks. 'Lalibela,' Sean replies, 'was intended to be a New Jerusalem in response to the capture of Jerusalem by Muslims. The Christians believed that since they were protected by the formidable mountain battlements around here, they would be able to repel the increasingly expansionist and militant Moslems. The site is home to 11 churches that were intricately carved out of rock in the 12th century.'

Monday, July 17, 2006. Lalibela. Once again, the dreaded scourge of diarrhea is doing the rounds, and I'm suffering from stomach cramps. Today we are booked to go on a tour of the churches, and soon after breakfast a guide arrives. As I'm in need of a break from the ongoing close proximity to my co-travellers, some of whom are extremely irritating, I decide to opt out and wander off on my own.

It is still early morning as I stroll down the main road, as a thin veil of mist recedes to reveal the stupendous natural grandeur of the surroundings, with the 4,200m peak of Mount Abuna Joseph dominating the skyline. A high school boy, Dessle Woldie, falls in beside me. 'Tell me about Lalibela?' I request. 'Of Lalibela's 8 to 10 thousand people, over 1000 are priests' he replies. 'Religious ceremony and ritual are usual here, with regular processions, fasts, and crowds of singing and dancing priests. My mother is one too.' When crowds of people begin to emerge from their compact dwellings, I find a path leading up into the mountains, and toil upwards in the thin air.

The trail leads along a steep ridge, giving a wondrous view of the encroaching peaks and falling terraced valleys. More and more people appear on the narrow pathway, most of them seeming startled to see me. An older man, bent double under a big pack overtakes me effortlessly, then two senior high school boys fall in beside me, determined to be my guides. They are Fiker Tadesse and Damena Ebabu (damena-16@ yahoo.com) of North Wollo, c/o Lalibela Post Office, Lalibela, Ethiopia. They live with host families in a small village higher up the path, but both come from another village, several days walk across the mountains from here. Every day they walk down to attend the high school, far below in the valley and they seem to be in marvelous shape.

There is a monastery further along a side-trail, and some old guy wants to sell me an outrageously expensive ticket, but I haven't even seen the place yet, so I decline.

The two boys guide me to their village of simple huts made of wood, stone and mud. There is no electricity or running water, but the air is fresh and unpolluted. They proudly show me their fields of barley, beans, lentils and eucalyptus trees. Both boys are desperately in need of sponsorship, which I'm unable to provide, so I give them US dollars for books.

When I take leave of the boys, they point me onto a narrow trail that will take me back on a circular route. As the path descends into a steep valley the terraced hillsides ring with the calls of small shepherd boys, as they crack their whips and wave to me. To the north the sky is darkening now, and beginning to look dramatic, the clouds are becoming dragon-headed warships, and across the horizon there are jagged tongue-lashes of light Later in the afternoon, as we gather beside the truck, a crisis arises. Sean and Christo had bought a small goat, with a view to transporting it on the truck's roof, until we run out of fresh meat in the north. Though this is standard practice in Africa, we are startled at the vocal opposition to this plan, mostly from John, Mary, Carie, and Marieke. 'When in Rome ....' I suggest. 'This is the way meat is transported in third world countries, where refrigeration is not freely available. You are not in your home countries with all the department stores selling refrigerated meat. Why don't you relax, have another drink, and let the guides do as they think best'. With his stiff upper lip all-aquiver, John retorts, 'We have a right to decide on how our meat is transported and presented'. Carie, who is dipping deeply into the gin, grows tearful. Christo shrugs his shoulders in resignation. 'Don't blame me if there is no meat later on', he says, as he grabs a large knife and leads the goat away. Carie accompanies them, and on their return with the slaughtered goat she's on the brink of hysteria. 'I'll never eat red meat in my life again' she swears (two days later she does). Tiring of her hypocrisy, I say, 'Why don't you grow up – where do you think the red meat you've been eating all your life came from?'

At sunset I retreat up the hill above the hotel to relax within the soothing balm of the breeze. There is some sort of festival taking place in the village streets below. I can hear loud music and I can see people dancing. Sean and Christo join me, equally in need of some 'inner space'.

Tuesday, July 18, 2006. Gondar. Our truck rumbles away just after 7 a.m. heading back the way we came from until we reach the juncture, where we turn right in a north-easterly direction. Along the way we see a few more abandoned Soviet tanks, vast plains of aloes, and flooded fields. There are also weird granite kopjes, with sheer rock pinnacles, and densely covered green hills.

When we stop for lunch along the way Sean has a few things to tell us about our destination for today. 'Gondar' he says, 'is famous for its castles and palaces, and it was the second largest city in the world during the 17th century. However, it went into decline after being sacked by the Sudanese in the 1880's. It was developed by the Italian occupiers in the early 1900's, and once served as the Ethiopian capital. Any questions?' 'Yes,' I reply, 'Can we buy beer there?' 'Don't worry,' he chuckles, 'There'll be plenty in the hotel bar'.

The frowning sky has a thunderous, bruised expression, as we enter this small, dilapidated, old city and make our way through its narrow crowded streets to the secluded terraces of the Terara Hotel.

Beer, Valerie and I pitch our tents in the hotel's overgrown grounds, while the others check into the hotel. Then the rain starts falling, as Christo battles to cook a large pot of soup. I have to take to the bushes in the rain later at night with a serious case of 'the runs'.

Wednesday, July 19, 2006. Gondar. Loud singing from the nearby mosque awakens us at 4 a.m. and continues throughout the day. After breakfast, a group of us wander into town to check things out. The main event seems to be at the massive mosque complex, which is thronged with people in white robes.

For a small fee we enter the Royal Enclosure, the so-called 'Camelot of Ethiopia', an area encircled by a high wall within which lie the remarkable remains of former castles, palaces, and churches dating back to the 17th century. As we wander through the remnants of these grand old structures, there is no doubting that Ethiopia's glory days have come and gone.

Out on the streets young people speak to us in English, and they all want a sponsor. We retreat into a cool café and order small cups of cinnamon tea. Later Carie and I try to buy a case of beer from a shopkeeper who speaks no English. Using mostly body language, I negotiate a good price, but then we learn that the beer is ours, but not the bottles. If we want the beer we have to leave the bottles behind – so no deal.

Thursday, July 20, 2006. From Gondar into Sudan. After breakfast we wave goodbye to John and Mary, who will not be going to Sudan with us. Jess, who will be returning to South Africa, does not make an appearance.

The winding, north-east bound road descends through valleys of twisted hills and rock rimmed mountains, gradually deteriorating into a 40/30/20 km per hour affair. Then the landscape changes, as we enter a green plain with yellow flowering bushes and small pink flowers.

The frontier area is sparsely populated, and shepherds with rifles guard their precious flocks of goats and camels, for inter-tribal as well as cross border raids are said to be rife.

When we reach the border area, several men, supposedly immigration officials, wave to us from beside a shantytown of structures made from wood and zinc. We follow a man across a littered, brown, muddy area, crossing trenches on wobbly planks, past piles of firewood, en route to the Ethiopian Immigration office. It is an earthen building, painted pink below and blue above, with holes in the roof. They don't have enough departure forms for Sean, Christo and me so we are processed first. There are a surprisingly large number of very friendly officials in attendance.

11

Sudan

THURSDAY, JUNE 20 continued. Two smiling officials process us in the Sudanese Immigration office, which is in a new building.

The road is in reasonably good nick initially, until the road-works begin, with the only traffic being big Bedford trucks manned by men in white robes. Our truck leaves the blocked road again, following a rough, dusty detour until it comes to a stop behind a line of trucks. The trucks are unable to negotiate the steep incline back onto the road, and many men help to push each truck up to the top. Sean, Christo, Beer and I help. When it's our turn, many men help us, and there is a loud cheering and waving when we take off again. There are no other foreigners, and certainly no other females on the road, so our ladies are a big hit.

Christo pulls off the road in the late afternoon, choosing a site at random, as there is nowhere near suitable for camping in this arid, semi-desert area. Behind us, large trucks hoot as they thunder by in clouds of twirling dust, while a shepherd drives a herd of goats through the surrounding gravel dunes in the twilight.

Luckily we have been stocking up on logs, storing them on the truck's roof, so we're able to make a cheerful fire, as the grim blackness of night settles upon the wilderness. As we're preparing dinner, two white robed men appear from out of the dark. They speak no English, but through hand-signals, we understand that their truck is stuck in the sand. Christo and I follow them back to their truck to assess the situation. It is so dark that we can hardly see each other, and have problems keeping on the road. Their truck has sunken down to its chassis in the sand, and our truck will not have the power to pull them free. One of them returns to our truck and has dinner with us, but does not want to leave, as the darkness is near impenetrable. Later we hear action out in the darkness, so I make him a flaming torch from a branch, and accompany him far enough to see that someone with a front-end loader has come to their rescue.

Friday, July 21, 2006. The way to Khartoum. We awaken to the sound of movement, and crawl out of our tents to see a shepherd astride a camel driving his flock of goats and donkeys through our camp.

The frequent roadblocks are an annoyance, as armed men in uniforms try to shake the drivers down for an on-the-spot fine for some supposed misdemeanor. With Sean in an advisory capacity, Christo soon learns the ropes. At the next block an 'official' suggests that a couple of US dollars could smooth things over. Christo hangs out the cab window beaming broadly at the men. 'I tell you what' he says, 'We're also a bit short of dollars. Why don't you take one of our blondes instead?' Startled, the men look up to where the smiling Carie and Marieke are waving at them. As they start arguing amongst themselves, Christo shouts 'Bye', and waves as he lets go of the clutch and we disappear in a cloud of dust.

The first hint of habitation we see are the grass dwellings of the desert nomads. Later we see mud huts and then homes made from bricks, and before too long we pass through the town Gedarer. The road continues in an easterly direction until we cross the Blue Nile at Wad Medani, where it turns northwards again.

It is summer time here in the northern hemisphere, and the sun's rays scorch the arid earth with merciless intensity. The inside of the truck is a pressure cooker, with the temperature reaching into the 40's (Celsius).

Later, big drops of rain begin to fall from the murmuring sky's murky countenance, but the threatening storm never materializes.

There is an unbelievable amount of trash on the outskirts of Khartoum before we turn onto Afriqyya Street and drive into the city, where we stop at a shopping centre for supplies. We are also able to exchange our dollars for Sudanese Dinars.

Khartoum lies at the confluence of the White Nile and the Blue Nile, and it is at the Blue Nile Sailing Club that we park and erect our tents near the edge of the brown, murky-looking river. It's stinking hot, and when we go to the ablution blocks to wash, Christo and I step under the shower fully clothed.

In the early evening the temperature is still in the lower 40's, as we follow Sean through the tree-lined boulevards into the centre, where there is a large white mosque beside a vast crowded area of bazaars.

It is in this area that we enter a restaurant of rough tables and benches to order fresh fruit juice and delicious shawarmas of spiced marinated lamb. When we begin to explore the market area, it becomes too complicated to stick together in the pressing throngs, so I drift off in the tide of the market's colourful hullabaloo. Later, as I'm trying to find my way back through the dimly lit streets, a big determined street dog takes after me, snarling in a threatening manner, and doesn't respond to the usual South African threat, 'Voertsek!' Luckily I spot a half brick in the gutter, and put it to flight with a good bouncing throw.

One cannot buy alcohol in this country, and Muslims caught drinking are flogged. We have a container of vodka mixed with squash, which at the current temperature is as warm as a recently boiled pot of tea, and not very appetizing. As most of our group members retire to their muggy tents, Sean, Christo, Marieke, Carie and I sit on a bench at the waterfront and add spice to the breeze. We talk about the 1966 film 'Khartoum', with Gordon Brown, the British general in charge of the city's defence, and Laurence Olivier as Muhammed Ahmad. The historic siege in the 1884 to 1885 period pitted the U.K. and Egypt against Mahdist Sudan. A prolonged drought lowered the level of the two Niles to such an extent that it allowed the attackers to wade through. In the course of events, the Khartoum garrison was overrun, and Brown and 7,000 (mostly Egyptian) troops, along with 4,000 inhabitants of the city, were slaughtered. I look out over the murky river face and try to imagine the din as hordes of bloodthirsty, sword-wielding tribal warriors surged over, and I shudder.

Saturday, July 22, 2006. Khartoum. Early in the morning, before the heat of daytime, Beer, Marieke, Carie and I wander into the city centre for a breakfast of juice, grapefruit, and egg burgers.

On our return we all follow Sean to the Aliens Department, in the maze of the city centre, where all visitors are required to register their names - a ridiculous requirement, as our names were obviously registered when we passed through immigration. This exhausting ordeal takes most of the day, as they initially refuse our attempt to register because we do not have a stamp from our hotel. Sean finds a friendly hotel manager who obliges, and then we have to fall in at the back of the queue again. A woman with mid-eastern features rudely tries to push in ahead of me, and starts shouting that I'm a racist when I do not allow her to do so. Heinz gives her a lecture on her bad manners. When we finally reach the front of the line they close for lunch, and it's only after 4 pm that we finally are done – a whole day wasted in an excruciatingly hot building with no cooling system.

As Sean, Christo and I are walking back through the inner city streets, a burly black man whistles from an alley to attract our attention. 'Hey yo wanna buy cold beers or ganja?' he calls. We decline, wanting to avoid trouble at any cost in this country.

At dinner time we are worried because Carie and Marieke are missing. When they finally come in out of the dusk they are visibly upset. They were arrested and detained for two hours, because Marieke took a photo of a mosque. They were shouted at, threatened with prosecution, and treated rather roughly, and were only released after they had been interrogated by the police chief - all this for taking an innocent picture of a building wherein people worship. What kind of people are they? Maybe a bit screwed in the head is our conclusion, after dipping into a few warm vodkas, as we enliven the late night breeze on the riverbank.

CHAPTER 11: SUDAN.

Sunday, July 23, 2006. It is rather ironic that in the most Islamic of all the countries we've visited, we're awoken by church bells from a nearby cathedral. Hopefully, this is a good omen, for there are going to be tough days ahead of us. Directly to the north, the Nubian Desert forms an immense natural blockade, the conflict zone of Northern Darfur lies to the west, and to the east there is the ongoing border problem with Eritrea.

On our way out of the city we pass over a high bridge with a great view of the convergence of the Blue and White Nile rivers. Threading one's way through the maze of roads and bazaars in the absence of road signs is a major problem, but the northbound route we're following soon leaves the city behind as it enters the desert. The pot-holed tar road eventually peters out into several alternative sand tracks leading northward. The real traveller supposedly chooses the least travelled way, but in this case, such a route could see you stuck in the sand for days, so we choose the main tracks. The sand track has a softer feel than the bumpy, pot-holed tar road.

Heinz is in agony as the truck's severe jolting is affecting his spine. I remember that there is a pack of anti-inflammatory tablets in my first aid kit and give them to him, as there is still a long way to go and this is no place for any of the group to break down.

Around us, the scrub and occasional thorn bushes eventually give way to flat, open desert. It is excruciatingly hot at midday, and the temperature must be in the mid forties. To our right the green foliaged banks of the Nile River form the north / south lifeline of the continent. The only signs of human habitation are the walled compounds of mud huts along the verdant riverbanks, with occasional shops where white-robed men smoke water pipes. From time to time the tar road reappears for short stretches, only to be eaten up by road works again. In the afternoon we follow the road to the water's edge, where we join a crowd of curious locals waiting for the car ferry to cross the river. The river is a strong-flowing muddy force, but the powerful ferry soon deposits us well downstream on the other side.

In the late afternoon our drivers spot a likely looking place for an overnight camp between the tall date palms along the riverbank. When our truck leaves the sand track and crosses over towards the riverbank, disaster strikes, every trucker's nightmare, the truck sinks into the soft sand, right up to the chassis.

The desert has eyes and ears. A group of white-robed men stroll over from a distant settlement and shake hands with all the males in our group, cluck-clucking in commiseration when they see the sand-locked truck. They only speak Arabic and soon wander off into the dusk as we begin to set up camp. As usual, I help Heinz and Olga who are both in bad shape, with Heinz suffering severe back pain.

Carie and I mix and hand out strong lukewarm gin drinks, for everyone is feeling exhausted due to the extreme heat, as the realization sets in that there is no AA to rescue our truck, our castle, which lies knackered in the sand. `Tell us about the Nubian,' I say to Sean, in order to break the silence. `In Arabic it's called As-sahara 'An-nubiya' he replies. `It's separated from the Libyan Desert to the west by the Nile River valley, and eastward lies the Red Sea. This is a vast rugged plateau of rocks and sand dunes, which is actually a remote eastern section of the Sahara Desert.'

After dinner, more drinks, and a strong whiff of the breeze we tackle the problem. Some of the females point the flashlights as the male members grab shovels and dig each wheel free. Then we place the steel grids built for this purpose beneath the wheels, together with all the small rocks we can find. Everyone stands back, holding their breath as Christo revs up the engine and releases the clutch. The truck roars and labours out of the hole, carried across the desert face by our jubilant cheers, then sinks back up to its chin in the sand. We retire defeated to stir the breeze on a distant dune.

To increase the circulation of air within the tents we've all removed the top flaps. This allows us to lie on our backs and look at the stars as we drift off to sleep, despite the claustrophobic heat of the stifling night air. As I stare up into the mystery of the universe, my tent is transformed into a magic carpet that swoops over the top of the palm trees and swishes up the Nile, to a dazzling welcome from a radiant princess in a Pharaoh's glittering palace.

Monday, July 24, 2006. In the Nubian Desert. At 5 a.m. the mighty lord and scourge of the desert is but a faint pink threat on the eastern skyline, as we go about our ablutions, and eat breakfast before striking camp. Then it turns into a desert style cage brawl – humans armed with shovels against a million billion grains of treacherous, sucking sand. Dig each wheel free, place the steel grids, pack stones for tread, rev up, release clutch, engine roaring, humans praying, -if you're not into prayer the desert will quickly change that- and pushing – up and out – wild cheers – disaster – repeat. By mid-morning we're buggered. The ascending sun is an unrelenting scorching force, and the exterior of the truck is becoming too hot to touch with the naked hand.

We hold an emergency meeting in the truck's dwindling shade. 'I'll go for help' says Sean, and armed with a bottle of water he strides back to the sand tracks and heads northward. By now our truck is so bogged down that it seems as if no power in the universe can save it, and Cairo remains a distant fantasy.

We lie back against the sand. Christo, Beer and I are exhausted, for along with Sean, we've been bearing the brunt of the digging. Then as the shady area recedes there is the first hint of hope – a distant roaring sound! Like a mirage of an invading space monster, the gigantic front-end-loader comes tearing across the desert. The driver, who has no English, produces a thick belt which Christo attaches to the truck. The monster roars and heaves, we hold our breath, the truck lurches forward then settles back into its hole. When the dust recedes we see that the belt broke. It breaks again. We tie another knot but to no avail. Sean and Christo set out to look for a chain, and to our consternation, the front-end-loader suddenly departs in the opposite direction.

It's almost midday, and as hot as a cooking cauldron within the desert's searing bake, as the temperature soars up into the 40's. Sean and Christo come back empty-handed, but shortly after the front-end-loader returns with some men in a 4-wheel drive pick-up truck. They have an enormous chain, which Christo attaches to the truck, and then in a fevered blur of dusty action we are out. We shake hands and wave goodbye to these true desert Samaritans and hit the northbound trail again.

This section of the road is still under construction, so the driver can take his pick of several alternative wheel tracks leading to the north. In the back of the truck we're lulled into a lethargic stupor by the monotonous landscape and hot waves of cloying, dusty air. Then there is a pause, a slight hesitation in the truck's rhythm, before it chokes and dies in the sand. Only some of us get out for a look, the others are too stunned to face reality, but there it is – only the truck's nose is sticking out of the sand. With the blazing sun directly overhead, this promises to be the ultimate test of character of the truck and its occupants'.

Out come the grids and shovels, once again we look for small, loose rocks to pack beneath the wheels and begin to dig. A few people are incapable of assisting, but some of the females take turns to help and before too long we're ready. Christo starts the truck, revs up, releases the clutch and steps on the gas. There is a mighty roar as we also throw our bodies against the back of the bucking truck and heave, using towels to protect our hands against the hot metal. The truck bursts loose in a brave bid for freedom, only to collapse onto its knees and sink back into the sand again like a dispirited mule. We gather around it in despair. If it were a beast and I had a gun I'd put it out of its misery. Now it looks as if it's we who need to be put down. How on earth are we going to get this truck through the desert? It has to happen. I go back to fetch the grids. One is sticking out of the sand, but I have to dig deep before I find the other, and struggle for a while to wrench it free from the sands' malicious grip. The situation seems to be hopeless, but it is at this point that three men in white robes materialize out of the desert and begin to help us. Although they speak no English, we soon realize that these guys are past masters at this kind of business, so I follow their instructions, and before too long we are out again. They also point us to the firmest tracks, and then we embrace these never-to-be-forgotten desert nomads who unhesitatingly came to our rescue.

There is a deathly silence aboard as our truck plows its way through the desert's endless fields of lifeless sand. I see that my co-travellers are depleted, and start singing that old hit by the band `America' from the 70's, `I've been through the desert on a horse with no name…' When some of the others join in, I change it to `Truck with no name'. `Why doesn't our truck have a name?' Marieke calls to the front. ``Its name is `Sweetness'", Sean shouts back, and the name sticks. Now that she is recognized as an entity, `Sweetness' will never let us down again.

The terrain becomes harder and stonier, with black rocky outcrops. I wince as I watch Heinz trying to brace himself against the bumps, and can see that though he's suffering terribly, he's determined not to complain. When we have a toilet stop, I wander out on the alien landscape and pick up one of the millions of dark stones. It's hollow, the shape of a pot-bellied cooking pot, and feels like heated iron. The air is thick, gaspingly hot, and unpleasant in the throat and lungs.

The route through the Nubian Desert

There is still no highway, so we thread our way through settlements, getting lost in the narrow roads of Berber. Our hot drinking water tastes awful, so the drivers stop wherever they see a roadside shop for everyone to buy a cool drink. They only sell fizzy pop, which is not good for my stomach but I guzzle it nevertheless. At each stop we 'dismount', unsure of our footing, like drunken cowboys, and stagger into the cooler interior of the shops, where all the locals gather around to watch. Many men seem to sit and chat in the shade all day while smoking water pipes.

Sean stops besides a small gathering of people beside a village. There, lying in the sand is a gigantic statue, which Sean says is of a Nubian King. Some people say it was toppled and dumped there by Islamic fanatics.

The desert's face changes again, becoming more severe, with no plants visible other than the occasional glimpses of riverside greenery. We follow the tracks deep into the desert until they eventually lead back to the riverside.

Sean turns off the tracks and drives across the treacherous desert face to stop beside the wide band of date palms along the Nile, within sight of small settlements to the north and south of us. As we unpack, a group of men come over to welcome us. Using international body language they indicate that we are welcome to visit their homes for refreshments. They hand raw dates out for us to chew on. This display of traditional hospitality is touching, and we thank them but do not take up the offer. The truth is that everyone is exhausted, and many of us are feeling unwell, with diarrhea doing the rounds. Sean is sick too, and retires to the roof of the truck.

I stroll through the bushes and clusters of palm trees till I reach the banks of the Nile, and I watch the mesmerizing, heady rush of brown water that is the very soul of these desert lands. As I bathe without bothering to take my clothes off, I'm tempted to let go of the reeds and drift off, to unite with water, sand and sky, in the river of life's eternal lullaby. Later, while sunning my wet body, I ponder on whether there are still Nile crocodiles in the Nile River.

Back at the camp, I help Christo make a small fire and prepare dinner with the scant provisions available. The only vegetables we have are tomatoes and onions, which are included in every dish, and also used for sandwiches. Neither vegetable is good for me, due to their high acidity, so I eat sparingly, with little appetite.

I pitched Heinz and Olga's tent near mine, where I can keep an eye on them, as they're both looking poorly. After sunset, everyone retires to their tents except Beer and I, who are on dishwashing duty. The stifling darkness brings no relief, as the intense heat settles over us in a suffocating chokehold.

I strip naked and lie on my back in the tent, looking up at the sky through the date palms, as it's far too hot to sleep. In the dark of night, a love serenade of intense passion brays through the desert quiet, awakening every soul in the near vicinity to its haunting loneliness. It is the white mule that some Arabs tethered to a tree near our camp. Seconds of deep expectancy tick by, before an answering song of equal emotional force and resonance rings back from afar. It is a promise of eternal love, despite the brutal odds of life. Though they're kept apart by humans, these simple beasts of burden call out for all to hear, that they have hearts of flaming passion.

Tuesday, July 25, 2006. Wadi Halfa. At dawn, there is a breathless beauty within the wild landscape, as the first rays of sunlight reflect from the dust in the air. Sean's face is pale and gaunt looking, as he and the sweat and grease-streaked Christo man the cab, while there is an unnatural quiet in the back, as each person mentally braces for the onslaught of the heat.

My condition has deteriorated overnight, as I have no appetite and feel ghastly. The road is hard and unrelentingly bumpy, taking poor Heinz to the limit of endurance. The dirt tracks have now left the looping course of the Nile, and are heading towards the Egyptian frontier. We stop along the way for lunch, but the sight of food nauseates me, so I recline in the truck's meager shade.

We press on and the interior of the truck is a hot-bed of festering discontent, as each person attempts to find an endurable position in the bouncing vehicle as 'Sweetness' lurches through the wilderness. Then as we pass over a crest, Sean's strong voice reverberates through the truck. 'Wadi Halfa!' he calls. At first I think he's joking, but then we begin to descend into a valley with clusters of brown buildings appearing beside the road, and before too long we enter a major settlement.

Consisting mainly of mud buildings, Wadi Halfa lies between tall outcrops of sandstone hills, bathing in the valley's blistering heat. A crowd of white-robed onlookers gathers around the truck as Sean gets out and goes to look for his agent. Mashan Sharti welcomes us to Wadi Halfa, and shakes our hands before leading us to his home within a high, mud-walled compound. He is friendly, and invites us into the shade of his spacious veranda, which also serves as a bedroom. His wife and various family members come out to shake hands with us, and serve us tea. It's 5p.m. and when he checks the thermometer in the shade the reading is 43 degrees. We also meet his brother, who is renowned for his mountain bike trips through the desert to Abu Hamed in the south. They tell us that once when they once had a rain storm in Wadi Halfa, hundreds of mud homes collapsed.

With all arrangements for the next day made, we drive out of town into the desert and stop at a scenic spot between stark sandstone hills. It's so hot that we all just collapse in the truck's shade, and wait for it to cool down somewhat before pitching the tents.

My stomach is churning and cramping, telling me that it's time to take a walk out into the desert. As I squat in a depression, I see a pack of sleek hunting dogs running by in formation, they do not see me, and run like phantoms of the wind until they're absorbed in the golden sunset.

It's dinner time but I'm too sick to eat. This is the end of the road for 'Sweetness', as we will be using alternative transport from here, so we have to empty our lockers and be ready to 'backpack' in the morning. The final act is to clean ourselves up, as we're all filthy. Each person is allowed to drain some water into an empty locker box from the truck's storage tank, and have a glorious bath under the starlit sky.

There is a vague feeling of sadness within us, as if we've run a long race together, but at the end there is no fanfare or celebration. Sean acquired a few beers in Wadi Halfa, but few of us are in any condition to party. In the course of the night I become intimate with the desert, as close as one in the throes of diarrhea can get.

Wednesday, July 26, 2006. The Nile ferry. Dawn in the desert is a time of immense natural beauty, as the barren sandstone hills come to life in soft pastel hues of mauve and pink. I awaken to stomach cramps and nausea, and treat myself to an Imodium, and I do acupuncture while the others have breakfast.

Mashan Sharti has gone to buy the ferry boat tickets, so we wait in his office until the sun cooks us out, and then we cross the street and order tea at an outdoor café. The proprietor is cooking fish on a large gas cooker and the greasy fish smell increases my nausea, so I return to sit in the truck where the temperature is pushing up into the forties. I'm feeling rotten as I listen to the foreign babble of Arabic voices around the truck. Every second man seems to be called 'Magmud', as I keep hearing this name. Marieke comes to see how I'm doing, and gets me to drink my oral rehydration salts mixed with water. When the interior of the truck reaches cooking point, we wander out to the outdoor market and buy apples and grapes.

We get a call to return to Mashan's home, where we take leave of 'Sweetness' with mixed feelings, and cram into 4-wheel drive vehicles with our luggage. At a further point, we have to change to the back of a truck which takes us to the Sudanese Immigration offices on the shore of Lake Nubia, the Sudanese section of Lake Nasser. Going through immigration and customs is a time consuming process, but luckily Mashan has all the connections, and his men squeeze us through the crowd as far as possible. Our passports are taken away from us and are not returned.

Finally it's time to board the multi-decked ferry. We're all heavily loaded but still have to help Heinz and Olga who have by far the most stuff, but are incapable of carrying much. Sean leads us up to the top deck, where most of us crawl in under the shade of the lifeboat. It's hot and uncomfortable on the steel deck, with a taut cable cutting through our space, but the alternative is to join the crowds in the airless crowded berths below.

Several hours pass before the boat is ready to depart, then suddenly there is the loud fanfare of honking ship horns, and the high-pitched ululating of many women. We peer over to see what's happening. A honeymoon couple has arrived with a large send-off entourage. The groom is decked out in a naval officer's uniform and is getting a 'naval salute', and then we eventually depart. The upper deck is finally fanned by the blessed movement through air.

The early evening brings even more relief from the flaming celestial fireball that now seems to be lodged on the western skyline. More and more white-robed men begin to appear on the upper deck until the place is crowded. They are silent and form orderly lines, all facing toward Mecca in the east, as they solemnly conduct their Islamic prayer ritual of kneeling and bowing, while the smelly, alcohol-drinking, pork-eating unbelievers skulk warily beneath the lifeboat.

When the men return to their berths it's time for dinner, but I cannot stomach anything, and only manage to take in another cup of water mixed with oral rehydration salts.

It is sunset, and as we stare out into the wild, ragged, sandstone mountain wilderness that forms the western shoreline, there is a vast sense of relief that we're beyond the clutch of those treacherous, sucking desert sands.

With Marieke and Carie beside me, we try to make ourselves as comfortable as possible, despite the steel cable which we cover and rest our necks against as a pillow. In the course of the night I have to make a run for the ship's nearly overwhelmed toilets.

12

Egypt

THURSDAY, JULY 27, 2006. Aswan. I awaken suddenly in the dim rejuvenation of dawn, rubbing my neck that is stiff from resting on a steel cable, and glance over my travel mates who are all scrunched into various uncomfortable looking positions. Something has changed, then it strikes me; I am feeling great! The nausea has finally passed and I'm hungry for the first time in days. It feels as if I've emerged from a dark tunnel. Yesterday has receded into a nightmarish blur, but this is a new day, I'm sailing down the legendary Nile River, and ahead of us lie Egypt, Israel and Palestine. We've passed through the continent's dark heart and are heading for the centre of the world. No force on earth can stop our ship of destiny.

Despite my newfound hunger, I can only manage a few crackers, a wedge of cheese, and an orange. Later some of us go down to the canteen to buy tea. The sun, an object of raw natural wonder, as it blossoms over the distant desert hill tops, blooms into a gaping dragon mouth. As we huddle in the available scraps of shade, we are joined by Mustafa, a young man from Aswan who interprets the intercom announcements for us. He tells us that the ferry passed over into the Egyptian section of the lake in the night, and that we are now in Egypt. We can collect our passports, which have now been stamped out of Sudan.

As the ferry approaches Aswan, things become rather chaotic aboard the boat as we gather our belongings, and join the crush of hundreds of people in the narrow corridors. The Egyptian Immigration officials board the ferry, and are determined to process us right here in a small office aboard the boat. As the craft is no longer in motion, with the sun overhead the temperature rises into the forties and tempers fray. There is pushing and shoving, and loud shouting in Arabic, yet from this seeming chaos, some form of order is born. All foreigners get pushed to the front, then all females, then all Sudanese, and finally the Egyptians.

It is only when every passengers' passport has been stamped that they finally open the pressure cooker ferry's doors, for us to spill out in a swill of sweat and luggage. Next we have to lug all our belongings down stairs, across the concourse, and up into the customs area where we have to be processed again. In the chaos we lose Heinz, Olga, and Carie, and it takes all of two hours before we are reunited and ready to proceed into Egypt.

We engage a couple of taxis to ferry us to the Nubian Oasis Hotel, which is situated in the souk, a colourful market area. The smiling middle-aged hotel manager hands out brochures which proclaim, `laundry service, free - all times' and `internet for free 24 hours a day' – wonderful!, but it's not all true. He also announces `this is your home away from home!' The rooms are OK and have aircons! Wow – the wonders of civilization! I'm sharing a room with Sean.

Later, after we have all washed up, we venture out onto the lively streets and treat ourselves to the delights on offer. I have a mango juice, a fruit salad, and two ice-creams. This thriving market area offers a fascinating variety of Nubian handicrafts, such as scarves, jewelry and baskets, and is full of the scent and colour of spices and perfumes. We return to the hotel and collapse on our beds.

In the evening Sean and I wander through the market area, running the gauntlet of salesmen until we find peace in a teashop. When we return to the hotel we fall asleep with the souk's wailing Arabian music in our ears.

Friday, July 28, 2006. Aswan/Luxor. In the early morning when I awaken to a soft bed with crisp white sheets, I'm struck by a bout of nostalgia. I miss my tent and its close proximity to the natural earth!

We go downstairs for a breakfast of bread rolls, jam, and tea before our group members depart on a local tour. Valerie, who never got close to any of us, leaves our group, never to be seen again. Sean, Christo and I go out into the streets for a fresh mango juice drink. I splash out big time and buy a half kilogram of black olives – to put some meat back on my bones. It's Friday, the Muslim day off, so the streets are quiet. `Aswan', says Sean as we stroll down the Corniche el-Nili along the waterfront, `is the ancient city of Swenet, which used to be the frontier town of ancient Egypt. It is also one of the driest inhabited places on earth.' There are many luxury boats and yachts berthed at the quayside, and across the river on the west bank the cliffs are surmounted by the tomb of Qubbet el-Hawwa, who Sean says, was a local saint. Bright-winged feluccas vie for scraps of river breath. With the temperature pushing 42 degrees we return to the hotel.

In the afternoon, Sean, Christo and I go up to the rooftop for a great view of the city, and a marvelous whiff of the breeze. When the others arrive back in a lather of sweat, we pack and take taxis to the train station for the 2-hour ride to Luxor.

Unlike Sweetness, the train doesn't bump, and the ride is a pleasant one that cuts painlessly through the desert's wild flow of undulating dunes. When we arrive at the main train station after dark, taxis ferry us down Sharia al-Mahatta Road to the Nefertiti Hotel near the main waterfront souks (markets). Across from the hotel's front door there is a small Bottle Store, where we immediately buy a batch of cold beers. We carry our luggage up to the third floor, where I share a room with Sean, and then we all meet up at the great rooftop lounge. The lounge has a balcony with a stunning night view of Luxor, the ideal setting for a long overdue party, as we've all somewhat recovered from the rigors of the trip.

Saturday, July 29, 2006. Luxor/Hurghada. In the morning we join a tour to the Valley of the Kings, and descend into the bowls of the earth to view the burial chambers of the grand rulers of an ancient civilization.

We escape from the ruins in the scorching heat of midday to the refuge of cold mango juice and lunch in a street café. Then we return to the hotel to pack and crowd into a small bus, together with five Chinese tourists. We're booked to take the longer route to Cairo, via the tourist resort Hurghada, on the Red Sea.

Our bus has to join a long convoy of tourist buses, and then we're off, with the drivers racing and overtaking each other at top speed. There are time-consuming bottlenecks at several checkpoints manned by men in white robes with machine guns.

Hurghada is a tourist trap of five-star hotels, restaurants and boutiques spread out along the shore of the Red Sea, and it seems that the travel industry is designed to bring tourists here regardless of their wishes. Our bus dumps us in the centre and the driver tells us to return in a few hours. We wander around and finally sit down at one of the outdoor places to order food and drinks. Sean, Christo and I squeeze through the buildings to take measure of the sea breeze.

The convoy finally proceeds northward again at about midnight. An hour later our bus is singled out at one of the roadblocks. The driver does not have a clearance to take us to Cairo, and has to turn back to Hurghada, despite all the heated arguments.

Sunday, July 30, 2006. Hurghada/Cairo. What a shambles! We get taken back to a small hotel in Hurghada at about 2 a.m. for a two hour sleep, after which we have to go to the bus station by taxi. As our Cairo bound bus follows the coastal road along the Red Sea, I try to imagine the biblical setting of Moses leading the Israelites through the parting waters.

Most of us are too excited to sleep, as our bus swishes in and out of the oncoming lane as it overtakes vehicles at a high speed. The bus turns inland into the desert, as dawn reaches out to us, revealing wild rugged sand dunes bathed in a soft lather of white morning mist.

CHAPTER 12: EGYPT.

We enter 'the Mother of the World', a city of about 18 million people with a turmoil of mixed emotions, for this is 'our' end of the road, for some of us the culmination of a trip across the continent from Cape Town. When we arrive at the bus station, Sean guides us to taxis, which carry us to the Sun Hotel on Talaat Harb Street, just off St. Eltahrir Square, in the centre of Cairo. We check in, and then get together for breakfast before retiring to our rooms. I'm sharing with Sean and Christo.

In the afternoon we all split up. Marieke is meeting her brother and sister, Heinz and Olga are recovering, Beer is going to see some pyramids, and Sean and Christo are looking for a part for the truck. Carie, Alexandra and I visit the Egyptian Museum, where one can spend hours looking at the archaeological glory of the past. I read more about the history of the city and find that the section of the city called Old Cairo was once the legendary, biblical city of Babylon.

Monday, July 31, 2006. Cairo. We decide to have one last bash together before parting ways forever, and meet in the Café Riche, which I become familiar with in the coming days. The walls of this quaint restaurant are lined with the portraits of famous Egyptian writers, with the Nobel Prize winner Nagib Mahfouz at the centre. It's time to wine dine and party, to wash the trail dust from our throats. We get back to the hotel in a drunken uproar, where the party continues into the night. Later some of us gather on the rooftop to savour the African breeze, and talk about the future.

August, 2006. Cairo and Alexandria. The trip is over and the party is done – everyone is moving on – it's time to get focused again. Beer and Marieke are keen to meet me in Holland, so I take a cab to the Netherlands Embassy to apply for a Schengen Visa which will allow me to visit 15 European countries. They block me at the gate and say I need to call and make an appointment. When I do this, a woman tells me that I cannot apply from Cairo, but should return to South Africa and apply from there. I try to explain to her that I'm a traveller and do not live in South Africa. She is not interested in my story, and says I must either prove that I have permanent residence in Egypt, or return to my home country and apply from there. So there it is: even though my father's ancestors are from Holland and my mother's from elsewhere in Europe, they are blocking my entry with a firewall of red tape. I give Western Europe a big middle finger and tap into the internet re visa requirements for Turkey. On a website it says that South Africans can apply for a visa on arrival.

I've got to visit Alexandria on the Mediterranean, where my Greek grandpa once worked as a cook for the British Army. On the bus I read through some interesting information I printed from the internet. An awed Ammianus Marcellinus, a fourth century Roman historian wrote about a tsunami striking the then thriving port of Alexandria in 365 AD: 'The sea was driven back, and its waters clawed away to such an extent that the sea bed was laid bare and many kinds of sea creatures could be seen. Huge masses of water flowed back when least expected and overwhelmed and killed thousands of people. Some great ships were hurled onto rooftops by the fury of the waves, and others were thrown up to 3 kilometres from the shore.'

The crowded inter-city bus deposits me at a bus station on the outskirts of Alexandria, from where I take a cab to Ramla, the large square running along the waterfront. From there I eventually find a place in the cheapish Kouja Hotel in Mahmoud El Falky Street.

In the afternoon I explore this lively city for hours, and enquire at several travel agencies about the possibility of travelling to Turkey by ship, but all are negative and suggest I fly. As the sun's glowering face is slowly engulfed in the sparkling waters of the western Mediterranean, thousands of people throng the promenade, seeking the relieving balm of the cool sea breeze. It is lonely out on the crowded streets, and I miss my co-travellers. Christo, a real character, was a good leader, his laid-back approach counteracted Sean's more volatile personality. Beer and Marieke were brave and uncomplaining, enduring hardships with equanimity, while Carie was tough when the going got hard, and put colour to many a blank hour.

Back in Cairo, I purchase a one-way ticket to Istanbul, and take leave of Africa after one last party with Carie, who is still in the Sun Hotel. The others have all gone.

13

Thailand

AUGUST, 2006. ISTANBUL / Bangkok. By the time the Turkish Airlines flight touches down in Istanbul, I have already studied the city map and done some reading, and I start to formulate a new plan of action. In this city I can arrange for a Russian visa, and access the country via Eastern Europe. At immigration I head for the 'Visas on arrival' counter, where the reception is hostile. 'South Africans cannot get visas on arrival' the female officer says and buzzes for the Immigration Police. She says the information I read on the internet was incorrect and probably outdated. When they want to deport me back to Cairo, I get really angry and refuse, demanding time to plot another course. Demet Doganay, the Turkish Airlines manageress is very helpful, giving me access to their computers, but we cannot find any country that issues South Africans visas on arrival in the direction I am travelling. With my Russian dream now in tatters I have to make a quick decision, and purchase a one-way ticket to laid-back Thailand.

August, 2006. Bangkok. Thailand welcomes me like a good old friend as I am stamped through immigration by a smiling official at the Suvarnabhumi Airport. It is well past midnight when I push through the crowd at Arrivals, and get a regular meter taxi to take me to Khao

San Road in the Banglamphu area. There is something familiar about the taxi driver, and then I get it when he starts the cab and turns on the music. He's an Elvis Presley look-alike! There are mounted pictures of him in Elvis-like gear on the dashboard, and we listen to golden oldies all the way into the city.

The expressway passes high above the city streets, subjecting one to a marvelous view of Bangkok's vast glittering metropolis of modern skyscrapers and old-style architecture. We bypass many familiar turnoffs, such as Bang Na, Dao Khanong, Din Daeng, Chaeng Wattana etc. before descending into the urban maze at ground level. At this hour there's not much traffic, and shortly after we pass Democracy Monument, 'Elvis' drops me off at the 'Burger King' end of Khao San Road after 1 a.m.

Even though most places have shut down by now, there is still a hum of activity as I stroll up this fluorescent wonderland of souvenir shops, second-hand bookstores, guesthouses, email cafes, travel agencies, restaurants, pubs, and massage parlours. When the road runs into the Wat Chana Songkhram Buddhist Temple complex I turn right and then left again into Soi (lane) Rambutri, until I reach the My House Guesthouse. There are no vacancies, as at Baht 190 (about $6), one gets a good, clean room with its own shower and toilet, and it's one of the best deals in Bangkok. I stash my backpack there and stroll back along Soi Rambutri to Popiang House's open-air restaurant, where I order a big Beer Chang and get really laid-back as I watch the comings and goings of the late night revelers. It's not until after 7 a.m. that I return to the guesthouse to find that there is now a room for me and I can hit the deck.

When I awaken after 2 p.m., the temperature is about 33 degrees out on the streets, as it is the rainy season in Thailand. I buy a sliced portion of fresh papaya from a sidewalk vendor, on the way to check my email. Back at the guesthouse I order a bowl of boiled rice soup mixed with minced pork and vegetables, and take stock of my situation again. The beauty of being in this location is that you're surrounded by travel agencies with visa services, and the cost of living is really low.

After sundown, I take a walk down past the Temple of the Emerald Buddha, and the Grand Palace, a glittering, golden array of grandiose structures cloaked in Oriental mysticism. When I return to the bustle of Khao San Road I go into a massage parlour and treat my desert parched body to an erotic, er, I mean aromatic, two-hour oil massage - mmmm! Back out on the streets it's all happening on the main drag and in the narrow alleys between the buildings, so I have a few drinks at a laid back Rasta bar, before settling on the sidewalk with a beer in my hand to watch the action.

Where to go to – what to do? I've got to make a plan! Though I've lived in the region before, I want to see more of the Mekong River, and then I've never been to Angkor Wat in Cambodia, or Nepal and India. I have heard that climbing in Nepal can be costly, as one may need a guide and special gear, so I email my old friend JP from Canada who has been there.

In the morning there is a reply from the charismatic JP. He's doing a tennis- coaching course in Toronto and is brimming with enthusiasm to coach in Katmandu. 'Meet me there in early October. It's a great time of the year to be up in the mountains. Check into the Khangsar Guesthouse.' he emails.

My plans begin to take shape. Step one, I need a visa for Laos, that mysterious, jungle-clad country lying on the northern banks of the mighty Mekong River. Next I have to check in with my old friends Pon and Annette, at Eagle House Guesthouse in Chiang Mai, northern Thailand. From there I'll travel to Maejo Agricultural University, in the countryside, to meet my former boss Ajarn (professor) Lalida Puthong, and my friend Aj. Rangson Chanta. After that I'll head northward into Laos.

14

Laos

WEDNESDAY, AUGUST 23, 2006. Northern Thailand. It is just after 7a.m. that I awaken to that old morning of departure thrill in my small Eagle House room. After a breakfast of fruit salad, toast, eggs and tea, I chat to Annette, the classy Irish lady who runs this guesthouse in partnership with her Thai husband Pon. Annette unlocks the safe and gives me back my money belt.

There is time for last minute shopping, so I walk out along the moat that protects the old inner area of Chiang Mai to the Tha Phae Gate area, which lies at the heart of the bustling city. I do the internet, buy bananas, peanuts and raisins, and then I'm ready to leave.

At noon I meet a small group of eager young Englishmen, who are also waiting for the minibus to the north. There are ten of us altogether in the vehicle, which follows the hilly route through the jungle towards Chiang Rai in the north. Later the minibus turns off towards Huay Xai in the northeast. There is a nervous silence aboard as the driver steers with reckless third-world panache, overtaking other vehicles on blind bends and racing buses, side-by-side up winding hills.

The road leads through verdant fields and jungle clad hills, with many fruit stalls and settlements of wooden dwellings elevated from the ground on poles. Our driver stops a few times at rural roadside centres where one can use the toilets or buy delicious, cheap Thai food.

It is just after 6 p.m. that we check into the PK Guesthouse, which lies just off the banks of the Mekong River in the laid-back town of Huay Xai. At the guesthouse we fill out the visa applications for Laos Immigration to make things easier in the morning. I make friends with Wolfgang from Germany and Sally from England.

We drink beers on the Mekong River banks until the dark sky overflows in a furious torrent of tropical rain, driving us back to the guesthouse where it's time to order dinner.

Thursday, August 24, 2006. On the Mekong River to Pakbeng Village. At 8 a.m. I join Sally and Wolfgang for a breakfast of bananas, eggs, toast and tea after which we are taken to Thai Immigration on the waterfront. After checking out of Thailand, we board a shaky narrow motorboat to be ferried across the river to the Laos Immigration post to have our passports stamped. When we exit immigration, we have to jump on the back of an old truck, which carries us to the ferryboat terminal.

As we are the first passengers to arrive, we can choose the best seats on the big old `slow boat'. Later the boat fills up with a mix of tourists and locals, and the aisle is stacked with an odd assortment of provisions, produce, and backpacks. The open-air craft has a roof and is made of wood, with rows of two seats on either side of the aisle. Aboard the boat, I make a reservation for a guesthouse, which is said to overlook the river in Pakbeng Village. A room with a toilet and fan will cost about $6.50.

At about 11 a.m. we depart into the fast flowing murky current, which is swollen with the deluge of seasonal rain. The brooding sky's murky complexion infringes upon the wild green jungle hilltops along the river, but mercifully it is not raining. The Mekong is a natural regional highway, which according to Wikipedia, the internet's free encyclopedia, runs from the Tibetan Plateau, through China's Yunnan province, and then on through Burma, Thailand, Laos, Cambodia and Vietnam. At over 4, 300 km, it is one of the world's major rivers. Apparently, the extreme seasonal variations in flow, as well as the rapids and waterfalls, make navigation exceedingly difficult. It also has an infamous reputation as a drug runners' highway, while some sections are said to be targeted by pirates, as it runs mostly through wild, jungle fringed frontiers, where law and order are tenuous.

Small boats chug by, ferrying goods to outposts, while occasional wooden huts perched on stilts can be seen, amidst groves of bananas and tall trees drenched in clinging ferns. Sometimes fishermen in little bobbing boats wave to us, as we wonder about the lives they lead.

Patches of cultivation appear on a flat area beside the river, and a Buddhist temple's golden façade peaks through the jungle greenery. The boat engine's monotonous throb is barely audible as the current does most of the work. Simon, an excited young man from Switzerland, is sitting beside me, as someone hands out lunch packs of fried rice and vegetables. From the back of the boat come strains of the Beatles' music 'I don't care too much for money – money can't buy me love.'

Large drops of rain begin to fall as lugubrious-looking clouds lean on the hilltops, bending in on the river. We scramble to undo and let down the plastic flaps. It is very dark on board as the deafening torrent of pelting raindrops overwhelms the senses, but it gradually fizzles into a light spray in the breeze.

The boat honks loudly at about 5 p.m., as it rounds a bend in the river, and there lies Pakbeng Village, consisting mostly of wooden structures which stretch from the waterfront up a two-fronted hillside. There is a large group of villagers present to meet and help unload the boat. In the gathering twilight, a man leads Sally and I, along with six Englishmen and a Canadian, up a muddy track to the guesthouse.

After checking in, I get to meet the local herbal merchant, who gives me an exceedingly good deal – he says local produce is the best. Then I see Sally and the others and join them on the restaurant deck, where everyone is having a drink, thrilled to have a bird's eye view of the Mekong. Across from us, the green, white-misted hills slope down to the muddy mass of water that whirls away around the next bend.

I order fried river fish and a bowl of vegetable rice soup, as the sinister sky-face grows dark and growls menacingly, with jagged silver zigzags sizzling the hilltops, before sheets of water sweep down from the breached dykes of heaven above. Several young men join me on the rim of the outer deck to take measure of the excellent local breeze. Below us, the frothing Mekong is an immense force of nature, as unstoppable as the destiny that life holds in store for each of us.

We retire to our rooms as the pounding rain threatens the electricity. When I lift the mosquito net covering my bed, the power finally fails, and I drift off in a bobbing Mekong dream-boat.

Friday, August 25, 2006. On the Mekong River to Luang Prabang. It is very dark in my room when I awaken to the sound of cockcrow and the drumming of rain on the zinc roof. I am the first guest out on the deck, where I order coffee with a banana pancake, and watch flurries of rain pepper the Mekong's steamy face.

Luckily, the rain lifts by the time we wander down to the waterfront and board our boat. Before long there is a large crowd of people on board, ready for the 8:30 a.m. departure, but for some unknown reason we don't depart until 10 a.m.

When we putter away from the shore, the current takes hold of us and sweeps us around the first bend, leaving Pakbeng Village behind as a warm memory. The river banks, with their steep jungled hillsides crowd ever closer, hastening the current, while the dark sky pelts us with intermittent squalls of rain. The prevailing colours are the river's muddy murk and the green of the hills, which continually change in shape and size, while the sky is shrouded in grey clouds, with dark, bruised complexions.

The local woman sitting beside me speaks no English, but she's expert at getting the rain flaps down quickly. It is not a good idea to hit on Laotion nationals, as the local law prohibits sexual contact with foreigners, and it is forbidden to invite a Laotion of the opposite sex to your room.

Our boat makes numerous stops at clusters of wooden huts where people are dropped off or picked up. Goods are loaded aboard till even the aisle is chock-a-block with merchandise. One wonders if these bags are filled with sugar, corn-meal, or just raw opium.

The river has a life of its own, forming whirlpools and branching into different currents. Large mounds of river debris and swirling eddies mark barely submerged rocks. One hopes that the local boat navigators are not from the same mould as the drivers on the national roads.

We are all suffering from sore bums after sitting on the wooden seats for such a long time, so it is a relief when the craft enters a wide section of the river to arrive at Luang Prabang in the late afternoon.

There is the usual chaos at the waterfront, but I soon sift through the guesthouse agents and choose the Merry Guesthouse, at $4 a night. Sally and Wolfgang decide to join me, so we share a tuk-tuk to the guesthouse, which lies on the banks of the Nam Khan River.

Luang Prabang lies on a small peninsula formed by the Nam Khan River's half-loop as it joins the Mekong. At the centre is Phu Si hill, with the rather exotic-looking golden coloured temple, That Chomsi, at its highest point. It is a large, rural, laid-back place consisting mainly of wooden structures, with many golden Buddhist temples. It was the royal capital of the Kingdom of Laos, until the communist takeover in 1975, and is now a UESCO World Heritage Site.

We are all on a bit of a high when we meet on the front porch and drink beer as we check out the riverside scene below. We watch a group of youngsters across the river. They are taking turns to climb a tree and jump from a high branch into the water. Later we stroll into town to use the internet, and have dinner in a restaurant. It rains hard sporadically.

Saturday, August 26, 2006. Luang Prabang. Sally joins me for a breakfast of banana pancakes and tea, after which we exchange money at a bank. $1 = Kip 10 000. Later we climb the rather steep steps leading up the back of Phu Si Hill, to the glittering gold-coloured extravagance at the summit. It's sweaty work climbing up the tree-shaded stairway in the balmy midday heat, but on reaching the top, there are superb views of the town, with its shimmering temples and scenic green hills.

We follow the path down the front of the hill to peruse the ornate interior of the Royal Palace Museum, which was formerly the residence of King Sisavangvong and his court. After the revolution, the king's son, Savang Vattana, and his family were exiled to an unknown fate in Northern Laos.

In the evening we meet up with Wolfgang and go to the theatre for a ballet performance, 'Sida's Trial by Fire'. The characters, include the beautiful Sida, Phralam and Phralak (the king and the queen), and Hanuman, the white monkey.

Afterwards we proceed to a restaurant on the banks of the Nam Khan River for dinner. I wash some rather bony river fish, and chips, down with beer. Later we go to the rather 'in' Lao Lao Beer Garden for more drinks.

Sunday, August 27, 2006. Luang Prabang. After breakfast at a nearby guesthouse, Wolfgang, Sally, and I contract a sawngthaew, (a pickup-truck taxi) to take us to the village Pak Ou, about 25 km upstream from Luang Prabang. Beyond the village we walk down to the Mekong waterfront, where a man and his son offer to give us a ride across the river to Tham Ting caves on the opposite bank.

'Do you think this boat is safe? It looks rather shaky', Sally queries (with good reason). 'They're in the business so I guess they know what they're doing' I reply. We board the boat, but its engine dies moments after the craft leaves the shore, and it's only the son's frantic paddling that gets us back before the current snatches us. The second boat angles against the current, and carries us across to a point below the mouth of the first of the caves, which all contain exotic Buddha images.

On the return trip the boat's engine stutters until it dies, much to Sally's consternation, as she says that she can't swim. Once again the young boatman paddles frantically, but he's no match against the power of the mighty Mekong. Luckily, another boat comes to our rescue and tows us to safety.

On the way back we ask our driver to stop at the "Whisky Village", Ban Xang Hai. Several street stalls display many bottles with various kinds of snakes of many sizes, all preserved in alcohol. There are also bottles with 'monster' scorpions and spiders, but we only buy small bottles of wine made from sticky rice. I open a bottle of the sweet tasting wine on the way back and pass it around, and by the time it's empty we all have a slight buzz. This type of alcohol is best consumed in small quantities.

On the way back we stop beside a large water buffalo and her calf, which are both submerged in a very deep puddle, with only their heads sticking out.

When we arrive back in Luang Prabang it's time to buy our departure tickets for tomorrow. Wolfgang is going directly to Vientiane, the capital, while Sally and I decide on a stopover in Vang Vieng along the way.

In the early evening, Sally and I climb Phu Si hill again to have a sundowner on the summit with the two Englishmen, Tom and Sam, and the Canadian, Lo. As the sun dwindles on the western skyline, the golden Wats, (temples) lying in its path seem to catch fire in a magical glow, as time stands still over this settlement that measures its history in thousands, rather than hundreds of years.

Tonight will possibly be our last evening together, so Sally, Wolfgang, and I take a tuk-tuk ride across the peninsula to the restaurants that line the Mekong shore, for dinner and drinks. Later another tuk-tuk takes us to the Lao Lao Beer Garden for more drinks.

Monday, August 28, 2006. From Luang Prabang to Vang Vieng. Wolf has left by the time Sally wakes me after 7 a.m. We both have slight hangovers, and go out for breakfast and pay our guesthouse bills. A minibus comes for us at 9 a.m., and then picks up several more people before hitting the road to Vang Vieng.

The driving is scary along the winding route, which passes through spectacular mountain scenery. Our driver blows the buses hooter at everything he sees, which includes other vehicles, water buffalo, pigs, dogs, cattle, goats, poultry, and scores of `free-range' children. On the seat behind us, a youngster `barfs' quietly into a plastic packet.

Many wooden huts that line the road are perched precariously on poles, with the valley falling away hundreds of metres below them – very similar to Ethiopia.

CHAPTER 14: LAOS.

Our van stops in the centre of Vang Vieng just after 3 pm, from where a tout leads Sally and I to the Chanthala Guesthouse, which offers fan-cooled rooms with toilets and hot showers at $3 a night.

After a quick lunch we exchange money and get a tuk-tuk to take us out to the Tham Jang Caves. While crossing a swing bridge on the approach to the caves, Sally pulls her camera out of her pocket and accidently drops her malaria tablets into the fast-flowing river below.

We shine our torches around as we wander deep into the partially lit caves, marveling at the oddly shaped stalactites and stalagmites. High up in the upper caves there is a magnificent view through a break in the limestone mountain, to the river valley below, which is bordered on the far side by sheer, green mountain peaks.

Vang Vieng, which is all lit up at night, is reputed to be quite a party centre, but there's not much going on tonight, and most of the dozens of bars seem to be empty.

Tuesday, August 29, 2006. Vientiane. Sally and I go out for breakfast, before boarding the bus to Vientiane at 9:30 a.m. The road gradually leaves the mountains behind and becomes less dangerous, as it enters a vast, flat area.

It's hot and humid when we arrive in the capital at 3:30 p.m. The city has grown a little since my last visit in 1998, with more tourists, guesthouses, and hustlers. We check into the Pathoumphone Guesthouse, then stroll down to the Mekong River for lunch at an open-air waterfront restaurant.

In the evening we have dinner in style aboard the Lane Xang cruise ship, which is berthed at the riverside. After a great meal of local cuisine, we stroll into town and have too many drinks at the Muzaik Bar.

Wednesday, August 30, 2006. Vientiane. After breakfast we go for a long walk, exploring the Mekong waterfront area. It has a laid-back, tropical ambience with most restaurant decks perched on poles above the river. Despite the fact that this is a communist country, there are numerous grand golden Wats, nestling between towering multi-limbed banyan trees.

It begins to rain heavily, so we go into a restaurant for lunch and then we return to the guesthouse. After Sally packs and checks out, I help her find the right bus to Hanoi. We are both feeling rather emotional when we say our goodbyes, but the path of life allows only the selected ones to walk the whole way together.

In the evening, I stroll down to the Mekong for dinner in a street café, before taking a long walk along the riverside to clear my head in the local breeze. The hustlers are out on the streets. 'You want hashish – ganja – opium – lady?' There's a lot of business out there for the right man.

Thursday, August 31, 2006. From Vientiane to Chiang Mai, Thailand. I wake up early, have breakfast and then walk across the city to the Talat Sao bus station. Bus number 14 takes me to the Friendship Bridge, where I pass through Lao Immigration. I hop onto a bus to the Thai Immigration office and once again have no problem entering that country. A tuk-tuk carries me into the frontier town, Nong Chai, from where I take a bus to the bus station in the neighbouring city of Udon Thani. Bad news! The next bus to Chiang Mai doesn't leave until 8 p.m. and then it will still be a 12 hour trip.

15

Cambodia

SUNDAY, SEPTEMBER 17, 2006. From Bangkok to Siem Reap. My trusty old alarm clock awakens me before 6 a.m. I pack and go down Soi Rambutri to a shop for bananas, peanuts and raisins, my usual road food.

After a breakfast of fresh mango, tea, and a toasted ham and cheese sandwich, I check out and go to the front of Tami Tours and wait for the 7:30 pickup. There is a European-looking young man with bleached blond hair, sleeping on the sidewalk. A drunken ladyboy, or `katoey', as these male-to-female transgenders are locally called, wanders over and gives me a back massage. When she gets amorous I have to move her on. My pick-up still hasn't arrived by 7:45, so I make a phone call from the nearby 7/11 shop. Someone comes to lead me to the bus, which is parked near Khao San Road. The bus is not too full, so I have an open space beside me, which is good as there's not enough leg room.

The 5-hour trip to the Cambodian border is rather uneventful. Aranya Prathet, the Thai frontier town, is a place where everyone is out to make a fast buck, a place where you should watch your wallet.

We pass through Thai Immigration then check in with the Cambodians. No problem as I have a pre-arranged visa. There is a long delay in the sweltering humidity, before a shuttle bus finally takes us to the local bus station, and then another long wait before a minibus comes to pick us up in the pouring rain.

The terrible, pot-holed road leads through what appears to be a vast swamp where rice grows wherever you look, and people live on higher ground in wooden houses elevated on poles. This is very unlike the orderly terraced rice paddies of mountainous South Korea. The water level is very high, as we're at the height of monsoon season. There are intermittent rain showers, and spectacular cloud formations massing in the disgruntled sky, as ragged jigs of lightning highlight the black horizon ahead. Despite the atrocious road conditions, the driver is a man who knows no fear, and things get really scary when we drive into a heavy rainstorm after dark.

Seven hours later, we stop to pick up a charismatic young Cambodian man who talks non-stop, trying to persuade us to sleep over in the Siem Reap guesthouse, which is our immediate destination. Our minibus suddenly slows down, as a crowd of people appear in the rain out on the road up ahead. Our driver edges through, until we see a young man lying spread-eagled on the road with a telltale white towel over his face. The locals say he was driving back after drinking in a bar when a truck struck his motorcycle.

We arrive in Siem Reap in the pouring rain and I decide to stay where we were dropped off, as the guesthouse only charges about $5 a night for a room.

Monday, September 18, 2006. Siem Reap. A motorcycle-taxi delivers me to the Naga Guesthouse near the centre of town. The place is old and run down, but cheap at $4 a night, and it has its own restaurant area. There is a safe in the room, and guests can provide their own lock.

First I need to exchange money, and I use my map to locate the most convenient place to do so. It is raining when I go out onto the streets, and I find that this is a hard town to walk in, as most vehicles are parked on the pavement, forcing one to step down into the streets, which are mostly under water. The only people on foot seem to be farangs,(foreigners), everyone else is on two-wheel vehicles - hundreds of them. Wherever I go I'm continually harassed by tuk-tuk drivers or motorcycle taxis.

The local currency is the Riel, and for $1 I get 4,000 Riel, but I soon find that this country has a dual system, and most locals seem to prefer the US dollar. After changing money, I go to the post office to send an ailing aunt some money, but I worry, as my Lonely Planet guidebook claims the local post office is unreliable. (I was to find out later that she did indeed receive the money).

The Stung Siem Reap River runs through the centre of town. Siem Reap means `Siam, (Thailand) defeated'. It's a cool, tree shrouded place where you can relax on one of the benches. The downtown area, Psar Chao, is crowded with shops, restaurants, and massage palours. I sit down at an outdoor café and order a beer and the delicious local speciality, lemon grass fish soup, with rice.

After dark I wade through vast puddles in the unlit streets leading into Psar Chao for dinner and a few beers. Later two local women come over to my table and ask if I want a massage. `How much?' I ask. They want less than $10, so we grab a tuk-tuk to my place, where I receive a two-for-the-price-of-one workover. Later I finish reading Harry Potter and the Halfblood Prince, but I don't like the ending.

Tuesday, September 19, 2006. Ankgor Wat. I have breakfast at 7:30 then leave by tuk-tuk at 8 a.m. The deal is that for $10 the driver will drive me to the main sites and wait for me till I'm ready to return. As my driver joins the swarming fray of two and three-wheelers on the pot-holed muddy puddled roads, I'm glad that I decided not to rent a bicycle.

Last night I read on the internet that the temples of Angkor were built by the Khmer civilization between 802 and 1220 AD, and from there, the kings ruled over a vast domain, stretching from Vietnam to China, and the Bay of Bengal.

It's about a 5 km trip to the entrance, where I have to buy a ticket. I read in some information brochures that Angkor Wat remains a significant religious centre, and that it was originally dedicated to the Hindu god Vishnu, and then later converted to a Buddhist temple.

As I wander through these magnificent ancient structures, which are the remains of a grand religious and social metropolis, I wonder at the fallibility of humankind. What on earth went wrong in this country? How could they possibly have gone from such a dominant civilization to modern day Cambodia, one of the poorest countries on earth, still recovering from the self-inflicted horrors of the Khmer Rouge?

The hordes of in-your-face salespeople at every site are very annoying, but I escape and am soon lost in the magnificent ruins. In some places the encroaching jungle blends with the ancient buildings, as gigantic banyan trees, their roots draped down like monstrous tentacles, grow on top of the remains of the temples.

Wednesday, September 20, 2006. Phnom Penh. A minibus gives me a ride to the bus company office and then I transfer and go to the chaotic bus terminal, where I manage to find a seat on a crowded bus. My window seat is uncomfortable, but luckily, there's enough foot space.

Through the rain-splattered window I can see vast, flooded paddies of rice, and small villages of wooden huts, all elevated on poles, and merry-headed palm trees.

After we arrive in Pnom Penh at about 3 p.m., a tuk-tuk takes me to the Boeng Kak (lake) area, a lively foreigner ghetto of winding streets and narrow alleys, with shops, restaurants and cheap guesthouses lining the lake. I check into the Same Same Guesthouse, which has a deck overlooking the lake.

After the temperature drops somewhat, it's time to explore the area. I soon find that the Boeng Kak area is a quieter little world within the greater area of Phnom Penh, where the roads are a race trek for two and three wheeled vehicles. As the sun sets and the evening progresses, young men peer surreptitiously from alleyways, cup their hands and call 'ganja – opium' or, 'you want lady?' Elsewhere it's the motto (motorcycle taxi) men who bug me.

I enter the laidback looking Tiger Bar and get to talk to the owner, Shan, a cool dude from Sri Lanka who's travelled all over Asia. He invites me up to the top balcony, from where we seek such comfort as may be contained within the breeze.

Later, as I'm getting into reggae music in a quiet corner below, Shan calls me to introduce two black South African men. We greet each other, doing the three-clasp, traditional African handshake and say 'Sabona' (hi). 'Unjani?' (How are you?), one of the men asks. My mind gropes back to my childhood days, and the answer in Zulu, 'ngisaphila' (I'm okay) comes to me in an instant, bringing cheers from the men, who are a bit homesick. As we drink beer together I ask them what they're doing here. They say they're traders. We talk about the military coup in neighboring Thailand and wonder if it will affect us.

Thursday, September 21, 2006. Phnon Penh: The Killing Fields. After having breakfast at 8 a.m., I do a deal with a tuk-tuk driver who will drive me the 15 km to the so-called 'Hell on earth in the 20th century', the 'killing fields of Choeung Ek'. In the 1975 – 79 period, when the communist Khmer Rouge regime took control of Cambodia, more than 20, 000 men, women, and children, including diplomats, foreigners, intellectuals, farmers, and others, were murdered there.

At the entrance is a tall structure, an oriental design of great beauty, a charnel house containing 8, 000 skulls of victims. There is a large glass cabinet, wherein the skulls are arranged in groups according to age and sex – e.g. females between 15 and 20, etc. The grim reality of the leering, eyeless skulls is a bit too much to stomach for long, so I walk out into the now-peaceful setting of the 'kilingl zone', and listen to the drone of piped male voices chanting Buddhist mantras. I sit on a bench beside one of several mass grave sites. I read from a pamphlet that most of the men women and children who were killed here were simply bashed with rifle butts, pipes, clubs, or bamboo poles before falling into the pits where their throats were cut. There is a plaque beside a tall tree with the words, 'Killing tree against which executioners beat children.' The most sobering aspect of this horror is that many of the killers are probably still alive and well today. It is said that most of the older Cambodians refuse to talk about those times.

My tuk-tuk driver negotiates the terrible road of bumps and muddy puddles, weaving his way through the myriad motorcycles back into the city, to drop me off at the Tuol Sleng Genocide Museum. It is a former high school that was converted into an interrogation, torture, and extermination centre known as S-21. It is a place of horror, despite the beauty and fragrance of the white-flowering Magnolia trees in the courtyard. I read that only 7 of the 17, 000 people that passed through here survived. The prisoners were interrogated and tortured until they uttered the names of every person they'd ever known, who were in turn arrested and so on. I walk through the small classrooms that were used as torture chambers. In some rooms there are still steel beds with the chains that held the victims. I take hold of a chain and try to imagine the violence and almost incomprehensible inhumanity.

I walk out into the courtyard and sit in the shade of the trees, overcome by the emotion of horror. The heavy aura is tangible, as though the moans, pleas and cries of unbearable pain are still hanging in the air, frozen in time, only fractionally beyond human hearing. Upstairs I find rooms with rows upon rows of boards with photos of the victims. There are pictures of old and young men, and women, teenagers, and children. Each one of them died in wretched agony – how could humans have done this to other humans? I feel numb, and lose track of time, until I become aware that darkness has descended, and I make my way back to the guesthouse.

After dark I return to the Tiger Bar and order a Masala Chicken Curry. Shan later invites me to a neat little alcove upstairs where he introduces me to Marie, his girlfriend from Denmark. She keeps rolling long herbal sacrifices to the breeze, and later two teachers and an interesting Chinese Malaysian man join us. Shan talks about the Cambodian Lottery, which he says is a kind of national obsession. It is a lottery about dream numbers. Every night everyone goes to bed and tries to dream about numbers, or about certain kinds of animals that represent specific numbers. Marie tells me that there is an urban legend here that if you eat watermelon and honey together you will die (I cannot imagine who would want to eat such an unlikely mix). I'm emotional, and drink another few beers, trying to forget the horror of the day. `We understand', says Marie. `We've all been there. If you want to stay sane you try not to think about it too much'.

Friday, September 22, 2006. From Phnom Penh to Kampot. It is a slow morning, beginning with bacon and eggs at 9 a.m., acupuncture to treat the hangover, and a motto to the bus station at noon.

CHAPTER 15: CAMBODIA.

The hot and humid conditions at the 1 p.m. departure soon change to light rain, and later there is heavy thunder and lightning with a torrential downpour, as we pass through the countryside of endless rice paddies and small, palm tree shaded villages. Our bus stops at every village to pick up and deliver passengers.

The road, consisting of a narrow tar strip, choked with motorcycles and a weird assortment of other vehicles, is a highly dangerous place. Along some stretches the tar has washed away, leaving monster potholes, while in some villages the entire main road is flooded. The driver often has to swerve to avoid wandering cattle, and once almost loses control after sideswiping a cow.

The bus reaches the Gulf of Thailand, and it is only when it turns inland again, that the only other foreigners on the bus, a French couple, realize that they've missed their destination, Kep, a small coastal town. A French speaking Cambodian woman interprets for them as they get dropped off in the pouring rain. A passing motto takes the man, plus their two backpacks, back to Kep, while the woman stands waiting in the rain.

At about 5:30 p.m. we arrive in the centre of Kampot, from where a tout leads me to Long Villa, a new guesthouse near the river and close to the market. For $3 a night I get a small clean room.

It is still raining when I go down to the open-air restaurant area for dinner after dark. As I'm enjoying Amok fish curry, a local speciality, I hear a young American woman and a German couple discussing a daytrip to the Bokor Hill Station tomorrow. I ask them for info, and then go to reception to sign on for the trip. Liana, the young American and I have beers with Colin, a fruity-voiced, middle-aged Englishman who sounds like someone in an English movie from the 60's. Liana tells us that she has recently started a new job with an N.G.O. in Phnom Penh. Colin tells us that Kampot was the scene of heavy fighting between Cambodian Government troops and the dark forces of the Kmer Rouge in 1974, with the latter eventually getting the upper hand.

Saturday, September 23, 2006. Bokor Hill Station. Liana and I have breakfast together before joining a mixed crowd of backpackers, French N.G.O. workers, and U.N. workers on the back of a pickup truck.

We cross over the Prek Kampong River, and after 7 km turn right to follow the winding, 25 km route. It is an atrocious road with the faint remains of tar making things worse. The track, which leads up the steep edge of the plateau, passing through thick jungle, offers brief, startlingly scenic views of the Gulf of Thailand below.

`Monkey', our driver, a small skinny chap with a great sense of humour, claims he was a soldier with the invading Vietnamese army who helped drive the communist forces out of the area. We stop for lunch at a viewpoint beside long deserted buildings, which he says were once occupied by the Khmer soldiers.

Next we wander through the skeleton of the Bokor Palace Hotel, which in its heyday was a summer retreat for French colonials from Phnom Penh. It must have been a grand place with its sprawling wings, great halls, spiral staircases, secret alcoves, and balconies with stunning views. The Lonely Planet guide book gets it right where they say the building is right out of the movie, `The Shining'.

After that we visit the stark remains of the Catholic Church, which have been trashed and desecrated with graffiti.

Sunday, September 24, 2006. Sihanoukville. I leave at 8 a.m., sharing a taxi with two attractive fashion design students, Emily and Alex, who are on their way back to Thailand. Sihanoukville is spread out over a large hilly area in the south west of Cambodia on the Gulf of Thailand.

A motto drops me off at the GST Guesthouse in the Ochheuteal Beach area, where I get a cool room with cable TV for $4 a night. I stroll across the road down to the crowded beach area, where a multitude of beach -bar-restaurants line the beach. The warm water is great for swimming despite the intermittent rain, and at high tide the water pushes right up to the bars' front steps.

In the evening, I take a long walk down the deserted undeveloped part of the coastline, but tread warily as there are rumors of foreigners being stabbed and robbed along here.

Monday, September 25, 2006. Sihanoukville. After an early morning beach walk and a long swim, I check out and take a motto to the further end of the beach to check into the Markara Guesthouse. My new room has no TV, but it's quieter here, and I'm close to the deserted beach area.

In the afternoon I take a long walk `down the wild side', to take in the fragrant sea breeze. On my return, a sudden heavy rain shower sends me running into the deserted bar shacks for cover. I dodge from shack to shack until I come upon a functioning bar. The two attractive young women working the bar are `Lynn' and `Two Hundred', (humorously), but there are no other customers in the area. I drink beer and eat chicken soup and then Lynn, who is an interesting source of information about Cambodia, returns to my room with me to `practice her English.'

Tuesday, September 26, 2006. Sihanoukville. After Lynn leaves on her motorcycle, I stroll down to Two Hundred's bar for breakfast. I wait for a gap between the intermittent showers to go for a beach walk in blessed isolation. I take in the splendid breeze, look back to the past and thrill about the trip that lies ahead. A furious torrent of rain soon drives me back to reality.

In the afternoon I head northwards to Serendipity Beach, and on to a rocky peninsula where I lose my yellow windbreaker.

Wednesday, September 27, 2007. Sihanoukville. As it is a nice morning I go for a walk, passing through the deserted beach area until I reach a fishing village beside a river. As I cross the bridge I see many men working on boats while the females repair the fishing nets.

In the evening I decide to visit Victoria Beach. It is dark and raining lightly by the time the motto driver drops me off along the road and points across a strip of land to a row of lights between the palm trees. I hurry down a muddy path to find there is only a bunch of tattooed, longhaired Frenchmen drinking at a bar.

Later the shark-faced barman directs me to the 'in' area up Weather Station Hill behind us. This place is a poorly attended tourist hangout with many overstocked pickup bars.

Thursday, September 28, 2006. Sihanoukville. It is raining again as I wander over to the restaurant for a breakfast of pork noodle soup. When the rain lets up I go for a banana shake at Two Hundred's bar, before going for a long stroll to commune with nature along the deserted beach area.

I say goodbye to the Gulf of Siam in the best way, by swimming out far into the warm, deep swells and floating out there for an hour or more, as I become one with elements of the sea, sky, and far horizons.

In the evening when I go for a farewell bar-crawl along the beach strip, and run into Rachael and Richard from Christchurch in New Zealand, a big party develops. Luckily we find that we're staying in the same guesthouse, as we wander back, giggling and dodging wayward palm trees for a last round in my room.

Friday, September 29, 2006. Return to Bangkok. It begins to rain lightly as the motto driver drops me off at the ferry terminal at the further end of town. I get a window seat beside a Cambodian couple with a baby on the two and a half hour trip to Krong Koh Kong Island, a wild frontier place renowned for smuggling, gambling, and prostitution.

I get stamped out at Cambodian Immigration and check in with the Thailand Immigration Office. From there I get a ride in a crowded minibus to the Trat city bus station, from where a bus takes me all the way back to Bangkok. The bus drops us of somewhere in the greater city area, but luckily a taxi is on hand to take me back to the Khao San area.

16

Nepal

Monday, October 2, 2006. Dhakar – Bangladesh. I awaken to the thrill of excitement within me, for today I will depart on the first step of a journey to the very heart of Asia, to wander through the legendary mountains of the Himalayas. Though I suppose I should be buying special gear, I decide to just `wing it`, with whatever I have in my backpack.

At 5 p.m. a minibus gives me a ride to Bangkok's new Suvarnabhumi Airport, where I check in at the Binam Bangladesh Airlines counter. The flight is delayed, but eventually leaves at 10:30 p.m.

When we arrive in Dhakar, I join a group of people at the transit counter. After a long wait we finally get whisked away in a shuttle bus to the Aero-Link Hotel somewhere in Dhakar. I make friends with an attractive young woman called Majo (pronounced Margo), a ski instructor from Argentina. We talk about Bariloche, the Argentinian ski resort which I visited in the 1980's, and finally get to bed after 2:30 a.m.

Tuesday, October 3, 2006. Kathmandu. Someone wakes me after dawn, and I'm feeling sleepy, as it's early here despite being one hour behind Korea. Majo and I have breakfast together with three Nepalese students who are returning home from Sri Lanka.

The Dhakar streets are teeming with bicycles and a colourful variety of two and three-wheeled taxis, while there are relatively few cars in the balmy heat of the chaotic 8 a.m. traffic.

Back at the transit check-in counter it's hard to understand the locals. The man at the transit counter says to me, 'You have no booking but I'll give you a boarding pass anyway', in his clipped Indian accent. I decide not to complicate matters by responding.

There is a long delay before we board the small aircraft. I have a look around from my window seat and see that there are mostly fairly dark-skinned, Asian people and a few Caucasians aboard. It is a short flight passing through magnificent cloud formations before we begin to descend into the Kathmandu airspace. I peer out through the window and get a glimpse of a sprawling city lying in a green valley between encroaching mountains. This is a very special place that was once thought to be the fabled and inaccessible Shangri-La.

After we arrive at the Tribhuvan International Airport I have no problem passing through Nepalese Immigration with my pre-arranged visa, grab my backpack, and exchange money. For $1 I get 71 rupees. Then I get a pre-paid taxi ticket (300 rupees), push past the guesthouse touts and ask my driver to take me to the Khangsar Guesthouse. It is an interesting looking city, with the cloudy sky opening momentarily to offer a stunning glimpse of a snow-capped mountain peak to the right. We drive alongside a large walled enclosure, which the driver says is the king's palace.

The driver, whose English is quite good, tells me that today the Nepalese people are celebrating Dashain, which commemorates a great victory of the gods over the wicked demons. He says that the 15 days of celebration occur during the bright lunar fortnight ending on the full moon. Throughout Nepal the divine mother goddess Durga in all her manifestations is worshipped with innumerable pujas, abundant offerings and thousands of animal sacrifices for the ritual holy bathing. Thus, for days, the goddess is drenched in blood.

Then we turn into the narrow crowded streets of Thamel, the downtown area, where adventurers traditionally stay before setting out into the far blue mountains.

I climb up to the reception on the second floor of the non-descript looking Khangsar Guesthouse and check in. They say that my friend JP has not arrived yet. I walk up to my $6 a night room on the top floor, and find that further down the open-air passage there is a rooftop garden with tables and chairs, from where there is a stunning view of the surroundings.

But where is JP? I go down into the street and check to see if there's any news in an internet café. As I'm strolling back there is a loud yell from a passing minibus, and there he is, hanging out of the window, his eyes sparkling with excitement within his handsome, dark-tanned, square-shaped face. Out bounces JP, tennis bags and luggage in hand. I can see the guy is looking fit, strong and healthy, ready for some serious tennis and trekking. He talks non-stop. His enthusiasm is contagious as his plans roll out over his tongue. We're going to follow the loop around the Annapurna Mountain circuit. Dammar, his former guide will be advising us, and will help us obtain the necessary permits, but first he wants to meet the president of the Kathmandu Tennis Club, who he's been in contact with, as he's offered his coaching services free of charge. JP is about 20 years younger than I am, but we've forged a long-lasting friendship, mostly under trying conditions in Korea, sometimes roughing it out in the wild mountains when not working bad schedules.

`Hey man, we've got to be in the right frame of mind for the trekking!' I suggest. `Don't worry dude', he replies, as he spots the local merchant of refined natural herbal supplements on the sidewalk. The merchant suggests we visit his home, and waves for a bicycle rickshaw-taxi. The three of us squeeze in and perch precariously at the back, holding on. Then the rickshaw wends its way down narrow streets into a poorer section, where it drops us beside a plaza between squalid looking apartment buildings. The merchant leads us across the plaza down a narrow alley into a derelict building. He goes up a narrow stairway then crawls through a hole in the wall. JP and I exchange glances as we wonder if he's leading us into an ambush. However I have my flick-knife handy, and with JP's immense, muscular physicality to back me up, I'm not too worried, and wink reassuringly at him. We go up a second low dark staircase, then he raps on a door. It is opened by a small quiet woman, who lets us into their neat one room box of a home. Asian style, she bows respectfully and places mats for us to sit on the floor. He offers us a sample of his wares, which we find to be awesome, and we place a big order. We return to the streets and walk back slowly while he hurries off in another direction.

An hour later we rendezvous back at the guesthouse. This time, the merchant is accompanied by his scar-faced, ponytailed wholesaler, who appears to be ill at ease in the company of foreigners and can't speak English. Up on the rooftop we check out the solid, dark-green compressed herbal paste that is said to bring about an increased sense of mental well-being when taken in small quantities, and we strike a deal. Now, armed with the secret balm of Shangri-La, we're ready to immerse ourselves within the magical trails and secret places of the Himalayas. We breathe deeply in the scented mountain breeze, and marvel as the clouds shift and the sky reveals shimmering snow-capped peaks across the valley.

It's a beautiful evening and fortune is smiling upon us. We wonder down into the city as the waning light of day highlights the sparkling array of curved silver ghurka khukri daggers and bronzed Buddhas on display in small glittering shop windows. Bicycle rickshaws whizz by like raffish war-chariots, while motorcycles, like viruses, buzz a weaving course through the narrow lanes, engaged in a perpetual game of dodge-ems with pedestrians.

As the evening asserts its presence, the unlit streets have an eerie unreal quality, lent by the fluorescent glow emanating from a multitude of neon signs adorning the sides of the aging, dark, grimy buildings. We drink beer in a rooftop bar, then as we wander down the street, a sign written in Hangul, (Korean writing) beckons from an alley which opens into a Korean garden restaurant. The Koreans treat us like royalty and ply us with drinks when we order our meal in their language – 'Kombae!' (Cheers!)

Wednesday, October 4, 2006. Kathmandu. I awaken to that profound feeling of well-being that comes from being where you want to be, and doing what you want to do. JP is also a great guy to be with on such an outing, as he's a bristling ball of enthusiasm and positive energy. A philosophy major, his world is governed by reason and logic, though he does at times tend to lapse into philosophical jargon which is a bit beyond me.

Out on the streets I buy vetkoek, (deep fried dough-balls) similar to what I bought in Africa, and bananas for breakfast. There is no sign of JP. As I'm checking out his map of the Annapurna Mountains, a smallish, extremely fit-looking Nepalese man appears at my open door. `Hi, my name is Dammar, I'm looking for JP, but his room is locked.' he says. Dammar, JP's former guide has an air of tough competence about him. After I introduce myself we decide to wait in the rooftop garden.

`Please tell me about the Annapurna Mountains' I ask Dammar. `Annapurna is a Sanscrit name for Goddess of the Harvest. She is also known as the Goddess of Fertility or The Provider' he replies. `The Annapurna Mountains are a series of peaks in a 55 km stretch of the Himalayas. Her peaks are some of the worlds most dangerous to climb, with a 40% fatality rate. Many of the victims succumb to avalanches, for which the mountain is known. The highest peak is Annapurna 1 at 8,091m.' he tells me. (Mount Everest is 8848m).

It is only after midday that a very jet-lagged JP emerges with a ravenous appetite. We go out to a rooftop restaurant and order that delicious, Indian lentil based dish, Dahl Baht (rice).

JP wants to see what the local tennis courts look like, so Dammar leads us on a 40-minute walk through the narrow bustling streets of Kathmandu. Some of the alleys we pass through are so tight that the buildings seem to close in overhead where wooden balconies with ornate, carved railings almost touch. There are a multitude of souvenir shops, street vendors, fruit and vegetable markets. When we get to the sports centre it's closed.

In the evening we have beers on the rooftop with Dammar, as we enjoy the stunning view while he tells us about the Annapurnas. He says that sections of the trail we're heading for are under control of Maoist insurgents, who are known to block the trail and demand `taxes' from trekkers.

Later the party moves into a Nepalese restaurant where I order a delicious mutton and spinach dish. The restaurant is festooned with brightly coloured shawls and cages of exotic birds, with the aroma of incense adding `spice' to the evening.

Thursday, October 5, 2006. Kathmandu. Today is a day for writing post cards, doing emails and exploring the city.

In the evening we visit the Korean restaurant again to find that they're celebrating Chuseok, which is the Korean Thanksgiving, so we join in the celebration.

Friday, October 26, 2006. Kathmandu. Dammar comes by early to accompany JP to the local tennis courts, where he is to play a few sets against a local professional.

After lunch we follow Dammar to the office that issues trekking permits. They require two photos, a completed application form, and 2,000 Rupees, (about $29) from each of us.

In the early evening we warm up with a few beers and `what not' on the roof, for we have a dinner date with Dammar at his place on the outskirts of Kathmandu. His real home is in a rural village where his wife and children live. He comes over to fetch us and hails a couple of cabs, but none of the drivers are willing to drive us out there, so we take a long walk through town to a bus stop where we get a ride. Another taxi ride later and we arrive in a slum-like neighbourhood. Many people stare as he leads us through several dormitory style buildings into a small room he shares with his uncle.

The room has two beds, a few bits of furniture and some pictures of women on the walls. Several family members crowd into the room, including his uncle, a young man called Vishnu, a younger teenager, and a woman with a kid. We open the beers we brought along as a lively party develops, for they are all curious about us, asking many questions with Dammar having to translate. I can see the fact that he is an international tour guide, and that he can speak English has given him a high social status in his community. (Two months later JP accompanied him to his village and spent about $500 on modernizing his home).

A warm atmosphere develops as everyone chats animatedly, while the kid overcomes his shyness and has a lot of fun with me, as I've done time teaching Korean kindergarten classes. They serve us two large plates of tasty chicken and rice, but we feel uncomfortable as we're the only ones eating while they watch.

Finally they see us off in a taxi back to Thamel, and a last hurrah, with a group of young backpackers on the rooftop.

Saturday, October 7, 2006. Kathmandu. JP and I get up before 6 a.m. and instruct a cab driver to take us to the sports grounds, where he is to give two top Nepalese tennis players a workout. It's a scary trip through the hurly-burly of the early morning traffic. The city is spread out over a large area. There are many 4-6 storey apartments but no high-rises.

This is the first time I see JP play tennis, and am surprised at the casual, athletic elegance he displays on court, as he seems to float, despite his burly physique. He easily holds his own, while taking on two promising young Nepalese men, as they send crackling sizzlers back and forth. JP loves tennis and philosophy with the same intensity, and lends his unique brand of passion to both.

Sunday, October 8, 2006. Kathmandu. In the morning we take a taxi to the central bus station to buy tickets to Besisahar, our destination for tomorrow.

Then it's time to do the final shopping for our trip. JP says I should buy a thick jacket as we have to pass through snowy conditions, but I decide to make do with my jersey and windbreaker as I'm on a budget.

Monday, October 9, 2006. Via Besisahar. My alarm, which is on its last legs doesn't awaken me, but fortunately I wake up at 5:20 a.m. and we scramble to get a cab to the bus station by 5:55.

At the ticket office, the man who sold us the tickets orders a young guy to guide us to our colourfully festooned, chicken-hutch shaped bus. We find that the bus is almost empty at this point and choose our own seats. Then when several people board the bus, the driver turns the key and we jolt into action. The bus follows a slow, circuitous route through the city and along the outskirts, with the two young touts hollering 'Besisahar – Besisahar' at every stop. The bus continually picks up and drops people off, but only a handful of us are going all the way, and we are the only foreigners on board

The bus finally leaves the city behind and emerges on the lip of a large, green hill-topped valley with terraced ridges falling away to the racing river far below. It is a long day in the cramped seating as people come and go, often cramming in with an odd assortment of luggage. There is a lunch stop where they serve us dhal baht.

After we pass through the village of Dumre, the road narrows considerably, resulting in a scary game of 'chicken' with oncoming drivers. On one occasion, neither driver will back down, resulting in an abrupt stop followed by a heated exchange of shouting, pushing and shoving between them and their seconds. Below us the racing river is dissected by numerous swing bridges, while houses are perched precariously amidst bamboo thickets and groves of papaya trees.

We pass through Phaliya Sangu and by mid afternoon we arrive in Besisahar, a small village lying between the green foot-hills of the Annapurna Mountains. As we stroll through this scenic village of many wooden structures, we see a police checkpoint at the further end of the main road where we have to register with our permits.

Then we're off, free to enter the Annapurna Conservation Area circuit, a legendary trail through the stunning Himalayan scenery that will take us over the Thorung La pass (5416 m), and back to the city of Pokara. It is a walk that could take weeks. The altitude here is 760m.

The track is rather trashed at the start, as we turn sharp right off the main road down into a small valley where we have to cross the swiftly flowing stream. Then the trail leads upwards, as it gradually ascends into the mountains. We see no other foreigners at this stage, but pass heavily laden Nepalese porters, and local women burdened by loads of firewood on their backs. Each pack is attached to a belt around the bearer's forehead which supports the brunt of the weight.

The trail leads alongside the swift-flowing, rock-fanged Marsyangdi River, - meaning 'Raging River' - in the local dialect, while further away green hilltops reach into the sky. To our left the heights of Telbrung Danda, 3140m, dominate the setting. We take time out to stop and check the view, breathe in the deep breeze and yell out loud – this is the real deal, and it's going to get a lot better (and sometimes worse). 'It's awesome mate!' I say to the beaming JP as we hit the trail again.

We pass by the small settlement named Khudi, where all structures are built from stone or wood. Then in the late afternoon we stop in Bhulbhule, (840m) and choose a guesthouse with a double room mouthing out onto a long balcony overlooking a small green valley. The outdoor ablution place is merely a cold shower against a wall, with a scrap of plastic curtain, while the toilet is of the squat variety.

The sound of the river sucking and chewing on the rocks as it rages through the rapids below dominates the evening quiet, as our host serves us cold beers and provides a cheap, functional menu. After dinner and a spell on the balcony, the exercise and fresh air take their toll, as we unroll our sleeping bags and collapse onto the hard beds.

Tuesday, October 10, 2006. To Bahundanda. I order an omelette and Nepali bread with cinnamon tea for breakfast, and by 8:00 a.m. we're ready to leave. Today the trail's incline increases dramatically, leading us by a few villages with small schools, where many people greet us with the words, 'Namaste' (Hello). A few foreign trekkers begin to appear on the trail, but always seem to disappear somewhere. Overtaking on the narrow track is not easy, and we get involved in a marathon session passing a muleteer and his convoy of heavily laden mules.

As we enter a small settlement, we see a teashop and stop for a drink. We see women wearing colourful shawls, and there are red wildflowers brightening the route, as porters stagger along under their burdens. Above the trail farmers attempt to coax a harvest from the stoney, terraced hillsides.

As JP and I both like walking at different speeds, I suggest that he goes on ahead and that we meet at strategic points up ahead. Later, as I'm approaching Bahundanda Village (1310m) the path branches with no marker to indicate the way to the village, so I follow the wider section. Then I hear my name being called, and a young Nepalese boy comes running to fetch me back. He leads me to the Superb View Hotel which is aptly named, as its elevated position up on a ridge gives you two different viewpoints over the valley. We check into a small double room for 150 rupees ($2). A bowl of vegetable noodle soup, a hot shower, a short rest and then I'm ready for a beer.

Wednesday, October 11, 2006. To Chamje. We have breakfast and check out by 8 a.m. To my dismay, the track soon begins to veer downward, losing most of the height we gained yesterday, until it reaches a swing bridge across the turbulent river that we crossed two days ago. We overtake mule convoys and overloaded porters, pass through villages with waving schoolchildren, and see spectacular waterfalls plummeting from giddy heights. When we have left all the backpackers far behind us on the muddy trail that is slippery with mule shit, we scramble up to a magnificent viewing point, to anoint the breeze with praise, and watch the bright butterflies abounding everywhere.

JP takes off again as he loves to do, while I stroll along at leisure, immersing my mind in the peaceful surroundings for hours. Then as I reach a place where the path leads through some enormous boulders, I come upon a group of hard-faced men who block the path and point me to a table where three men are seated. 'Welcome to Tamuwan Autonomous Republic', says one of them as he hands me a leaflet that states, LONG LIVE – MARXISM – LENINISM – MAOISM & PRACHANDAPATH! LONG LIVE – TAMUWAN AUTONOMOUS REPUBLIC!

'Please tell us where you are going, because we need to calculate your tax bill' he says. 'You've got it wrong' I reply. 'This is Nepal and I've paid my taxes, look, here is my permit', producing the permit issued in Kathmandu. Several men step closer in a hostile manner, and realizing that I'm outnumbered as well as outgunned, I shrug and take out my wallet. I am pissed, as they want me to pay 1,200 rupees, which is a big bite out of my budget. A man gives me a receipt, which someone signs for Buddhi Ram Tamu United District People's Committee Tamuwan Autonomous Republic. Well now, I've met the Maoists and I'm not too impressed, as the term 'highway robbers' comes to mind.

A little further on I come upon a few buildings perched on the side of the track, overlooking a powerful waterfall that cascades down the rock face across the gorge. Around the next bend I come upon JP, polishing off tea and dhal baht on the front porch of the Natural View Guesthouse in Chamje (1430m), which consists of nothing more than a few buildings. He's already checked us in. 'Did you run into the Maoists too?' he calls. I turn back to the trail and make a rude sign. 'Oh well', sighs JP, 'I tried to explain to the dude why their policy is flawed, but he said he's not from the political wing'.

After I've had a bowl of noodles we grab a couple of beers and backtrack to the waterfall, as at 2 p.m. we're done for the day and ready to party.

Thursday, October 12, 2006. To Bagarchhap. The moment I awaken I know there is a problem, as my knees are aching, and seem to have seized up. I rub them vigorously and try to flex them as they're all I've got, and the only alternative method of transportation in this region is horseback.

I manage to hobble down to the restaurant and order Nepali bread, fried eggs and tea, while rubbing my knees continuously, which seems to help. On my way out I buy a walking stick for 30 rupees. Our total bill comes to 650 rupees.

The trail leads steadily upwards for two hours. There is a mixed group of foreigners and Nepalese people and we finally start to move downwards to a swing bridge across the river. Several waterfalls cascade down the mountainside to feed the roaring Marsyangdi River's savage surge of power. As we overtake a German-speaking couple halfway across the swing bridge, a convoy of ponies begins to cross from the opposite direction, giving us all a few hairy moments as we flatten ourselves against the side cables of the swaying bridge.

After we've left all the other trekkers in our wake, JP, who is ahead of me, disappears from view, and I'm alone for ages, at times wondering if I'm still on the right track. I pass through several small hamlets, and at one stage I'm accompanied by two pretty young Nepalese women.

Later as I round a bend, I'm startled to find that the trail ahead has been demolished by a landslide which has plummeted right down into the river, and that one needs to keep a cool head while passing on the crumbling slope.

During one of my increasingly frequent rests to massage my knees, I'm startled at a human-like call from the steep mountainside above me, but am unable to establish if it's a cat, bird, or goat – or maybe the fabled wild Yeti of the Himalayas? The track is very muddy, and at one stage we have to climb down a ladder. The beasts of burden have to follow a long alternative route.

While passing through Dharapani, I see a swing bridge connecting it to a small village on the opposite river bank far below. I suddenly notice a man waving and gesticulating frantically from the village below and am confused. It's too far to see clearly, but he looks like JP. I turn back and take the path down to the swing bridge with some village boys yelling 'no – Ghorka'. To my great disappointment there is no sign of JP in the village below, so I trudge all the way back up again.

A half hour later I enter Bagarchhap, (2160m) to find JP relaxing on the front porch of the Marsyangdi Hotel, where he's already secured a room for us . After I demolish two bowls of vegetable noodles, we grab a couple of beers and wander up to a viewing point to wind down from the stresses of the day. This time I keep moving my knees to ensure that they don't stiffen up again.

On the trail to Bagarchhap

Friday, October 13, 2006. To Chame. During the night, I massage my knees at every waking moment and when morning comes, I'm pleased to find that they're back to normal, despite it being Friday the 13th. We take to the trail at 8 a.m. taking a steep upward turn and continuing to climb for the next hour. JP goes on ahead and several younger people pass me, only for me to overtake them later.

Once the path levels out, convoys of ponies and mules clog the trail, and I am held up considerably while trying to get past a herd of goats. The deep blue sky shuffles, and rearranges its white-puffed cumulus clouds to reveal breathtaking glimpses of Lamjung Himal's (6932m) icy peaks shimmering in the sun. Far off to the right, like near-impregnable fortresses of nature, lie Kuchubhro (5910m) and Kang Guru (6990).

For most of the day, the only people I see are porters or muleteers, and each bend in the trail leads to a new challenge. Suddenly dwellings appear between the trees, and before too long I come upon JP resting at the front of the New Shangri La Hotel in Chame (2670m).

As we ascend the trail each evening is becoming increasingly colder, and to counter this effect JP has bought a bottle of local Rum. After a shower and a couple of shots of Rum and whatever, we're done in, and hit the sack by 8 p.m.

Saturday, October 14, 2006. To Upper Pisang. We awaken early, feeling refreshed in the pure, cold mountain air. As we step out and marvel at our surroundings, the sun's first rays fall upon the shimmering icy veil of the mountain goddess Annapurna, 2 (7939m) aloof in her near-impregnable isolation.

I take care of the bill while JP hits the road for an early start. On my way out of Chame I pass by rows of prayer wheels, with prayer flags flapping in the wind. This morning there are more people on the track than usual, with many porters and convoys of hardy, mountain packhorses. Once again there are many bugs on the trail. The trail is cut out of a slanting cliff face, with many sheer drops to the frothing river down below, and is no place for someone with a fear of heights.

I reach Lower Pisang (3200m) by noon, and from there it's a killer walk to Upper Pisang, (3300m) where I berate JP good-naturedly for having chosen the highest lying hotel. 'Yea – but check out the view dude –

isn't it awesome?' he responds, and I have to agree. Directly behind us lies the white-headed Pisang Peak, (6092) while across the valley the twin peaks of Annapurna 2 and Annapurna 4 challenge the celestial gods for dominance of the sky.

The hotel, which is made entirely of wood, is a small affair, run by an elderly couple who only have a few words of English, and our room has two beds and nothing more. The old woman gives me a jug of heated water, which I carry to the ablution shack down the trai. I wash hurriedly, as a cold wind cuts through the planks.

The trail leads between the bedrooms and the restaurant, which is built on a platform supported by poles. One good shake should see it tumbling down the hill. The restaurant is divided into one room with a seat built around a table, and a cosy little kitchen with a wood fire in the centre. Tin plates, mugs, and an odd assortment of utensils adorn the walls. They serve us cold beers and warm bowls of noodles, as we rest up and take in the view.

As the sun disappears behind the peaks, JP and I walk up to a temple situated higher up behind the hotel for a few spiritual moments in the refined mountain breeze.

Back at the hotel, we find that another trekker has arrived with her guide. She is a Korean woman who calls herself ' Sasha'. Outside, the chilly air carries flurries of light rain, as we crowd around the fire with the old couple and Sasha, and her guide, who seems to dominate her.

Sunday, October 15, 2006. To Manang. It is very cold when we step outdoors to the awesome spectre of the first sunrays bathing the icy Annapurnas in a dazzling, eye-blinding radiance. A yak bull in a nearby kraal stretches his lungs until his bellows are amplified down the mountainside.

Before leaving at 7:30 a.m., we grab a quick breakfast, huddled around the fire, but I have to return 10 minutes later to fetch my walking stick, with JP going on ahead. Today's trail is relatively flat as it runs beside the river, following a narrow corridor through the mountains.

The terrain changes dramatically as we forge deeper into the mountains, which are becoming stark and barren, with spectacular, wind-carved sandstone formations. There are few trekkers, with the main traffic consisting of porters, convoys of mules, and herds of goats. Many black crows enliven the atmosphere with raucous cries.

As I reach the village of Braga there are a number of yak bulls bellowing and dueling in a field adjoining the walkway. Across a shallow valley I can see the rooftops of Manang, (3540m) and before too long I reach a gateway with a sign: WELCOME TO MANANG.

On my way in, JP and I miss each other, and it takes me a while to find him, as I stroll through this typical Nepalese mountain town where almost every dwelling is built of stone and wood. Each house has its own store of firewood, either neatly stacked on the roof or on a ledge. At the centre of Manang is a white square brick structure, with the Islamic half-moon at the top of the dome, a Buddhist prayer wheel halfway down, and at the bottom the Hindu prayer wheels. The surrounding mountainsides are of stark barren rock, as hard as the people who live here.

JP has checked us into the Tilicho Hotel, where we order tasty yak stew and beer. Then we have hot showers and find a spot on the rooftop for a brief party before passing out early.

In the dead of the night we are startled out of our beds. There is a rolling thunderous sound, and the whole building is shaking. 'Avalanche!' shouts JP above the din, as we rush out into the freezing night air, but it's too dark to see what happened.

Monday, October 16, 2006. Manang. As we had previously earmarked Manang for a rest day, we wake up in a state of eager anticipation. It's party time! First we have a good breakfast, then we go into a shop to buy Scotch and beer before walking back through Braga. We cross over the next bridge and walk across fields towards the mountainside, passing by a water mill astride a stream, and follow the course of the rocks and water threading into the mountains. It is glacier water, tumbling down from the magnificent frozen heights of Gangapurna (7454m) directly above us. Across the valley, is the spectacular sight of the Chulu peaks, reflecting brilliant particles of virgin light in the early morning sun. This is snow leopard country, and I keep a lookout, for such a sighting would be the ultimate prize.

I dip my hand into the ice-chilled stream and drink deeply of the pure water. We crack open beers and shout 'Cheers!', as JP prepares a toast to the gods of the Himalayas. 'Do you realize that it's Monday morning and that most of humanity is bitching at the yoke of the day?' I say to the beaming JP. 'Dude', he says, as he pours us each a big shot of Scotch, 'this is a once in a lifetime opportunity, let's make the most of it!' We both raise our glasses to the reality of now.

Later, when the afternoon winds descend and sweep through the valley we return to Manang, buoyed by the sweet wings of intoxicated euphoria. On entering the town, we find a small crowd of people blocking the narrow road, as two huge yak bulls duel on the slippery cobblestones.

Tuesday, October 17, 2006. To Yak Kharka. We leave at 8 a.m. to join the porters and it's really cold. As we ascend the corridor leading deeper into the stark mountains, a few trekkers soon get left behind. The trail has been hewn out of the mountainside and offers stunning views of Tilicho Peak (7134m) in the Grand Barrier Range across the valley. The path is narrow but not too steep.

After about three hours I find JP at the Gangapurna 'Hotel' in the small hamlet, Yak Kharka (4018m). There is an icy wind blowing, and many porters are huddled around talking, too cold to sit down for a break. We get a small corner room with a stunning view overlooking the approach to Yak Kharka.

We order food. JP has dhal baht and I try the local soup as we compare notes. The biggest problem is that we're sweating due to the physical exertion, and when we unzip our outer jackets, the wet inner clothes become extremely uncomfortable in the chilling wind. After lunch we crawl fully clothed into our sleeping bags for a nap and to warm up.

An hour later we've recovered, and we decide to climb to a viewing point. I wear my full 'suit of amour', which consists of a T-shirt with a long-sleeved shirt over it, my jersey, a sleeveless windbreaker vest, my grey windbreaker, and jeans over long shorts. On my head I have a complimentary 'Western Union' cotton hat which was given to me while doing a cash transfer in Bangkok. I have no scarf or gloves. The trick now is to let enough air in so as not to overheat and sweat.

We climb high up until the little settlement lies exposed below, and all humans and their pitiful dwellings are dwarfed by the sweeping grandeur of the Annapurnas.

As we descend, a group of people arrive with an army of porters and erect their tents in an open area in the centre of Yak Kharka. They are obviously on some tour. Then a big surprise; there to greet us is Dammar, who is guiding an Australian couple; David and his wife. We go indoors and order scalding mugs of mint tea and a bottle of Raksi, a local firewater. Dammar tells us the news on the porter 'grapevine'. Apparently, some German-speaking foreigners refused to pay the Maoists 'taxes' and were beaten up.

Wednesday, October 18, 2006. To Thorung High base camp. We awaken to a pale blue early morning sky, and blessedly, the knife-edged wind has dropped. The trek follows a desolate corridor, which the ferocious elements of nature have carved through the naked sandstone mountains over the passage of time. Far below us runs the pulsating heartbeat of the Jharsang Khola River. Clumps of low, red and green coloured bushes cling tenaciously to the falling mountainside. To our right the Chulu peaks are wondrously silhouetted by the ascending sun's piercing rays.

The trail cuts precariously along the steep slope, and a sign warns of rock falls and avalanches, but there's not much one can do to avoid them if they should happen. The wind comes up again, cutting cruelly at our exposed parts. Other than trekkers and porters, there are no mule or horse convoys as the trail is too dangerous.

By the time we reach Thorung Phedi (4450m) we're beginning to sweat, something we've been trying to avoid because of the biting wind. Most trekkers seem to check into guesthouses here, but on Dammar's advice, we continue. Golden rays of sunlight sparkle on the frozen peaks of Putrun Himal (6466m) and Genjang, (6111m) to our right, as we cross the swing-bridge over the Kona Khola River, where the trail veers westward. Directly ahead of us lies the glittering white-faced challenge of the 5416m Thorung La Pass, which cuts between Khatung Kang (6484m) and Shya Gang (6032m) on the left, and Yakawakang, (6482m) on the right. JP leads the way along the narrow path that zigzags up hundreds of metres until it reaches a 'base camp', where we check into an outside room of stone, mud, and rock at the Thorung High Camp Hotel. There is no shower and only a filthy outdoor toilet, but it's far too cold to wash anyway. Lines from an old poem come to mind, 'Where the wind cuts like a whetted knife.' (J. Masefield). It's only mid-afternoon, but we're so cold that we crawl into our sleeping bags and pull the ragged duvets JP borrowed from the hotel, over ourselves.

After we've recovered somewhat, we find that Dammar and his clients have arrived and are in the room beside us. Outside in the waning light there is a scene of great natural beauty, as streaks of lightning flay the embattled skyline, while peals of thunder roll through the valleys. Later, Dammar, David, and his wife rap on our door. They've come to visit us, to partake in a ritual salutation to the mountain gods. After dark, we venture out into the freezing cold to meet in the restaurant for a desperately needed warm meal. The wind is smiting our solid stone dwelling with flurries of frozen white flakes, covering the area in a thick blanket of treacherous snow.

Despite the extreme weather, I have an ongoing duel with rats, which keep trying to raid our provisions throughout the night.

Thursday, October 19, 2006. Over the Thorung La Pass to Muktinath. I wake up at 5 a.m., and soon after Dammar is tapping on our door. He is bright and hearty and seemingly unaffected by the freezing conditions. We step out into the white wonder-world, unsure of our footing. It has stopped snowing but the broody looking sky has a heavy expectant look.

After breakfast, JP lights the sacrifice before we hit the trail. Initially there is a bit of a jam of people slipping and stumbling up the steep, narrow pathway. The climbers, who are all fitted out in ski-jackets and state-of-the-art gear, stare curiously at me in my windbreaker and yellow Western Union cotton cap. I have one hand in my pocket, with a handkerchief wrapped around the other, which is holding my walking stick. Ahead of me, a man drops his camera, which slides far down the slope. His Nepalese guide scrambles down in an attempt to retrieve it, then loses his footing and disappears downward, lost in a flurry of flying snow. At one stage there is a bottleneck at an incline, and when I'm next in line the guy ahead of me loses his footing and comes sliding back towards me. I brace to stop his descent, and then give him a shove before clawing up myself. The path is treacherous due to the slippery combination of mud and ice, and off the trail, the snow is ankle deep. At this stage, a mere slip could result in a person going into an uncontrollable skid down the mountainside, with disastrous results.

An icy wind is sweeping down the slope, and it's becoming increasingly difficult to concentrate on each step. Though my right hand is wrapped in a handkerchief, it is going numb from the cold, and it's becoming difficult to hold onto my stick, which I finally throw down beside the path.

Later the crowd thins out as the path widens at places, and we begin to pass large groups of tiring people. All movement is slow and rhythmic as breathing is constricted due to the altitude. After some time I find myself alone, as most people have fallen way behind me. JP is somewhere ahead of me.

I stop to take a photo and marvel at the vastness of the bleak, white landscape around me, where one is utterly at the mercy of the elements. The nearest people I can see below me are like insects, slowly crawling up the trail, while I'm gradually catching up to a smaller group of climbers up ahead. The silence is profound, and I'm aware that if I were to wander off the trail into the mesmeric beauty of the Annapurna's secret places, my body would soon fail me, yet my soul would soar through the majestic peaks above.

The path suddenly veers to the right and disappears over a neck which I hope is the top of the pass, but I'm disappointed. An hour later as I inexorably close in on the group ahead of me, they break into wild cheers of celebration, and despite exhaustion, I see that we've reached the neck of Thorung La, (5416m). (Later, on our return, JP and I read that on Thursday, October 26, 2006 a Swiss man, Thomas Nikles, was killed here in an avalanche, and another Swiss trekker and two Sherpa were injured).

I'm in a slight daze as I wander along the crest and down to some buildings in a dip, where people are congregated, and I am delighted to find JP, who has just managed to procure two mugs of steaming tea.

Once we've regained our strength, we decide to get going before the climbers form a pack again, which would mean having to descend hundreds of metres down a pathway which is not only steep slippery and snow-bogged, but also barely visible. There are some porters ahead of us so we try to follow in their footprints, but the path beneath the snow is treacherous and often divides. My knees begin to take the strain and my boots do not seem to have a good grip in the mush, and I slip and fall several times but luckily, I don't hurt myself. When we overtake the porters, they get into some kind of frenzied climbing duel with us, even though they're far more heavily laden than we are. Later we leave them behind when they turn off to a settlement somewhere.

Then we finally reach the bottom of the pass where the descent becomes more gradual, with a grand view of the glacier fed river below us. We later climb up to a viewing point where the turbulent river flattens and races through a vast area of islands. We're very tired and my knees are sore, but we're on a big high, for it's now downhill all the way. We fire up a toast in the pure mountain breeze and take to the trail again, with JP off ahead as usual and me following at a more leisurely pace, each within his own abstract reverie.

I stroll along daydreaming until I notice a small hamlet off to the right up on a hillside, and wonder at the peoples lives, how they've survived here for centuries in this harsh climate. There are no power cables leading there, so these people make do without accessories such as heaters, TV's, computers, washing machines, etc.

There are very few people on the trail as I wander along with my eyes fixed upon a town on a very distant hilltop, while trying to cope with the descent. When I pass by a small hill, I suddenly become aware of a path branching off to my left, to a far closer, newer looking town. There are no people in sight to ask which one is my destination, Muktinath, so I head for the closer one.

Within the first clump of buildings there is the Bob Marley Hotel and The Doors Pub, so I suppose I'm on the trekkers' trail, and have arrived in Muktinath (3800m). There is no sign of JP as I follow the road around which most of the town is built, until the road begins to climb up a hillside. He suddenly appears ahead of me, coming out of the Hotel North Pole where he has gotten us a room.

We are exhausted and sip beers as the events of the day play back through our minds. An hour later Dammar arrives with the Aussies David and his wife, who are equally in need of emergency beers. There is something very familiar about the walking stick David's wife places against the wall. 'Where did you get that stick?' I ask her. 'It was very strange', she says. 'Some guy ahead of me on the trail suddenly threw it away, just at the place where it was most needed'. When she finds out that it used to be mine she insists I keep it. We drink a toast to the coincidence.

It is snowing lightly outside, and by the time we've had hot showers and more beers we're almost sleepwalking, and we crawl into our sleeping bags – kaput.

Friday, October 20, 2006. To Jomosom. We have breakfast with the Aussies and say goodbye to them and Dammar, as they will be going on a side-excursion, and our paths will not cross on the trail again.

We hit the ever descending trail at 8 a.m. I'm very pleased to have my walking stick back, as the temperature is somewhat warmer and I can comfortably hold it without needing gloves. Though it is great not to be confronted by the never-ending energy sapping ascents, walking downhill also has its disadvantages. My knees begin to ache from the continuous jolting.

Once again there are many porters on the trail. These guys are the unsung heroes of the mountains, carrying in supplies to the most inaccessible places. Often they are small men dwarfed under monster packs, yet their greatest delight is to engage in a walking duel with backpackers, who may only be carrying a daypack since they usually have their own porters.

By the time we reach Kagbeni, (2800m) a scenic little hamlet, we've descended 1000 metres. We stroll through the town and once we reach the tranquility of the open trail it's time to clamber up to a viewing spot for moments of reflection in the refreshing breeze.

Back on the trail JP pulls ahead, while I get tangled in a large group of Japanese trekkers, and it takes me a long time to overtake them on the narrow path. The wind picks up, blowing relentlessly from the front and sending my cap flying. The path keeps descending until it joins the very wide riverbed, where the green-coloured water flows strongly in several channels.

My knees are almost creaking by the time I enter Jomosom (2710m). I pass several hotels and shops along the main drag, before I reach a bridge across the Bhurung Khola River, which dissects the town. It is not clear where JP may be, so I cross the bridge and walk along the opposite side until I reach a roadblock manned by soldiers. I cross the river again via another swing bridge and later meet JP who is looking for me. He has found a room in the rather expensive Om's Home, at 200 rupees per person. It begins to rain.

There is a big dining room on the first floor so we shower and have a bit of a party. When the lights suddenly go out it takes us a long time to find our room in the dark.

Saturday, October 21, 2006. Jomosom. We sleep till after 7 a.m., as today has been scheduled as a rest day, which is just as well, as my knees are hurting. We have a lazy breakfast, hand in our laundry, and check in with the Police and Tourist Authorities as required.

Next we buy two beers and go for a walk. We cross the river and watch two small airplanes descend over the surrounding mountain peaks to land at the local airport. Once we're out of town we leave the path and climb up a hillside through fields of mielies, (corn) where locals are working.

Higher up on a crest of the mountain slope we enter the village of Thini, which appears to be untouched by tourism or change. Like everywhere else, every dwelling is constructed from rock, with the flat rooftops laden with firewood, which seems to be a measure of the owner's wealth. Most doors are closed, but when we peer into an open one, it leads into a courtyard which can be accessed via several other doors leading into adjoining buildings. Children spot us and run up asking questions and shouting 'Namaste' (greeting).

The wind picks up and blows strongly as we leave the village behind and climb higher into the mountains. Directly above us towers Mesokantu La, (5099m) in the Muktinath Himal range, while below us we see old ruins.

Back in Jomosom we play table tennis, eat, and rest. Our room has a TV so we watch Animal Planet and National Geographic. I go out to buy lip-ice, as my lips are cracked and dry.

In the evening it begins to rain again and the power keeps cutting out. We pick up our laundry but it's still very wet. It's time for another early night.

 Sunday, October 22, 2006. To Lete. Our laundry is still wet by the time we leave at 8 a.m., but this cannot delay us, as we're on an unstoppable roll down through the mountains.

Today the descent is not as dramatic as usual, also it's a lovely day to be strolling through the mountains with Nilgiri North (7061m) looming to our left, and Tukuche Peak (6920) visible across the yonder hills. The trail which is a narrow corridor between the mountains, is especially quiet because there are no porters out on a Sunday.

We eventually pass through the pretty little town Marpha, which lies beside the fast flowing river that perpetually dogs the trail. We see no trekkers, only several motorcycles, (the first we've encountered) and a tractor pulling a trailer full of villagers, who all wave and shout 'Namaste'.

JP and I leave the trail to catch a whiff of the hilltop breeze, before he hurries on ahead while I wander merrily along. The wind picks up and blows directly from the front, spoiling the deal. Then the trail begins to ascend all the way to Kokhethanti, (2995) before dropping down to the river again.

By 2 p.m. I catch sight of JP up ahead, walking beside two Nepalese women. We pass through Kalopani (2530m) and continue on to Lete, (2480m) a nearby village where we choose an upstairs room in the empty Hotel Magic Mountain. This is a very cold place, as it lies between a number of snow-capped mountains. Luckily, there are hot showers, and our smiling landlord serves us hot meals and cold Everest beers. We retire early as it has been an exhausting day.

Monday, October 23, 2006. To Tatopani. It is very cold when we wake up, but we open the frosted hotel windows for a blow of the breeze, for we need to be in the right frame of mind to tackle today's very long walk.

As usual, JP hurries on ahead, while I stroll along with my head in the clouds, as the path leads across a picturesque swing-bridge over the river. Then the traffic picks up along the narrow muddy track, as I start banging heads with oncoming caravans of heavily loaded mules, horses, and donkeys.

I walk through the small hamlets of Ghasa, Rukse, Chhahara, Dana, and Guithe, with glimpses of the towering icy heights of Baraha Shikhar, (Fang) (7647m) looming like a mysterious, white-domed fortress to the left.

Seven hours later, after several dashed hopes, I walk into Tatopani, which is strung out along the riverside, with wooden dwellings set amidst leafy trees and blooming red poinsettias. A porter who can speak a little English is walking beside me and tells me that Tatopani means 'hot water' in Nepali. Suddenly there is a loud yell, and on looking up I see JP waving a beer at me from the rooftop of the Hotel Himalaya.

I am absolutely buggered, but manage to stagger up and chug down the cold beer, while marveling at the scenic setting, as we stir the fragrant breeze. A short while later I collapse on my bed, absolutely done in, but an hour before sunset JP is tugging at me and pleading for me to follow him. 'Where do you want to go?' I ask. 'It's a surprise', he answers. 'Please believe me Dude, you've got to come – you'll never regret it'. 'This had better be good' I growl, as I drag my trail-damaged body up and follow him into the town, and then down a path along the rocky riverbank.

After walking a couple of hundred metres we see a steaming pool beside a shack, where several people, including some females, are relaxing in the water. We wash ourselves with soap under a tap of horrifically cold water, and then plunge into the hip deep pool. It is pure bliss, as the healing hot spring waters envelope us in a soothing, heavenly balm. 'This is the real deal Dude – I told you you wouldn't regret it!' says the smiling JP. 'You've sure got that right' I murmur, as every ache seemingly evaporates within the steamy mist. Then things get even better as JP spots some guys selling beers from the shack, and before long we are beaming at each other, as we bash our bottles together and drink deeply. Darkness falls from the sky above, but the distant stars bring scant illumination, as it is pitch black away from the candle-lit pool. When our stomachs begin to growl we gather ourselves, change into dry clothes and contemplate the dark return route. A young Nepali couple with torches offers us a deal. For 300 rupees they'll escort us back to town.

Then it's party time back in the crowded hotel dinning room. Outside there is some local event, as we can hear Nepalese music and singing. The power keeps cutting out, but undeterred we continue to drink beers as the landlord provides candles. In the course of the evening I persuade JP to stay over here an extra day.

Tuesday, October 24, 2006. Kalopani. It is still dark when we wake up, as the rising sun only appears over the encroaching mountaintops after 10:30 a.m. After a slow breakfast we stroll out of town and descend to the riverside, where we open a beer and brace the breeze. There we skip stones on the river face. JP with his powerful tennis arm gets the prize for the furthest skip, while I get the award for the most skips with one stone.

In the evening we wander down to the hot water springs again. Initially it's too hot, but after sunset it cools down somewhat. People arrive and join us. There is a European blonde and a pretty Japanese woman to add spice to the laid back atmosphere. JP and I buy beers and spark the breeze, others join us – it's fun all around.

Wednesday, October 25, 2006. Kalopani. JP struggles with guilt as I persuade him to stay yet another day. After breakfast we buy beer and water and then leave the town behind, as we follow a footpath through the fields leading up to the small hamlet of Topang, which is far removed from the tourist trail. People stare at us and groups of teenagers wave and shout 'Namaste'. A friendly man comes out of a building to chat. He says he's the local English teacher.

On our way back we notice a spectacular waterfall plummeting down the steep mountain face above us, and decide to climb up towards it. The path soon peters out and the slope becomes dangerously slippery, with thickets of blackjacks a curse. We stop climbing and relax, enjoying the marvelous view. Rising high into the cloud-shrouded sky behind us is the white-studded peak of Annapurna South, (7219m) while parts of Topang cling precariously to the mountainside, vulnerable to the sweeping elements.

In the evening it's time for the pool again. By now we are the local veterans of the late night show.

Thursday, October 26, 2006. To Pokara. We pay up and start the long walk out of the conservation area and on to Beni, from where we can take a bus. It is a moderately easy walk with the scenic path following the course of the river.

The trail leads through Bagar, Tiplyang, and Raghuthat, where we hear there's a possibility of a jeep ride, but decide to give it a miss as the jeep has an engine problem and there's a crowd of people waiting. We walk on and on, muscles fatigued and minds unfocussed, yet the trail demands persistence, as it passes through Galeswor, and finally reaches Beni, in the early afternoon.

At the bus stop we're told that the last bus for the day is leaving now. It's full, but I shout at JP to follow and stop it as it as it begins to pull away. We climb up onto the roof, where a couple of Nepali men and four foreigners are seated. There is a kind of railing which spans the roof and is hard to sit on, but the air is fresh and there's a great view! Then comes the scary part! The local driver, a fearless man, follows the course of the single lane road at top speed, with utter disregard for blind bends, driving as if he's taking part in a championship-racing event. The road is a narrow strip, gouged out of the steep mountainside, which falls hundreds of metres down from beyond the roadside.

The bus suddenly comes to an abrupt stop. A car has broken down in the oncoming lane and there is no place to pass it. There is a long period of arguing and shouting before a group of men man-handle the car to a wider section beside the road. JP raises himself onto his knees, then ducks frantically as an overhead cable narrowly misses his head.

A feature of the local driving is the continual honking of the buses' hooters in a ritual greeting to every other vehicle it encounters along the way. The sound is not unlike that of elephants trumpeting. It is a four hour ride with prolonged stops in Baglung, Kusma, Phedi, and

Sarangkot, before we reach the crowded suburbs of Pokara, which lie beneath the full splendor of the Annapurnas.

Then there is the chaos of arrival, and soon we're in a taxi bound for the downtown Phewa Tal Lake area. We walk down the main drag, deal with touts, and somehow come upon a splendid room on the rooftop at the Hotel Gorkhali Dee, with a great view over the lake and the magical mountain setting beyond the city. The great part is that it's at a really cheap price, and right now neither of us is in too much of a hurry.

Now it's time for a big party to celebrate the end of a hike of epic proportions! I look at JP's animated face, and realize that without his inspiration and motivation I might not have made it all the way back. 'Cheers JP my mate – you've been an excellent guide – let's hit another big one again sometime!'

Wednesday, November 8, 2006. To Birganj on the Indian frontier. I am now the sole occupant of Khangsar Guesthouse, room 403, as JP has moved into a hotel near the tennis club.

After shopping and checking my email in Thamel at midday, I drop by the travel agency to pick up my bus ticket. When I look at the ticket I'm shocked to discover that due to a 'miscommunication' I'm due to leave tonight, and not tomorrow night as I supposed. I go up to my room and find that JP is waiting on the rooftop. As I pack he prepares a sacrifice to the Himalayan gods – with us it's never too early for a party. We go downtown into Thamel and order food and drinks on a pub's roof with a view of the city around us. Then we return to the guesthouse for a final ritual celebration on the roof. 'Cheers JP!' 'Goodbye Dude!'. We're both hurting as we've been through so much together, and with the transitory nature of our lives we do not know if we'll meet again.

My travel agent sends two young men along to guide me to the bus by taxi. When we arrive at the bustling bus terminal, they have a long argument with the driver, who tries to overcharge them. They lead me to the bus company office, where a man is assigned to show me to my bus. He leads me through the crush and puts me in an excellent position behind the driver, with plenty of legroom, despite the hard upright nature of the seat. Then, with a great hue-and-cry, we take off into the night. `Goodbye Kathmandu – I'll never forget you!'

The bus eventually reaches the outgoing road and continues through the night in a convoy of honking trucks and buses. I open the newspaper, `The Himalayan', that JP handed me as we parted. The headlines read, `Peace at last!' It appears that the Nepali government and the Maoists have finally signed a peace agreement. I hope I qualify for a tax refund!

17

India

Thursday, November 9, 2006. Birganj/Raxaul. (From Nepal into India). It is still dark when I awaken with a start at 5 a.m., as the bus jolts to a halt somewhere in Birganj, the so-called 'gateway to Nepal'. Everyone disembarks and disappears, leaving me alone in the dark street. I heft my backpack and wander down the road until I find a young 'taxi' driver who gives me a ride to the centre of town on his two-wheel horse drawn cart. There he hands me over to another driver, who indicates that I must wait. The cart gets loaded with bags as another passenger takes the seat beside me. He can speak a little English and says that he's a Tibetian refugee. Then we take off with the horse galloping at a good clip down the road, as the dim surroundings slowly come to life and the sun creeps up onto the edge of the far-off horizon. I asked the driver to drop me off at the Ashok Guesthouse, as I was instructed to pick up my train ticket to Calcutta there.

The driver suddenly turns down a side trail and drops me off at the guesthouse where I receive my ticket. A young woman gives me a cup of coffee and tells me to wait. At about 7 a.m. another horse-cart taxi takes me to the Nepalese Immigration post on the Indian border, where I check out.

When I check in at the Indian Immigration office, I am shocked to find that my visa only has three days left on it, as it was activated on the same day it was issued by the Indian Embassy in Bangkok. This is ridiculous, as a visa is usually only activated when you enter the country. My Indian visa has two dates. Date of issue: 14-08-2006, and Date of expiry: 13-11-2006. When JP and I discussed it before, we assumed that the visa had to be used before the expiry date, in which case it would be valid for three months after entry. When I put this to the immigration official he looks confused and says, 'They issue many different kinds of visas so maybe you're right, but I suggest you go and check with the tourist police when you arrive in Calcutta'. 'Ok' I reply as he stamps me in.

A bicycle rickshaw delivers me to the Raxaul Train Station, where I have a reservation for the 10 a.m. express to Calcutta, or rather, Kolkata, as it's called here. The station area is very crowded, and when I produce my ticket I'm relieved to be allowed into the building. My first class ticket allows me certain benefits, so I go upstairs into the 'retiring room' where I make use of the toilets and showers.

As I'm waiting I look around at the station's grand colonial style structure, and recall reading the internationally renowned travel writer Paul Theroux's book, 'The Great Railway Bazaar'. It gives a real life account of his four month journey through Asia by train, including a detailed description of the Indian rail system. At the time of reading the book I had no inkling that I too, would one day be travelling through India by train.

There is a very confusing scene when the exceptionally long train eventually arrives, and hundreds of people and porters descend onto the platform, jostling and shouting as they try to find their coaches. People are helpful, and I soon find my name on a list stuck to the side of a first class compartment.

The first class sleeper coach has six berths in each compartment and I take a top bunk, as I'm sharing with an Indian family, none of whom can, or will, speak English. There is the excitement of the departure and then I settle down, making a place for my backpack. My taste buds crawl all over my mouth when the Indian family opens their lunch packs of chicken curry.

It is gloomy on the top sleeper, as the windows are frosted over and there is no view at all, so it's impossible to tell if it's day or night. The train stops at regular intervals with people coming and going. I stay on my sleeper, reading and writing, as I'm overcome by a temporary wave of depression. There is the visa issue that I'm going to have to deal with on my arrival, while finding my way around in the human jungle of Calcutta, with its 15 million plus people. I'm feeling weary, tired of travelling continually, and some part of me craves for a kind of permanence. Travelling through India will be a huge challenge, as it is possibly the most culturally diverse country on the planet, and at this stage I'm not sure if I have the enthusiasm and energy for such a trip. Then there is the crucial matter of my dwindling cash reserves – I suppose someone my age should be saving money, not spending it. I lie on my back looking up at the roof - a cockroach appears...

Though I was told that we would arrive in Calcutta at 11 p.m., it doesn't look like we will, as people are making up beds and seem to be settling down for the night.

Friday, November 10, 2006. Kolkata (Calcutta). It is still dark when I wake up, but the train is moving. An hour later at 6 a.m. we arrive and our coach is flooded with porters, whom I disappoint, as I have yet to learn that in India a 'gentleman' never carries his own bag. As I head for the exit of Howrah Station there is some commotion in the crowd to the right of me. A big, tall man is shoving a smaller, mustached man. The next day I read in a front page article in 'The Statesman' newspaper, 'Assault- 'Eastern Railways CPRO assaults an electronic media reporter.'

I heft my backpack through the crowded turmoil of the station, and negotiate a 100 rupees fare for the taxi driver to drop me off in Sudder Street in the Chowringhee area. The taxi passes over the Hooghly River and down under an overpass, where two men are enjoying an early morning crap beside the road.

When the taxi turns into the Chowringhee area and drops me off near the Catholic Church in Sudder Street, my first impression is that the place is a slum. Although the buildings look ancient and are covered in grime, the streets are lively, with rickshaws, taxis, and a few backpackers, who seem to be looking for accommodation. A tout leads me to the

4th floor Ashok Hotel, (again), where I get a cheap, dirty-looking room with a double bed, toilet, and shower for 200 rupees. In India, when you're checking in, the hotel reception demands to see your passport and visa when you fill out the very detailed guest book.

After I've cleaned myself up I decide to take care of business first, and get a cab to take me to The Foreigners Registration Office in A.J.C. Bose Street, where I have to wait until their 11 a.m. opening time. A friendly man listens to my story and inspects my visa before consulting with his partner in Hindi. 'You're absolutely right', he says in that inimitable, Indian style of speech. 'This visa is good for three months from date of entry'. I'm vastly relieved to hear this. 'Can you please write that down together with your name and telephone number?' I ask him. 'No, I cannot do that, but you don't have to worry – your visa is OK' he assures me, and I take him at his word – why shouldn't I?

I find my way back to the hotel on foot where I wash my clothes and start looking ahead. But first things first – I'm starving, so I go down to a small eating establishment in the street where the proprietor can speak a little English, and order mutton curry with Nan, a delicious Punjabi leavened bread. As I'm eating, a pleasant looking Indian woman asks if she can share my table as the place is crowded. She tells me that she's a homeless beggar and that her 'takings' on the street allow her to eat once a day. Her name is Farieda, and she says that there are more than 70, 000 people living on the city streets. I watch the proprietor patiently handing out low denomination coins to a never-ending stream of beggars, and realize it is a way of life, and that for the beggar and the giver there is no other way.

In the evening I take a walk around the neighbourhood and I am almost overwhelmed by masses of people, including the beggars who are continually in my face. The somber, dark facades of the buildings look as though they've never been renovated. There are street urinals and water outlets where people wash themselves. People are colourfully dressed despite the poverty. Many women are overweight with bare midriffs. Then I make eye contact with a taxi driver who ushers me into his car. His name is Salim and he says his brother is a gardener, as he offers me a bank bag full of excellent local herbs for Rs. 1,400. We settle on Rs.500. Then I spot a formal looking drinking establishment on Sudder Street with a sign, 'Pub', where I try the local Kingfisher beer.

I lie back on my bed and listen to the sounds around me. There is the whirring of the fan, cars hooting in the streets, the muffled voices of people, and unidentifiable metallic sounds. My window offers a view of the squalor below. There are squatters who seem to live on the rooftops, and I can see many people bedding down on the street. As in Nepal, there are big, grayish-black crows everywhere.

Saturday, November 11, 2006. Calcutta. I awaken at around 6 a.m. to a raucous crow-chorus out on the rooftops. There is life out on the streets: hawkers, backpackers, commuters and the homeless - while rickshaws and taxis cruise about in search of fares. A man working from a café that is merely a hole in a wall serves me a good breakfast of banana lassi, coffee, and a toasted cheese sandwich.

Back in my room, I have a good look at the city map and plot the course I'm going to take to the Eastern Railways office, as I need to make a reservation to Bhubaneswar, near the east coast, which I've decided on as my next port of call.

Walking within the teeming throngs of humanity in the vibrant streets of Kolkata, is an eye-opener. The shops stand shoulder-to-shoulder, street vendors throttle the sidewalks, the roads are living monsters of thunderous traffic, the outstretched hands of beggars cry for help, there are public urinals, and homeless people are washing themselves and their clothes at water pumps. I reach the central area and see public buildings which were once magnificent, but look like they have never had a face-lift since the colonial era when they were constructed. It looks as if one good shake would be enough to see most of this old city collapse. Many of the street names have links to the colonial past. There is a Shakespeare Street, and the railways reservation office is in Fairlie Place.

I am too early and have to wait for the office to open. Then I fill out a reservation form for a trip to Bhubaneswar tomorrow and wait in the line. A friendly female official helps me, and persuades me not to buy an Indrail Pass, as it's not economical, unless I'm planning to spend most of my time on the trains.

In the evening I go to the 'Pub' for a drink, before returning to the little restaurant where I order a chicken masala curry dish. Farieda, and a woman with a baby, harass me, begging for money.

Sunday, November 12, 2006. To Bhubaneswar. It is cool and overcast as I wander around the area, trying to find an open internet café. The Springbok rugby team played Ireland yesterday and I have to know what happened.

I stop at the hole-in-the-wall for a breakfast of lassi, toasted cheese, and coffee. The soup kitchen has opened at the ancient church near the end of Sudder Street, and hordes of people are lining up for a free meal. The crowd is lively, with boys playing cricket in the street with a tennis ball and a stick. The attention I receive is fierce, clutching hands, mothers thrusting babies into my face, everyone needs help – it's like being back in Africa. To make eye contact is an invitation to conversation, and it is mentally draining to ignore people while you wish you could do something to change their lives for the better.

Finally I find an internet café that's open – terrible news, the Springboks lost – how is that possible? I mull over this travesty while having lunch of an omelette and tea.

Then it's time to check out and take a cab back to the crowded chaos of the Howrah Station. I establish that my train, the Coromandal Express, leaves from platform 14 at 14:50. I fill out a section in a book to check in to the first class waiting room.

An interesting feature of Indian life is that rich, or upper class people never carry their own luggage, porters do. There are always scrawny looking men in red shirts staggering by under impossibly heavy loads. Wherever I arrive porters always come running, only to be disappointed when I put on my backpack.

When the very long train arrives, I search the name lists on the coaches and find that I'll be in the second to last one. As I sit down a woman thrusts her baby into my face – I'm not impressed. Then it's 'take off' time again as I sit beside a window and watch the passing scenery, as the train passes through the slums until it reaches the outskirts of Calcutta. There are many squalid looking squatter settlements beside the tracks, where ragged children play cricket, and I even see monkeys swinging in the trees. Sharing the compartment with me are several middle-class looking men.

On board there is a never ending succession of tea, coffee, and vendors selling snacks and food. There is a man who offers to shine shoes, and a man walks by selling delicious tasting samoosas from a bucket. The train rapidly cuts through the lush countryside of West Bengal. There are numerous small settlements beside dams, green cultivated fields, palm trees, vast ponds of water lilies, and generally water everywhere. Then we leave West Bengal behind as the train enters Orissa State.

It is dark outside when we arrive in Bhubaneswar at 9:30 p.m. I step out into the chaotic street medley of public transportation and a tout on a bicycle rickshaw gets my attention with his offer of a room at Rs150 in the Hotel Atithi Nivas. Sitting in the back of the rickshaw, I feel as though I'm part of a high-speed computer game, as my driver claws his way into the bedlam of evening traffic and vagrant cows.

After checking in and taking a shower in my small room, I feel thirsty and ask the manager where I can drink a beer. He points to an establishment across the road which is full of men drinking beer. I order a Kingfisher and a plate of Masala Naan, but only manage to eat one slice, and I have to chase my second beer as they close very abruptly, with the place emptying within minutes.

Monday, November 13, 2006. To Gopalpur. It's a new day and I have to make a decision regarding where I'm going to go. According to my Lonely Planet guidebook, Puri, with its Jagannatha's temple, and Konark's Sun Temple, are the main tourist attractions in the area, but I choose to go to Gopalpur-on-sea, which seems to be off the tourist track.

In the early morning I go for a long walk deep into the slum area alongside the railway lines, where people somehow eke out an existence. Stray cows wander around at random, eating whatever garbage is unsuitable for human consumption. People live in shack-like dwellings in abject poverty. On my return, the hotel manager arranges for a motorcycle rickshaw to see me onto the right bus. The driver takes me on a long ride through the hurly-burly of the morning traffic, weaving his way through a herd of homeless cattle that have somehow gotten themselves entangled with the traffic at an intersection. He weaves a crazy trail through the city to a point on the main route, and hands me over to another man who eventually waves the right bus to a standstill. He enters the bus with me, pushing me onto a seat beside a woman with a young girl of about nine, who has to move onto her mother's lap. I open my bag and give the kid a chocolate bar, which she handles delicately, as though it is a fragile treasure.

It's a colourful ride, as the conductor hangs out the open door at every stop shouting, `Berhampur, Berhampur!' - our immediate destination. Before long the ancient old rattletrap of a bus is hopelessly overcrowded, yet vendors somehow squeeze through the crush, flogging peanuts and bananas.

At midday the bus arrives in Berhampur, a vibrant, chaotically crowded place, where it comes to a halt at the central bus station. I try to enquire where the bus to Gopalpur is but nobody seems to understand. Finally, I stroll out and walk down the main road, where a young bicycle rickshaw driver gets my point, and takes me on a hairy ride through the crazy free-for-all traffic, 90% of which is bicycles or motorcycle rickshaws, and buses.

He drops me beside an ancient looking contraption that is packed with people, and speaks to the tout who has a red band around his head and is shouting, `Gopalpur, Gopalpur!' at the top of his voice. He pushes me onto the bus, pulls some poor sod off his seat, and places me there within a group of young women in brightly coloured saris. My backpack goes on the roof. The ticket costs about 20 US cents. I offer my seat to a young woman who is standing in a bent position under the low roof, but she laughs and refuses to move.

As the bus leaves the turmoil of Berhampur behind, it comes to me that travelling in India is less about sightseeing than it is a study of humanity, as one experiences life in its fullest intensity. The bus turns down a narrow road en route to the seaside, cutting through the ubiquitous tropical banana and palm trees.

The trip ends abruptly as we come to a halt at the top end of a street that is lined with shack-like shops, which meanders down by a lighthouse to the sparkling blue oceanfront. I wander down the road but unfortunately miss the sign to the Holiday Inn, and carry on until I reach the government run Panthanivas Hotel. I am not charmed at the Rs.400 they want for a room and manage to get them to agree on Rs.360. It is a really nice room, and when I order vegetable soup and fried fish, the food and service are excellent.

After a quick shower I stroll across the sand dunes onto the beautiful coastline of the Bay of Bengal. To my right there are numerous groups of villagers, crowded around their fishing boats, which have been dragged out of the water. To the left lie the dwellings of Gopalpur, with some kind of tiered seating area above the main beach.

I meet a weird Italian guy who is sun tanning. He looks like a scarecrow with a very prominent nose and adams-apple. His name is David, and he explains how I can get to the very laid-back Holiday Inn where the accommodation is cheap. He says the swimming here is dangerous, and advises me not to go in deep but rather to swim up and down the shore.

As I continue towards the main beach area I see several Indian families relaxing in the sun, but only some of the men are in swimming costumes and few people venture more than hip-deep into the water. Three beggars come charging across the sand with upturned palms. I pretend not to understand, and shake their hands before continuing on my way. An Indian family who are watching laughs, and the father runs over and shakes my hand too.

On the main beach, there are several Indian families, all of whom are dressed up. The 'lifeguard', who is carrying a stick comes down to meet me and insists that I visit his office. He tells me that as this is only a part-time job, and it's poorly paid, he cannot afford to get married. He talks about drownings on the beach but I have difficulty following his English.

After sunset I enter the lobby of the Kalinga Hotel, which is on the fringe of the beach, and enquire about beer. The courteous waiters lead me upstairs to a grassy deck overlooking the sea and serve me a big Kingfisher beer. Below me the waves roll in, crashing onto the beach and to my left Gopalpur's dim lights glow invitingly. Off to the right, just beyond the high, dark beach dunes, the closely packed communities of the 'fishing people' are spread out along the coast. Directly across the bay (Bay of Bengal) lies Myanmar, while to the southeast are Malaysia, Thailand, and Indonesia. The island of Sri Lanka lies to the south.

I walk back along the deserted beach, with the lighthouse's revolving light probing into the secret places of the night. In my room I marvel at the two white sheets on my double bed – this is a first since leaving South Africa.

Tuesday, November 14, 2006. Gopalpur. I check out at 8 a.m. and lug my backpack over to the Holiday Inn Lodge. It consists of several rooms around a courtyard. At the gate I meet a scrawny old guy who introduces himself as Mr. Singh, and tells me that he lives in a building outside the enclosure. 'Where is the reception?' I ask. He blinks a few times and says, 'It's not that type of place, you can just speak to me', and leads me to a big room with a four-poster bed, toilet, and shower.

I walk down the coast and go for a long swim. The beach has a sudden, deep drop into the ocean, but the water is warm and the waves are great. An old Indian man joins me, but I find later that he is a beggar. David is also on the beach with a crowd of local people around him. He's a flamboyant character who loves to entertain the locals with his skillful juggling act. He says he's a professional clown and that his stage name is Giulivo. He watches over my things while I go in for another long swim. One big drawback here is the amount of human feces on the beach. The problem mainly seems to be men from lower castes who come down to the beach for their daily crap.

In the evening David and I join a French woman, Claudia, who is staying in India for 6 months, at Krishna's restaurant behind the Kalinga Hotel. Krishna, a jovial plump Indian man serves us fresh seafood and Knockout beers. He places the beers under our chairs, and asks us not to let the Indian customers see that we are drinking alcohol as it may offend them. Claudia, who is attractive despite her prominent nose, has a cold demeanor. She startles us when she says she has grandchildren. There are two lively little girls with long black hair serving as waitresses. They are free-spirited little waifs who cannot speak English, but dance with wild abandon each time an Indian song is played on the stereo. Krishna says they're from the fishing village, where people are desperately poor. Then the lights short, and Krishna, with scant regard for safety procedures, stands on a stool and pulls live wires out of the wall, and soon changes the entire lighting unit. At the end of the evening, my share of the bill comes to Rs.361, which is about $6, – a big night out by my current standards.

Wednesday, November 15, 2006. Gopalpur. I awaken early and walk by the imposing Hindu temple, and on through the village as it slowly comes to life. A street vendor sells me a mixed bag of bananas, apples, and mandarins for Rs.50. Then I spot a barbershop where I revert to my 'Ghandi' hair-style.

Back at my room I find a small Indian waiting on the porch. His name is Ranjang and he's the local herbalist. It takes me a while to follow his English, as he likes to chatter away all the time. When I ask him why his arm is bandaged, he tells me that he was cut with a knife by a group of men who tried to rob him while he was taking an evening stroll on the beach. Luckily, he managed to run away. We make a sacrifice to the Bengali breeze, and then he wanders off to chat to my neighbour David, and some of the other Italians who keep arriving.

It's time to check out the local scene. As I amble past the back of the lighthouse I see a group of boys playing cricket with a tennis ball and a wood plank. There are dogs everywhere, mangy stray mutts, each holding and defending its territory for all its worth. At the garbage dump beside the hotel, there is often a free-for-all between dogs, pigs, goats, and cows, each to its own taste. A group of women in eye-catching saris step elegantly along the beach, carrying the day's catch of fish in woven baskets on their heads.

Krishna serves me fried chicken pieces rolled in roti. When I go for a swim, David is on the beach again, with the usual crowd around him. This time there is trouble. It's a dispute about the price of peanuts, and now a young hothead wants to fight an older fisherman.

In the evening David uses Krishna's kitchen to cook us Italian spaghetti, while Krishna pot-roasts a chicken to go with it. Claudine joins us for the feast. Then there is the after-party at the Holiday Inn.

Thursday, November 16, 2006. Gopalpur. I awaken to the smell of Ranjang's herbs, and join him out on the stoop. A cleaning woman gives my room a once-over, and when she's finished she cups her hands and says,'baksheesh?' David joins us, and later we go down to a beachfront café for coffee and biscuits. This is where I meet the Indians Shawn, his wife and two little girls. He says that he's a navigator on leave from his ship. He's an extremely likeable man, seemingly well-travelled and knowledgeable, though there's something strange about him and his family. Something I can't put my finger on. Maybe it's that he doesn't really look Indian, but rather Eurasian, while his one little daughter has almost Afro-style curls. His wife is pretty but rarely says much. The girls are shy but very cute. Shawn writes his name and address in my notebook, S. Rosario, H. No. 33/3 S.R. Signals, Ameerpet, Vengalrao Nagar, Hyberabad, 82. Email:cruisetop26@hotmail.com.

David and I follow the coastline until we're amongst the fishing folk and their boats that have been dragged ashore, beyond reach of the chopping surf. It's a scene of daily communal activity, as some groups are gathered beside their boats sorting the days catch, while others are straining at long ropes as they haul in their fishing nets. There are sailing boats far out at sea, with their dashing sails of red and yellow flying in the wind. Painted on the side of one of the boats are the words, 'Jesus is my save'.

Today's catch seems to be good, so David and I buy eight small swordfish for Rs.100. Everyone is happy except Krishna and his cook who we ask to prepare the meal, which they serve with lemon and rice.

In the afternoon I venture deep out into the surf for my daily workout. The water is rough, with side currents, and though there are good waves you have to watch out for the dreaded dumpers that will pound you straight down onto the seabed. When Shawn and his family appear, I try to teach the two little girls to swim and we have a lot of fun in the shallows.

Later when I emerge from my room, I find that Shawn and his family are partying with my Italian neighbours and some Indian guys, who are all great partakers of Ranjang's wares. Shawn invites us for a drink on the upper deck of the Kalinga Hotel. On the way there Shawn and I turn off into the backstreets to the notorious hole-in-the-wall wine shop, where we buy beers and a bottle of McDowell's Rum. Shawn tells us interesting anecdotes about life aboard ships, and suggests that he could easily get me connected through his shipping contacts if I wanted to experience life at sea for a year or two. It all sounds very exciting, as I'm always up to a new challenge. Later the party descends on Krishna's place for dinner before we continue at the Holiday Inn.

Friday, November 17, 2006. Gopalpur. As Shawn and I both need to exchange money I share a taxi to Berhampur with him and his family. When we stop in the town-centre, his wife says we must meet back at the taxi as she and the girls are going shopping. Shawn and I go to a bank but the exchange rate isn't very good. He says he's going to look for a friend who does black-market exchanges at a far higher rate. He suggests that he'll take my dollars along and get them changed for me too. I should wait at the bank in case he's unsuccessful. When he doesn't return after some time I have a bad feeling and wander back to the taxi, but they have gone. Something seems wrong, so I take an auto-rickshaw back to the Kalinga Hotel only to hear that they've checked out. Then I understand that I've been cheated by professionals. I had taken a real liking to Shawn and had trusted him, mainly because I thought it highly unlikely that a man accompanied by a gentle wife and two great kids would be a swindler.

Do I want to see the man being arrested in front of his family and dragged off to jail? No, but I'm a little angry, and deciding to pursue the matter I go to the Gopalpur Police Station. They say I should report the case to the Berhampur police, so I go there by auto-rickshaw. Nobody can understand me at the central police station until my driver interprets. A policeman leads me upstairs to the station commander Captain Nitinjeet Singh, a tall, suave, well-spoken man dressed in plain clothes. He's the real deal and gets to the bottom of the matter at once. 'We've got to stop them' he says. Accompanied by three policemen armed with machine guns, we race to the train station in a police vehicle. Halfway through the train search we have to stop as the train is leaving, so we go and check out the bus station, as well as a few classy restaurants and hotels.

Captain Singh says I must report the case to the Goplapur police and that he'll continue to work on it. The senior officer at Gopalpur is initially reluctant, but a phone call from captain Singh quickly changes his attitude. Police officer Rama Sahu opens a case and promises to do his best to bring about justice. As part of the procedure they ask for my passport and enquire about the validity of my visa. I patiently explain what the tourist police in Calcutta said and they accept that.

In the evening Krishna and some other locals join us for beers. Everyone is astounded to hear about Shawn, and the feeling is that he'd do well in Bollywood – India's version of Hollywood.

Sunday, November 19, 2006. Gopalpur. It is early in the morning when I go down to Babu's shop on the beachfront for a coffee and biscuits. I find a fairly recent English newspaper on the table and read that there has been a massacre of low cast Dalits, sometimes called the 'Untouchables', in the Indian caste system.

As I'm returning, I am startled when I peer into a busy construction area and see that the labourers are all female, working in colourful saris in the heat of the day. They work with casual, unhurried elegance, retaining their femininity despite the grim surroundings.

David the clown, who has been entertaining the children, and the people of the fishing community, leaves in the afternoon and is replaced by another David, also from Italy.

Monday, November 20, 2006. Gopalpur. The sound of cannon fire awakens me, and when I find Ranjang out on the stoop with all the young Italians doing their ritual tokes, I hear that it is the Indian Navy training out in the Bay of Bengal. I cannot imagine who they think would attack them from there.

At around noon, Subash, a likeable young local guy gives me a lift to Berhampur on his motorcycle. We stop at various places for oil, petrol, and brake fluid, before riding through the country hamlets into Berhampur's chaos of two and three wheelers. Bigger vehicles plow through with hooters blaring, like sharks passing through shoals of sardines.

Our first stop is at a finance company where Subash's brother-in-law is the MD, and after much filling out of forms they exchange my traveller's cheque. The next stop is at an internet café, owned by friends of Subash. There is an email from Soon Young at the International Pub in Changwon, Korea. 'Come home for Christmas' it reads, and I experience a wave of homesickness, as that's about the closest I have to home these days. When I've done my emailing one of Subash's friends says, 'we'd like to have an educational meeting with you', and soon I'm surrounded by serious young men trying to sell me an IT package: www.ebizel.com – check it out. Our final stop is to buy a mosquito net, as I'm being chewed by mossies every night.

Saturday, November 25, 2006. To Visakhapatnam. I get up early and go for a quick coffee at Babu's before paying up and saying goodbye to old Mr. Singh. He asked me to write something about Goplapur for him as he had heard that I'm a writer, so I give him a copy of my scribbling, mostly done under the influence:

GOPALPUR

The country road descends into a medley
of Orissan styled bazaars, boutiques and quaint, homely abodes.

Tiered in layers of white 'n red, the lighthouse looms,
winking its even welcome to weary seafarers returning from the deep.

A laid-back beachfront of cafes 'n vendor stalls,
a little peoples' playground, and idle cows on the sandy shore.

The Sea Pearl, Kalinga, the Holiday Inn, and Krishnas,
with lovers riding rickshaws in the lingering sunset haze.

Amidst the white-toothed grins of handsome dusky men
a sign proclaims, 'Gopalpur Police – how may I help you?'

Elegant dark-haired beauties sway too and fro in a dazzle
of saris in rose 'n lemon, lime, and deep sky blue.

An unbroken vista of curling, foam-peaked waves
caressing white-sanded curving shores.

On ocean crafts of creaking wood, hardy sea-folk
strain at oar and rudder through the tumult of the surf.

Far horizons of dashing fishing dhows in candy striped sails
unfurled in the Bengali's balmy breath.

Gentle, sweet-smiling locals lure travel weary wanderers
into this eternal romance of land and sea.

An auto-rickshaw takes me back to the railway station in Berhampur, where I buy a ticket to Visakhapatnam. It is a pleasant five-hour trip through the scenic countryside of green hillsides, sugar palms, and rice paddies.

On arrival I shoulder my backpack through the crowds and instruct a skinny old guy on a bicycle-rickshaw to take me to some cheap, Lonely Planet-recommended hotels. He wobbles off into the swath of traffic like a spindly old butterfly drifting into the flight path of a flock of swooping swallows. I can see from the surroundings that this is not what I want, but there's no turning back as we fly down Main Road through the congested, slum-like city. The recommended hotels are all full, but someone gives my driver directions to the bug-infested Lakshmi Durga Hotel, where I get a cheap room with a TV. Once again, there is an argument about my visa.

I go for a long walk, exploring the narrow, crowded streets of smog-grimed, run-down buildings. The good point is that despite the abject poverty, there is no sign of gang activity, and although travellers should naturally watch their wallets, the place doesn't seem to be dangerous.

A street vendor with a liquidizer sells me a glass of fresh papaya juice. Then I spot an email café. The news from home is worrying. Mom is in hospital because she was on the wrong medication.

As I'm picking my way back through the shabby buildings there is a small sign that says `Bar', over a low doorway. A man leads me down a dark passage into a dingy windowless room in the building. Other than a bunch of tables and chairs, there are no decorations or adornments in this dim, cheerless room. I have a beer and ask for another to take with me.

The clerk at my hotel's reception offers me a menu and I have a delicious Chicken Biryani and rice dish delivered to my room.

Sunday, November 26, 2006. Visakhapatnam. I walk about at random, losing myself within the urban maze. Though the shops and internet cafes are closed, the streets pulsate with life, and I have to watch my step, as there is always a jingling rickshaw or buzzing motorcycle weaving through the crowds. Many restaurants have the word `Tiffin' on the door.

After checking out the hotels, I move to the cheaper and newer looking Jupiter Hotel, where they once again argue about my visa, saying it has expired. This is becoming very annoying. The good point is that there's a TV room, where I can watch South Africa thrash India in a live game of cricket, and there is an open liquor store across the street.

Monday, November 27, 2006. Visakhapatnam. I'm running low on cash so I take an auto-rickshaw to the Bank of India, where they give me a very good exchange rate. The rickshaw ride through the early morning traffic must be something akin to partaking in a death-defying chariot race in the days of the Roman Empire.

On my way back to the hotel I begin to recognize the area, and I jump out to buy some fresh fruit. The street vendors are selling mandarins, bananas, pomegranates, coconuts, apples and some other fruit I don't recognize. Back at the hotel there is a rugby game on TV and I'm absolutely delighted to watch South Africa beat England.

After dark I enter another bar which is boisterous and crowded. A man pushes me through a doorway into a backroom where there is a more genteel atmosphere, with men sitting at tables drinking scotch and water. They avoid eye contact so I have a beer and don't attempt to strike up a conversation.

Tuesday, November 28, 2006. Via Vijaywada. At 6 a.m. my auto-rickshaw ride to the railway station is early enough to miss the morning rush-hour traffic. As I'm so early there is no difficulty buying an open ticket to Vijaywada, but the clerk is rather obtuse, 'wait at platform 3 or 4' he says. As I'm sitting on a bench waiting at platform 3, a small Indian man beside me looks my way and asks, 'have you met Jesus?' He's Pastor Wycliffe Sagar of Dantewada, Chatthisghar (07864 – 284729). We chat, and then after he listens to an announcement on the public address system he says I should board the train that's arrived at platform 4. I do so, and the moment it departs I realize it's going in the wrong direction. The female conductor puts me off at the next stop, Simhachalam Station. I'm pissed off as I have to wait another hour for a train back. When in India always expect the unexpected. Hundreds of cheering men, all dressed in black with garlands of flowers around their necks enter the station and board the train. A man with needles, thread, buckles, and various tools does an excellent job stitching my small daypack. Then, as I'm forced off my seat because I have no reservation, he leads me to another coach. When the conductor, who speaks no English, arrives, I understand that I'm on the wrong train again and jump off. Though there is an 'Enquiries' window, nobody can tell me where to wait, but somehow I get onto the 11 a.m. express to Bangalore, which goes via Vijaywada.

I have a wooden seat in the 'second class' section, but it is an undisputed window seat, across from a young man who can speak English. I buy a bag of tasty samoosas, and check out the scenery. There are the usual slums along the tracks, with people shitting openly, water buffaloes lying with their bodies submerged in deep pools of water, and clotheslines with colourful saris streaming in the wind. There is the regular din aboard, as vendors pass through the carriages shouting 'Samoosas' or 'Chai', (tea) as we pass by vast sugar cane fields, groves of sugar palms, wild bananas, and villages amidst the green hills. Boys play cricket wherever there is an open space, women breast-feed babies, and grey herons search for food in the swamps.

Somewhere along the way we pass over the mighty Godavari, a sacred Hindu river, as I watch two eagles involved in a spectacular aerial duel. It is harvest time, and whole communities are out in the fields of cane and rice. I see a boy sitting on a buffalo's back in the centre of a dam. The sunset lends a mystical aura to the surroundings, as it hangs over the hills on the horizon like a spectacular red moon, until it is mysteriously lost in the mist.

The train gets really crowded, with people sitting in the aisle. Sharing my seat is a grinning, skinny old man. There is an air of expectancy, something has got to happen. Then suddenly buildings appear along the tracks, and we arrive in Vijaywada just before 6 p.m.

I immediately work my way through the hordes of people to the chaotic ticketing counters, and make enquiries regarding a ticket to Hospet, which is more than halfway across the country to the west, en route to Goa. I am told to purchase a 'general ticket' for tonight, but when I join the right queue it never gets shorter, as people keep joining friends in the line in the scrum at the front. A serene looking old Indian man who is standing around watching proceedings, tells me to go around and enter the ticketing office via the back door. I'm reluctant to do this, but he grabs me by the arm and leads me there. He opens the back door and when he speaks loudly to the harried clerks, one of them helps me right away. I shake hands several times with the man who says his name is Mr. Adams. 'Well, thanks again Mr. Adams, because if it were not for you I might well still be out there in that line!'

I board the train at 7:45 p.m. and get the top bunk in the aisle in a cheap second-class coach. A young Indian woman on the top bunk across the passage from me asks if she can borrow my Lonely Planet guidebook. With the overhead fan rotating at top speed it grows surprisingly cold, and I'm glad to have my sleeping bag on hand. My total expenditure today, including train fares is less than $10.

Wednesday, November 29, 2006. To Hospet and Hampi. I awaken to the music of the train's click-clacking wheels and the carriage's swaying motion. The window offers views of fields of brightly blooming sunflowers framed by mist-shrouded hills. It is very wet outside with water everywhere. When I buy a local newspaper from a man on the train, there is a satellite image of the Godavari River in flood, and an article about it flooding its banks and causing havoc in the inland states. The train stops in the middle of nowhere, we wait in silence, then it crawls slowly forward into the station at Tornageslla. When it comes to a halt it is besieged by a bedlam of filthy beggars, some with no arms, crawling ones, blind people, and samoosa, coffee and chai sellers, all clamouring for attention.

When we arrive in Hospet, a large rural town at around 9 a.m., I ask an auto-rickshaw driver to take me to a few Lonely Planet recommended hotels, but they are all full. 'Why you want to stay in this place?' my driver Ranga, enquires. 'Everyone is going to Hampi'. 'Why should I go to Hampi?' I ask. 'Hampi', he replies, 'is the site of a large historical ruin that was once the magnificent capital of the powerful South Indian Vijayanagar Empire, said to be founded by Harhara and Bukka in 1336 A.D. You've got to see this place!' 'OK, buddy' I say. 'Let's go!'

He drives along a narrow road out into the countryside of green fields and rocky hillsides, with ancient relics of structures from the past appearing along the roadside. Then we pass through granite-domed hills to enter the awesome, boulder-strewn setting of a small town lying on the banks of the holy Tungabhadra River, amidst the solemn ruins of the past. Everywhere one looks there are boulders. There are hills that consist entirely of boulders.

Ranga is intent on taking me to some guesthouse where he has connections, but I'm having none of that. This place is the real deal. 'Drop me off right here' I say, tipping him handsomely before wandering into the vibrant streets around the magnificent main tower of Virupaksha Temple.

There is a man with a peculiar way of speaking at the tourist office. He gives me a great brochure for Bangelore City. 'But this is Hampi!' I say to him. 'OK' he says, and gives me a smaller one for Hampi. It says that 'The city once had opulent palaces, marvelous temples, massive fortifications, baths, markets, aqueducts, pavilions, stables for royal elephants, and elegantly carved pillars. This was a city whose merchants offered diamonds, pearls, fine silks, brocades, horses – and according to one Portuguese visitor, "Every sort of thing on earth." Wow – it sounds as if it were one hell of a place, but all that remains are the impressive ruins, while the wild landscape of granite kopjes and monstrous boulders add to the mystique of the setting.

I check into the recommended Shanthi Hotel (after the usual argument about my visa), but am not too happy with my room as I have to share bathrooms and toilets.

As the late afternoon sun wanes, bathing the surroundings in a luminous pink haze, I follow the trail along the banks of the holy Tungabhadra River in the uncertain twilight. Below on a flat rock beside the river, two dusky beauties in lovely saris are washing their long black tresses in the water.

An old man in a dark cloak with a long stave in his hand is wandering along the road ahead of me. He is following a big ambling bull, but when he sees me, he cups his hands and gesticulates vigorously, while making the inarticulate sounds of a mute. I'm pleased to follow their path as it is unlikely that there will be snakes on the trail behind them. To the left there are remnants of a temple-like structure amidst gigantic boulders, while to my right there is thick, jungle-like vegetation. The only sounds that can be heard are the friendly chuckles of a stream, and the inconsistent hoot of an owl. The old man and the beast turn off and follow a path towards some dwellings, where the sounds of music and chanting can be heard, and I decide to go back.

The half-moon is riding high between the clouds, highlighting the main temple's sacred centre, which towers over the wild jumble of boulders. I stop to smell the flowers, and wonder at the divinely inspired zeal that led to such magnificent creations. I feel that as humans with spiritual dimensions, being essentially of water we are sparkling particles of the universe. As the wild clouds riding the sky-face above, and the 'sacred' waters following the river course below, I am part of the greater 'whole' which is eternally changing forms and regrouping. I try to imagine being a thunderous cataract, a wild foaming, typhoon-lashed sea, or an electrified black cloud in a momentous thunderstorm that rips the heavens in flaming shreds, and instinctively know that elements within me have been there. For I am a drop of water formed from the current of life.

A dark, growling beast within me drives me back to Hampi, demanding to be fed. I go up to a rooftop restaurant where a friendly young waiter who says he's from Nepal serves me mint tea with Palak Panir, which is goat cheese in a spinach sauce.

Thursday, November 30, 2006. Hampi. In the morning I pay the local barber a visit for a head shave, before having my photos burned onto a cd. After checking out several possibilities, I move out to the remote family run Paradise Gardens, which is a bunch of very basic bungalows of bamboo and thatch, lying in a grove of tall trees beside the river. My room has only a small table and a mosquito-net draped bed, and there are outside toilets and showers, but it is a great setting. The restaurant is a low wooden deck with a marvelous vista of the river below, and the incredible hills of boulders beyond. Parmesh, the owner, serves me a tall papaya lassi before I head back into town again.

Back in the centre of town, I take photos of a man feeding an elephant, and a snake charmer with his 'dancing' cobras. I can't make head-nor-tail of the tourist map and decide to follow my instincts.

Somewhere out between the kopjes I scramble up the back of a boulder the size of a house, to find that it is part of an amphitheatre, with the ruins of an ancient temple lying beyond. The ornate façade of the temple is intricate, clearly the work of past masters, but it is in a state of disrepair. As I relax in the shade, with the essence of the breeze in hand, the haunting melody of flute music begins to pipe from a hidden place out in the wild jumble of boulders beyond me. The magical notes open a gateway into the past, and it is as though there are ghostly figures dancing in the temple courtyard.

Between the rocks there are patches of vegetation, with long lustrous stalks of grass, ferns, and a variety of cactus plants. A woman dressed in robes appears between the ruins. Maybe she is the guardian, collecting baksheesh from visitors.

The hillside behind me blurs in the mellow sunset. As I follow a different path on my way back, the route passes over a knoll where there is some kind of shrine. The baksheesh collector, an old woman, allows me in to see the figure of Hanuman, the monkey king. She scowls when I give her a token tip of only Rs.10, and as I walk back, a sudden whirlwind whips sand into my eyes. Could it be the work of a mischievous monkey spirit?

A steep staircase of rock ascending on my left lures me up into the boulders. From halfway up there is a great view of the Tungabhadra River's rocky islands disappearing into a maze of green banana plantations in the distance. Suddenly I'm startled by ferocious growls and screeches up ahead, and continue cautiously until I see a number of monkeys peering out of a cave above me. I shout, 'it's OK buddies, you can keep the whole hillside to yourselves', and turn back.

Back at 'home' I order green tea, samoosas and beer. There are several other travellers in small groups, and later some local Indian people arrive for dinner.

Friday, December 1, 2006. Hampi. It is still dark when I get going at 5 a.m. and follow the course of the river until I reach the Vithala Temple, where someone sells me a small cup of coffee. Then I decide to leave the main trail, and scramble along a naturally formed pathway leading across the wild jumble of rocks that tumbles down to the serene waters of the Tungabhadra. As I approach the riverbank, walking across slabs of rock, I note that various rocks have inscriptions, or images of Hindu gods chiseled out of them. The path leads over gigantic, carved columns of granite, all in a jumble amongst the other rocks. Although they must individually weigh 1000's of kilograms, it looks as though they've been carelessly flung aside. At the waters edge there is a chamber built from granite slabs, which blend into the environment. Above the doorway there are two elephants carved out of the rock with their trunks raised over a Hindu god. Inside, various god-figures are chiseled out of the walls, and at the back of the chamber, a black hole leads to another room.

As I breathe deeply in the fragrant breeze of dawn, the first light of day reveals temple ruins on the hills to the left and right of me. High up against the small mountain of rock behind me are Parthenon-like columns of granite, with roofs of rock slabs. The river is rippling with playful otters, and there are brown water birds with white wings, and small, marvelously swift, blue-winged, white-chested birds with black heads.

I look around. It is not a completed picture. There is a story of life here that was started but left unfinished. Near me there is a female goddess carved out of the naked rock, and there are several inscriptions on the rock faces. Many of the huge columns of rock have had their shapes altered for some uncompleted purpose. What happened - why were they abandoned? To move such monstrous slabs of rock must have taken a force on par with the industrial cranes of today. I read in the tourist information brochure that in 1565, the Muslim kings united to attack and overthrow the forces of King Sadasivaraya, whereafter the Empire of Vijayanagara was looted by the marauders for six months.

Saturday, December 2, 2006. Hampi. Though it is still dark, I'm up and about at 5:30 a.m., and eat my usual banana before going for coffee and biscuits at the old street vendor beside the king's pool in town. His only English is 'good morning', but that's enough, and his coffee is good.

The town is in the first awakening of its usual bustle, as I stride down the main road until I reach the 'monolithic bull' at the end of the road, where the trail continues between two hills of boulders. There is another trail to the right which is signposted 'Matanga Hills' leading up to a gateway at the top. Two Indian men coming down the trail stop me, and one says in a singsong voice, 'This trail is too dangerous, don't go up there alone, there are gangsters in these hills.' They look startled when I smile broadly and say 'Thank you very much!' before continuing, but now that I'm forewarned, I make sure my catapult and knife are handy.

Then I take a turnoff to the left and follow a steep path, which leads upward into the wild jumble of rock behemoths. There is a cave to the right with a Hindu god carved out of a slab of rock within, but there are also signs of human habitation, which is not good.

The path leads up and up, with steps cut out of the rock in places, while at others there are staircases of small rock slabs. I follow the final stage of the path that leads upwards along a sheer drop, until it reaches the flat top of a monster boulder where there is a small temple-like structure. Far below, crowds of Indian pilgrims can be seen streaming out of town towards the religious sites. I wedge myself between two boulders for a spiritual moment in the breeze, as I wonder what life was like for Indian people in the days of the Vijayanagar Empire.

With the thought of gangsters in mind, I decide to 'evacuate' as I don't want an encounter high up in the sky on such a narrow lip of rock. Going down is easier, and I get into a flowing rhythm of descent. Near the bottom, there are two villainous-looking men hiding behind rocks on either side of the trail, peering downward, but I am unstoppable, like a river tumbling down the rapids and I leave them reeling with startled expressions on their faces as I flit down to the main trail.

Later in the afternoon I return to the same area but do not take the turnoff to the Matanga Hills. I follow the path that veers to the left, which leads me into a vast area of rocky outcrops lying between clusters of thorn bushes. When I reach a high point and survey the wilderness around me, I am dismayed to see an Indian man dressed in a navy blue tracksuit, surreptitiously watching me from behind a rock on the top of another vantage point. I take evasive measures and lose myself high up in the rocks.

With the cool breeze upon me and an unparalleled view of India's spiritual heartland, I'm unprepared for the uninvited company that drops in. A big ape appears over the further rim of the wide rock in front of me, then another and another, until there is a whole troop of them, cool as downtown dudes, but watching me surreptitiously as they unobtrusively edge closer. As I do not want to panic them on such a precipice, an unhurried retreat seems to be the best option, but as I move towards my vertical retreat several apes begin to growl and move threateningly forward. I will be totally exposed while climbing down, so there is no other option. Out comes the catty, (catapult) and I reluctantly 'put a shot across their bows', which results in a panic-stricken stampede away from me.

Sunday, December 3, 2006. Hampi. Today is the universal day of rest for people in many cultures, a day when humans traditionally turn to their gods or reflect on their lives. At the break of day, I find myself beside the radiant waters of the holy Tungabhadra River, absorbing the residual cosmic energy from the enormous slabs of granite rock beneath and around me. A traveller's karma is one of perpetual movement. Many people choose paths of action while others stagnate in meaningless lives. Some rivers flow into the sea, others run into dams, yet without energy there would be no life. Each particle of water is inherently compelled to move, to reform and regroup, forever seeking to become one with the ultimate power of the oceans. India is a land of spiritual people, while across our universe there are seekers everywhere, people who wish to rise above the world's earthly and materialistic temptations, to find the mystical place called 'Heaven' where the Great Spirit of all of life is centred. Yet not all rivers run into a great ocean, and I wonder where the path I am following is leading me.

Wednesday, December 6, 2006. Hampi. Early in the morning I decide to tackle the 'gangster' hill again, but this time there is no sign of 'the evil ones'. Along the way I overtake five scared-looking Indian schoolboys, who fall in behind me. They can all speak a little English and ask me many questions. After we reach the first temple, I scout around and find that there is a hidden pathway leading higher up to another bigger temple. When we explore it, I come upon a faqir, (holy man) in deep prayer and I quietly retreat.

As I stroll into Hampi I see a mahout feeding banana leaves to his elephant. Then a large group of men in black robes arrives, and they take turns to go down on one knee before the beast, as it solemnly places its trunk on each man's head, as if it is bestowing blessings. The men each hand over money to the mahout. Then I follow them down to the river, where the elephant immerses itself while the mahout gives it a scrubbing. This takes place alongside an Indian mother and her two lovely longhaired daughters, who are bathing in the holy river.

Beside the Tungabhadra River

In the evening there is a lively festival in Hampi. Parmesh, my landlord, says that the people are celebrating the engagement of the god Shiva to the goddess Parvati. The streets are alive with colourful stalls selling curry powders, dyes, sweets, bangles, and all sorts of handmade goods. I hear a loud drumming sound as a wildly dancing crowd of people enter the town. In the lead is a woman with a blank, hypnotised look on her face, beating a drum-like instrument, monotonously, rhythmically. She is followed by a man wearing a fierce-looking mask, who prances around collecting money. It is a lively scene, with crowds of colourfully dressed people, cows on the streets, and monkeys swinging from the rooftops.

Thursday, December 7, 2006. To Goa. It's time to break the hypnotic spiritual hold of Hampi's exotic temples, and move on to Goa, the home of hedonism, with its palm-fringed, white sandy beaches on the shores of the Arabian Sea. I go to a travel agency and purchase a ticket to Mapusa, in the north of Goa. I read on the internet that Goa was a Portuguese colony for about 450 years, until as recently as 1961, when they were ousted by the Indians.

I spend a few reflective moments beside the sacred river, before taking off on an auto-rickshaw, which I share with Pia, a good looking German woman who's going the same way. We join a mixed group of tourists and Indians waiting for the bus at Paulo's Travels. When the bus arrives, I find that my 'luxury seat' has no foot space, but the conductor says that for Rs.50 I can upgrade to an upper sleeper-bunk. The bunk is too small for me to lie full length, but then I notice that the double bunk across from me is unoccupied, so I swing across the aisle and move in.

It is not a comfortable trip. The road is atrociously bumpy, the driver honks at everything that moves, and other vehicles honk back, which keeps us from sleeping deeply, and the air-conditioning is freezing. It takes a delegation of several passengers to convince the driver to turn it off.

Friday, December 8, 2006. Arambol (Goa). There are loud cries and lots of hooting to announce our arrival in Margoa, in the south of Goa, before dawn. The next stop is in Panaji, the capital, and finally in Mapusa, the 'gateway' to the north. I meet up with Pia again, who is also heading for the coastal village Arambol. We manoeuvre through the early morning clamour at the bus station to discover that the taxis to Arambol are expensive, and that the best way is in the cheap, crowded local bus. The bus wends its way through lush tropical vegetation, stopping for passengers at several villages along the way, before we get sightings of the brilliant, blue Arabian Sea. Then there are raucous shouts of 'Arambol, Arambol!', and we hastily disembark to find ourselves beside a big church in a small country town. We follow a road that leads down towards the beach, through tall coconut palms and scattered rural dwellings amidst the verdant plant life. Near the beach there is a turnoff to the Piya Guesthouse, and Pia immediately says, 'Follow me, that's my place!' Piya's offers a variety of accommodation, including cheap rooftop huts of bamboo, which we choose. When we check in the woman at reception says, 'Ah, but your visa has expired!' I sigh and say 'That's not right. Let me explain…' She shrugs and checks me in.

The guesthouse lies in a lovely rural setting of quaint old cottages with gardens, palms, banana trees, and free-ranging pigs and poultry. Across the road is Piya's open-air restaurant, where one can order all kinds of cheap Indian and seafood delights.

Even though its 'winter' in this part of the world, in the balmy midday heat, everyone is expected to take a siesta' –so that's what we do. In the late afternoon Pia joins me for a stroll down between the gardens and the old, colonial-style mansions, towards the beach. We cross over a wide sandy area of coconut palms and then we are on the wide, white-sanded beach, with low lazy waves rolling in. It's an idyllic setting. To the left the beach dwindles away into the haze, while off to the right the white sands run into strange, peaked rock formations below a steep hillside.

Pia watches over our things as I go for a long swim in the warm water. The waves are rather small, but as far as I can ascertain there are no devious currents at all, and you can swim out as far as you wish. Water's my thing – I love to swim deep out into the ocean until I'm totally alone, where - floating for ages - I become immersed, at one with the rising and falling liquid motion, as the water merges with the sky.

The Goan sunset is a transcendental gateway into the very soul of the universe. It settles on the far edge of the ocean in magnificent celestial splendour, bestowing peaceful karma on the mysterious Indian shores. On the beach, a dark long-haired man is singing ballads in Hindi to the mesmeric accompaniment of a bongo drum, as an odd assortment of people gather in the golden halo of sunset. Many people kneel, others dance - some topless - while a few juggle with balls, do hula-hooping, staff-twirling, or just sit and stare out into the ocean. Directly to the west of us lie the Arabian Peninsula and the troubled Middle East, and further back skulks the dark continent of Africa.

Pia is glad to see me back, as I lead her in a ritual sacrifice to the breeze of destiny. The people slowly disperse as the drum falls silent, and only when we are alone do we realize how dark it has become. As we stumble along through the coconut trees she finds a small light in her bag, and we somehow find our way through the jumble of buildings and gardens to Piyas, where we order beers and dinner. Goa is famous for the liberty the authorities allow the guests, and the restaurant area is thick with the smell of hashish, as many people are smoking openly.

Saturday, December 9, 2006. Arambol. It is delightfully cool when I get up at 6 a.m. and awaken Pia. There are still few signs of activity as we follow the road that leads to the main beach area. We find that Arambol consists of the old part, up at the church where the bus dropped us off, as well as the new touristy area of shops and guesthouses behind the bar-restaurants that line the beach. Piyas is out on a side-road, somewhere in the countryside between the two.

As the track we are following spills out onto the flat, golden-sanded beaches we see several people. Some are jogging while others are engaged in yoga and other apparently spiritually related rituals. Each stretch of sand is the domain of a different pack of stray dogs that 'work' the beach front. To our left a herd of cows roam casually along, doing 'mopping up', eating anything from fruit peels to newspapers.

Pia and I head for the strange rock formations to the right, and follow the narrow walkway around the side of the hill with its white cross, which dominates the beachfront. It leads by colourful vendor stalls, small guesthouses and restaurants with platforms above the sea. At the further end of the trail, there is another small beach within a frame of rocks and hills. A small lagoon emerges from a deep, mysterious rain forest within a narrow valley. On our way back we climb up to a table and chairs under a thatched cover, situated on the side of the hill above a restaurant. A young waiter comes up to take our order and serves us mint tea, toast, eggs and fruit.

Back at Piyas it appears that many of the foreigners who hang out in the shaded restaurant area are semi-permanent Goan residents, and pride themselves on being ultra-cool. Usually they have partially shaved scalps with long, plaited hair, studs, tattoos, cool robes etc. Some are in the business of massage, tattooing, ayurvedic healing, meditation, and other enterprises. The majority seem to be from Europe. They all have motorcycles, and sometimes take off with much revving, but mostly they just hang out.

Sunday, December 10, 2006. Arambol. The peal of church bells awakens me before dawn. Goa is of course a former Portuguese colony, and I believe about 26% of the population are Christian.

It's a pristine morning. I wander down along the beach below the hill for a cold fruit lassi drink in the open-air restaurant overlooking the lagoon.

Soon the warm water is calling, and I begin my daily swimming routine as my motto is, 'get the body in shape and the head will come along!' The shore surf only allows for some low level body surfing, but it's a joy to swim out deep and float in the large swells.

During the morning I check out the local scene, and at sunset I return to see about the herbs that are offered by the young Indian men from a small village over the hills.

Monday, December 11, 2006. Arambol. I get up early for a long swim and later I meet Pia for breakfast at a walkway restaurant. Mmmm – banana pancakes, mango lassi and mint tea sounds good! As we're eating an Indian man points out to sea, and we suddenly become aware of the dolphins frolicking in the waves.

As I'm getting into my midday siesta, I become aware of the sound of people arguing in Afrikaans in an adjoining rooftop bungalow. It is a young immature couple from South Africa, who have brought their mental baggage along with them.

Evenings are an early affair in Goa. After a two-hour spell out in the water, a meal of rice and fish masala, drinks, and a ritual burning of the herbs with Pia, I'm ready for bed.

Tuesday, December 12, 2006. Arambol. As usual, I get up at the crack of dawn and I walk along the coast until I reach the second beach where there is only one early stroller. There is a path going along the further side of the lagoon, which leads me into the monstrously tall trees of the rain forest. An unexplored forest is like a precious chest that holds a rich trove of priceless jewels. The path follows the sparkling little stream that feeds the branching pools of the lagoon, but I soon find it's best to stick to the lower section. Two Indian men pass by, and judging by their attire, I guess they're here for spiritual purposes. As the sun rises above the treetops, it becomes steamy below, and I'm glad for the shade as I take a rest on a rock in the stream. I blow rings in the breeze and watch the winged world of magical dragonflies, beautiful butterflies, and small, colourful birds flitting through the leafy trees and bushes.

Later I stop and rest below an immense banyan tree with huge protruding roots, which form nooks suitable for bedding down in. It appears to be used as a shrine to the Hindu gods, as there are several articles of religious paraphernalia placed around the tree. Then I hear chanting, and I see that there are some structures up a path to the right. When I surreptitiously check it out I hear an English sounding voice, perhaps preaching, but the speaker occasionally stops speaking to utter wolf-like howls. I guess he's been out in the bush for too long, and decide to give the local guru's place a miss.

The path seems to end here so I follow the rough course of the stream, which leads through big red boulders as the hillsides converge. It is a good place for private reflection, as there are no humans to be seen or heard.

When evening comes, I am once again floating out deep within the gentle swells of the Arabian Sea. From the beach comes the throbbing sound of bongo drums carrying into the night, while the usual groups of performers are entertaining the small gathering of people.

Wednesday, December 13, 2006. Arambol. Happy birthday to you! It's that time of the year again – a good time to celebrate! Pia gets woken up just after 5 a.m. and has to join the action.

First we walk along the beach, paddling through the spent waves' foamy reaches. We come upon a territorial dispute between the beach strays, and when I break it up one of the dogs tries to bite me. I kick sand into its face sending it into a coughing, sneezing retreat.

It is still dark when I lead Pia up the steep path to the top of the hill, where we see men in white robes gathered beneath a tree – it's the Tai Chi class. We sit down at the viewing point beside the white cross for a snack of bananas and apple juice. To round things off we burn a sacrifice to the breeze, as the sun creeps over Goa's eastern rim, bringing into focus the vast vista of misty palms, golden beaches, and the immensity of the sparkling sea to our right.

Goa offers me a gift. A big black dog suddenly appears out of the haze of dawn and walks up to me, unconditionally offering its lifelong friendship. I hug it and tell it that though we're soul mates, we bachelors have to go our own ways.

With our appetites on the rise, we're the first customers at our favorite restaurant with its open-air deck on the edge of a small cove. We order coffee, mint tea, toasted cheese, fruit salad, and coconut shake.

In the late afternoon I swim out as far as I can in one go, and I find myself amidst a shoal of flying fish. It is quite a shocker when one smacks down on my chest as I'm floating in a state of meditation. When the sun begins to melt into the shimmering ocean, the drum beat summons' me back to the distant shore.

Thursday, December 14, 2006. Arambol. Today is a sad day as I have to see my new-found friend Pia off. Part of my enjoyment in her company stemmed from the obvious pleasure each aspect of life here brought to her.

I decide to follow the seemingly endless coastline to the south, passing by the long-haired Frenchman in his prayer-like pose, as he awaits the dawning day, and I carry on through the ankle deep surf, past many open-air beachfront 'restaurants' and wandering cows. There is the usual lot of fishing folk, taking tally of today's catch, while some of the females repair the nets as men tinker with the boats. This fishing community is more affluent than those I encountered at Gopalpur, as they use more sophisticated motorboats, are better dressed, and generally look less scrawny. Then there is a shocker. A ghastly looking one metre long sea-adder with a small V-shaped head washes out onto the beach before me. It is a venomous looking reptile, which everyone gives a wide berth. How many of them are out here in these waters I wonder?

Friday, December 15, 2006. Arambol. The sound of loud Hindu music awakens me before dawn. The lyrics sound something like, 'Bu bu bubesahar…' This is the best time for a walk and a swim so I hit the path around the hillside to the lagoon beach.

Today I have to make a major decision, as Piya, the Indian woman in charge of the guesthouse, is pressing me as to how long I'm staying, as there's a big demand for accommodation over the Christmas period. I should be out there on the road exploring India, but somewhere along the way I've lost my drive, and for now I'm happy to hang out here. To keep Piya happy I pay for a further 11 days, and now that I've committed myself it's as though a weight has slipped off my shoulders.

After a long swim I make it back to my towel and see that the lagoon beach is nearly deserted. A man approaches me in the twilight. It's Moona, the herbal merchant man – time for Christmas shopping!

Saturday, December 16, 2006. Arambol. This day was formerly known as 'Blood River' day in South Africa, and was celebrated as a national holiday. It was in 1838, in the days of the conflicts between the Zulu and Boers, (farmers of European descent) that a group of 400 Boers, led by Andries Pretorius, encamped in an ox wagon lager on the banks of a river, defeated around 10, 000 Zulu warriors. Today it is still a national holiday, but now, more appropriately called the 'Day of Reconciliation'. It is also a difficult day for my family, as I have received an email telling me that today, Mom, who has not been well, is going to be moved to a retirement home, where she will live out her remaining years.

A pack of stray dogs runs up towards me as I stride down the beach. They've learned that I'm always good for head and chest scratches or a rough-and-tumble in the sand. I am getting to know them individually. My favorite is a small brown dog I first named Beach Bitch, but she looked hurt, so I renamed her Beach Baby, which she seems happier with.

Any dog that enters from adjoining territories will be attacked by the pack of dogs that hold sway there, but Beach Baby uses me as a shield to pass through several hostile areas. This almost gets me involved, when a couple of dogs try to outflank me to get at her. Together we scramble up the inclined path beyond the lagoon beach, and ascend up into the hills above the cliffs. When the path eventually descends again it leads to another beach, which is deserted other than for a couple of restaurant shacks. We follow the tree-lined beach until it reaches a large river. This beach area also seems to be the unofficial toilet for the Indian men who seem to materialize from the interior.

On my return I follow the coast and Beach Baby proves to be adept at boulder scrambling, as we work our way back along the rough lower route. When I come upon a small cove I'm delighted to find several cowries, and a also find a place in the shade of a leafy bush that will become my private retreat in the coming days.

Sunday, December 17, 2006. Arambol. Today is my international communication day. My first call is to South Korea, as it's my good friend Soon Young's birthday. I get through and speak to her and the artist Mi Ok. 'Come home to Korea!' they both say, but Korean Immigration may have different thoughts on that. My next call is to South Africa, where Mom has been moved to her new home, but it seems as if it's going to take time for her to settle in there.

After a midday siesta, I take to the beach and swim far out into the alien world of the sea, where I'm at home amongst the elements, in an eternal state of flux. I float off into a dream wherein I'm a solitary whale shark, forever cruising through the exotic seas amidst the corral reefs and islands of the tropics.

Monday, December 18, 2006. Arambol. On the way out to my distant cove retreat I pick up a new friend, a fine looking beach dog with white and brown patches whom I call 'White Tail'. I get a little stressed when he wants to leave me to attack the group of apes that are always lurking somewhere up on the cliffs, as he doesn't realize that he is no match for them. Along the way I lose my yellow 'Western Union' cap that was my headwear in Nepal.

In the afternoon I climb high up into the hills beside the main beach and sit above the cliff tops to enjoy the stunning view as I catch the balmy breeze. High above me there is a paraglider, soaring up into the incredibly blue expanse, and two eagles, large and brown-bodied, with white heads and white chests, are hovering, slowly rising.

On my return I go for the buffet dinner at the Arkan Bar, where I fall in with the Germans Wilhelm and Herman. They say we should go to the Coco Loco Bar to hear an Indian band playing, but they've already finished by the time we get there. Another German called Michael arrives. He's a professional musician at the Surf Club, and rolls several reefers, which he passes around as we drink beer and chat. When we discuss travel plans I mention that I'm going to Rawalpindi in Pakistan, to follow the ancient Silk Route via the new highway across the Karakoram Mountains into China. `I've been there but you cannot do that at this time of the year. The pass will be closed because of the heavy snow', says Herman, squashing my immediate plans.

Tuesday, December 19, 2006. Arambol. There is some disturbance out in the dead of night causing all the neighbourhood dogs to bark loudly. My landlord gets up and shouts `Hit, hit!!' to no avail.

When the raucous cries of crows awaken me again before dawn, I set out along the beach to see the fishing people in action. Several boats have already returned with the morning's catch, which consists mostly of rather small fish. When I stand beside a boat to watch the proceedings I'm surprised to see a man tossing several of the smaller fish to the stray dogs, which devour them on the spot.

As the sun peers through the palms that fringe the beach, people begin to appear, all engaged in their favourite activities of jogging, yoga, posing, prayer, stretching, etc. etc. – this is Goa!

Wednesday, December 20, 2006. Arambol. As I'm strolling along the beach at dawn a black stray who looks all beaten up falls in beside me, obviously intent on using me as a foil to cross `enemy lines'. His camouflage doesn't work, and a pack of strays closes in on us, involving me in the ensuing free-for-all. I have to whack at them with my day bag, and eventually shoot one with the catty when he has a serious go at me. A little further on I shout at an Indian man who is having a crap on the main beach, but as a probable serial offender he is not easily put off.

By the time I reach the end of the beach and begin to crawl over and under the boulders to get to the cowrie cove, I have a new sidekick who I call `Eagle', as he has the same white, brown, and black colours as the local eagles.

On my return I duck into the `rain forest' to escape the blistering midday heat. There beside the stream a couple of Indian men are plastering their bodies with yellow clay, which I suppose is good for the skin. Then I come upon a fat man lying on his back under a tree, singing `Hare Krishna' very loudly. When I reach the giant banyan tree there is the sound of communal singing interposed by sporadic howls, coming form the 'wolfman's' hangout.

Saturday, December 23, 2006. Arambol. Today my mission is to find the source of the stream that feeds the lagoon. Maybe it originates from a magical fountain that contains the elusive elixir of life! On my way along the course of the stream I notice a couple of hippy-like figures emerging form the wolfman's place, but I avoid them amongst the boulders of the stream.

There is a deep, rocky riverbed winding between big boulders into the dense vegetation, but the stream eventually goes underground, as it is not the rainy season now. Then the course of the water comes to an abrupt halt at a solid rock face. When I climb up the side, I find myself at the top of a hot, deserted plateau of long grass and deep thickets of mostly thorn bushes.

As I try to work my way back towards the coast, it becomes increasingly difficult to penetrate the dense vegetation, so I take to a green gateway of soft bush leading back in the direction of the valley. It later transforms itself into a stream within a cool green tunnel of vegetation, which I'm able to descend without too many problems. Along the way there is a flat rock with the large letters 'BA', formally engraved in a square.

At first the only sounds to be heard are those of small birds flitting through the branches, but then I become aware of far-off singing and the smell of wood-smoke and ganja. Three men sitting beside a shrine beneath a banyan tree seem to be startled when I suddenly appear and greet them. 'How did you come from there?' an Indian-looking man asks. 'I'm exploring the area' I reply. The Indian man continues singing as I talk to the other two, who might be Eurasian and could be from anywhere. One says he's from Chile but grew up in Sweden, the other is a greasy looking character who has a switchblade that is half concealed beneath the mat we're sitting on. They have an exotic looking shrine with an image of the Hindu god Shiva against the tree. 'Tell me about Shiva?' I ask. 'Shiva is a moody god' the Indian man replies. 'Because he often changes his mind, there is no real truth' another continues. Their attitude becomes slightly hostile when I don't bow to their shrine as is proper, but rather greet it with a 'hi there' and a half-salute. A German couple guided by another Indian man comes up from the valley below, and I can see these guys are actually trying to extract baksheesh as a donation to Shiva. In the rambling, religious indoctrination that follows, I ask where Jesus Christ, Buddha, and Muhammad fit into the order of things, but find that Shiva's disciples are not in the mood, and I'm expelled.

Sunday, December 24, 2006. Arambol. Piyas is the local foreigner hangout and the restaurant is open from early till late. There are long communal tables where you can meet people, or smaller, private tables for more intimate gatherings, and the garden area, where the biker crowd like to get together.

The beach areas are more crowded than usual, as bus loads of Indians have arrived from the interior and are out for picnics and fun on the beaches. For a good deal of the day I'm out of reach, far out in the sea, only returning to dry land for food and a siesta.

In the late afternoon, I climb up the hill overlooking Arambol and sip at a small bottle of Goan 'Honey Bee' brandy, as I watch the magnificent sunset and listen to the far-off sound of drums. Some people have erected an illuminated cross at a high point overlooking the town.

Monday, December 25, 2006. Arambol. Merry Christmas! My internal alarm wakes me at 5 a.m. and I head up into the hills to watch the sunrise, and before long, the clamouring of church bells ring in the day.

Lunch at Piyas, siesta, phone calls to the family, and then I'm off to the beach again. I swim far out and drift in the swell until the drums begin to sound in the twilight, where the silent throng of people is gathered on the beach.

Sunday, December 31, 2006. Arambol. It is time to take leave of Goa. I visit all my favourite places, and scramble over the rocks to the secret cove where I add cowries to my seashell shrine to the sea gods. As I lean back against a rock and look out to sea my wet sidekick snuggles up against me. These stray dogs that roam the beaches, always on the look-out for food and love in equal measure, touch my heart as my mind involuntarily drifts back to the beloved dog of my childhood days. It was shortly before the final exams in my senior high school year that I came home one day to hear that my lifelong companion and greatest friend, old Chippy, had been put down. As I returned to our familiar haunts deep within the African bushveld to hold a wake for a fallen comrade, I sensed his presence, and knew that Chippy would always be somewhere up ahead, looking out for me. The sun wept crimson tears on the translucent skyline, as it sank back beyond a dark shawl of cloud, and the moon smudged the kopjes with melancholy, and withdrew, leaving me alone in the gloom. It was then that I began to understand why wolves howl.

In the evening I return to my hangout above the cliff face overlooking the sea. As I watch the eagles soaring high above the ocean, there is a rustling sound in the bushes, where a troop of curious monkeys is peering in. `Hi guys!' I say, but the little ones flee. Fishing boats putter in from the deep waters below the stars. Now it is time to have one last party down in the town!

January 2007. To Mumbai/Bombay. The call of the road has become ever stronger, and can no longer be ignored. I've paid up and said my goodbyes by the time the motorcycle-rickshaw man comes to pick me up for a long ride to the bus station. I have a sleeper berth in the express bus, and this time I have my sleeping bag on hand to combat the fierce air-conditioning.

I read in my Lonely Planet guide book that Bombay is now called Mumbai, after Mumbadevi, the patron goddess of the city. It is a wicked jolt to be transported from the peace and quiet of Arambol into a city with a population of 13 million plus people.

A taxi carries me across the Mumbai peninsula, via Shahid Bhagt Singh Road, which offers brilliant flashes of the azure waters of the Arabian Sea, passing the monumental structure of the so-called Gateway of India, to drop me off along the downtown Colaba Causeway.

A backpacker's first priority is to find suitable accommodation. I try a couple of Lonely Planet recommended places but they're full. It is when a tout of about my age offers to lead me, that my problems begin. `Yes, we have a room for you' says the man at the first place's reception. The price is reasonable, but when he checks out my visa he pushes my passport back to me and says, `Your visa has expired, I cannot let you stay here'. 'Let me explain how this visa works', I say, but he is not interested.

After this happens at several hotels, I become frustrated and ask the tout to take me to the nearest police station, as I want to get this matter cleared up. We go to a nearby police station where a very friendly officer meets me but says he cannot decide on such an issue, and gives my guide directions to the Tourist Police. At the Tourist Police office I have to stand in a line before I can put my case to a stern-looking female officer who processes me. After looking at my visa and listening to my story she says, 'This visa expired shortly after you entered India.' I shake my head in frustration and say, 'Why don't you call the tourist police in Calcutta, they will confirm that they told me my visa is valid for 3 months after entry?' She shakes her head and says, 'This is Mumbai, we are not concerned about what people say in Calcutta. Your visa has expired and I'm going to give you 24 hours to leave India.' And that's that, nothing I say can persuade her otherwise. 'How am I supposed to find accommodation, can you give me a letter to say I'm OK for tonight, as I've checked in with you?' 'No', she replies, 'Accommodation is your problem, and you have to return to our office at 10 a.m. tomorrow morning' - and I'm dismissed.

I pay my guide and go into a travel agency where the only option available to me is a flight back to Bangkok tomorrow evening. There is not enough time to get a visa to any other country. My immediate problem is finding a place to sleep. This is not the kind of city where one can sleep on a park bench. Then I have an inspiration, and look in my diary where I find my old pal Ravi's phone number. He is a member of the IP (International Pub) family from my Korean days, who I believe now lives with his family in this city. I call the number from a public phone and hold my breath as it rings. Then Ravi's familiar voice comes onto the line. I briefly explain that I'm in Colaba and am having problems, and ask if he can put me up for the night. 'Meet me at the Cafe Churchill in one hour. It's on the Colaba Causeway' he replies. I hurriedly search for a bank where I can exchange a traveller's cheque before setting out to find the café.

As I'm striding down the sidewalk through the bustling crowds of people I suddenly hear my name being called, and there is my old friend Ravi, looking as though he hasn't aged a day since I last saw him. He makes a quick phone call, and before long his chauffeur comes swooping out of the traffic to pick us up, and my immediate problems are over.

In a city like this it pays to have a professional driver, as we settle down on the back seat while he steers the vehicle along Marine Drive through the voluminous torrents of traffic. To the left lies Chowpatty Beach, and across the bay is Malabar Point.

Ravi says that Mumbai is one of the world's top ten centres of commerce, and that it houses India's Hindi film and television industry known as Bollywood. It takes a long time to reach his home, as he explains that most people live to the north, because the southern areas of the city command among the highest rates in the world.

We stop to pick up a couple of beers, and then he introduces me to his lovely wife, daughter, and son. His wife keeps serving tasty dishes to go with the beers while we catch up on old times. When things quieten down somewhat outdoors, Ravi takes me for a spin in his car to show me around the neighbourhood. Then we return home for more delicious dishes. This sure beats fending off muggers in a park!

In the morning I join him and his driver, who powers us into the turbulent ocean of early morning traffic. When we reach his office I'm truly sad to take leave of a real friend, a friend in need! Then I take off into the current again as he has put his driver at my disposal.

At the Tourist Police Office, the female officer is a little friendlier today as she asks how I survived the night. 'We believe that the misunderstanding regarding your visa's expiry date was an honest mistake, so you will not be blacklisted' she says. 'Please pay the fine and then you're free to leave'.

So here I am, shouldering my backpack along Colaba Causeway – a deportee! A taxi picks me up. 'Mumbai International Airport please', and away we go, swimming against the tide of traffic. 'Good bye Mumbai and India – sorry we have to part like this!!'

18

Déjà vu

January, 2007. Bangkok. It's déjà vu! I'm back in a taxi, high up on the expressway with the glittering nightscape of Bangkok City zooming into focus. The time is nearly 1 a.m., and I'm on my way to the Khao San Road area again.

My fiftieth year has come and gone, lost in a hazy blaze of trails through Africa and Asia. When the taxi drops me off I wander up towards Rambutri Lane in a daze. Incredibly there is a room available at My House Guesthouse, where I leave my bag in room 306 and go up to the top balcony for a whiff of a breeze in the muggy night. Below me the twinkling night lights of Bangkok are calling. I stroll down to Popiang House. 'Will it be a big beer Chang?' asks the smiling waiter. Maybe I've been here before.

Later a young couple from the USA join me at my table. They are Don and Sarah from San Francisco. 'Hey, what's up man? You've got this strange smile on your face', enquires Don. 'Like you've discovered some rare treasure', adds Sarah. 'I'm looking ahead into the future', I reply. 'The future is so uncertain, are you a clairvoyant?' she asks. 'No', I answer. 'But each one of us has the power to shape the future through our current thoughts. By visualizing our future course and unwaveringly following that goal we can make it come true.' 'Yeah, but many difficulties, bad luck or some random event can stop you from getting what you want,' says Don. 'Think of life as a river.' I reply. 'There are difficulties from time to time, that's true, but the river of life keeps flowing, from its source, it keeps flowing just as a river keeps flowing because the flowing itself is a universal principle of life. You flow with the river and your life is the river; you flow from your thoughts and your life here and now, towards your dreams. If you have a cherished dream and follow it with all the power of your being, you will create a current of energy; you invoke The Universal Law of Attraction, which brings unforeseen elements into play and propels you to your goal, despite the hardships'. 'Cheers to that!' says Don, as we raise our glasses and drink to a sparkling future.

There is an exceptionally balmy atmosphere, then suddenly a tremendous clap of thunder captures our attention, and it is as though the sluice gates of heaven have opened as torrents of rain pour down. There is water in the air, there is water everywhere. I feel so connected. I notice a map of Asia, open on my table, which under my gaze spirals into a kaleidoscope of the future. I look to the north as the present blurs into images of the golden pagodas of Bagan in Burma, the legendary Great Wall of China, prancing horses on the Mongolian steppes, and on into the shimmering, icy vastness of Siberia. I see exotic monasteries and the lonely snow-clad peaks of Tibet, and to the northeast there is a vision of the Korean 'Kingdom of the morning calm', where gold-plated Buddhas in ornate temples are nestled deep within the mysterious, misty mountains.

'One more big beer, Chang' suggests the understanding waiter. I nod slowly. Revellers stagger in and out, people come and go, and in a few hours it will be dawn. It is as though I am drifting ... drifting. Ahead of me lie two courses, the main-stream or another way. Then I sense a sound, at first undefined, it comes to me, it calls – it is a wild call, a clear call, a call that may not be denied – it's the call to enter another side-stream of life. Will you come along with me?

#1 AUTHOR'S NOTE: Although there have been unconfirmed sightings of Koos in Palau Borneo; Tadzhikistan; Morocco and Easter Island, his current whereabouts are unknown.

#2 AUTHOR'S NOTE: Readers are welcome to view my photo album on www.facebook.com or contact me at: mystellaland@yahoo.com

Introduction

Folklore Performance and the Legacy of Joel Chandler Harris

In the summer of 1882, still flush with the popular and critical success of *Uncle Remus: His Songs and His Sayings* (1880), Joel Chandler Harris was waiting to catch a train in Norcross, Georgia, twenty miles northeast of Atlanta. Harris explains in detail the unique experience he had that night, and he made sure to include this important episode in his introduction to his second book, *Nights with Uncle Remus: Myths and Legends of the Old Plantation* (1883). The train was late, and darkness had already fallen when Harris overheard several black railroad workers sitting in small groups on the platform and perched on crossties, cracking jokes at each other's expense and laughing boisterously. Harris sat down next to one of the liveliest talkers in the group, a middle-aged worker. After enjoying their banter for awhile, Harris heard someone in the crowd mention "Ole Molly Har'." Suddenly inspired, and "in a low tone, as if to avoid attracting attention," Harris narrated the tar-baby story to his companion, "by way of a feeler."

Harris reconstructs in some detail what occurred next, a folkloristic event any ethnologist today would swap the SUV for. The lively man next to Harris kept interrupting the tar-baby narration with loud and frequent comments—"Dar now!" and "He's a honey, mon!" and "Gentermens! git out de way, an' gin 'im room!" Suddenly, Harris's audience of one grows exponentially into a storytelling community of thirty.

> These comments, and the peals of unrestrained and unrestrainable laughter that accompanied them, drew the attention of the other Negroes, and before the climax of the story had been reached, where Brother Rabbit is cruelly thrown into the brier-

patch, they had all gathered around and made themselves comfortable. Without waiting to see what the effect of the 'Tar Baby' legend would be, the writer [Harris] told the story of 'Brother Rabbit and the Mosquitoes,' and this had the effect of convulsing them. Two or three could hardly wait for the conclusion, so anxious were they to tell stories of their own. The result was that, for almost two hours, a crowd of thirty or more Negroes vied with each other to see which could tell the most and the best stories.

Harris notes that some of the black workers told stories poorly, "giving only meager outlines," while others "told them passing well." And then he adds that "one or two, if their language and gestures could have been taken down, would have put Uncle Remus to shame." Harris, always the astute observer, stresses that a storyteller's language and gestures must interact with the audience's emotions to create a truly memorable oral performance.

That evening, Harris goes on to explain, he heard a few stories he had already included among the thirty-four animal tales in *Uncle Remus: His Songs and His Sayings*. He also heard several that he had previously "gathered and verified" but had not yet published. Yet "the great majority were either new or had been entirely forgotten." Then Harris shares an insight that reflects on the collective psyche of his fellow storytellers and, even more importantly, on his own conflicted self. Harris explains that the darkness that night "gave greater scope and freedom to the narratives of the negroes, and but for this friendly curtain, it is doubtful if the conditions would have been favorable to storytelling." Furthermore, "however favorable the conditions might have been, the appearance of a notebook and pencil would have dissipated them as utterly as if they had never existed."

Like a professional folklorist, which he never claimed to be, Harris knew the inhibiting effects on his human sources of introducing the reporter's pad in a natural, unforced, oral-performance setting. Gifted with a remarkably discriminating ear and auditory memory, however, Harris carried off the Norcross stories in his head as surely as he had stored away the Middle Georgia black folk tales he had heard from Aunt Crissy,